Ravishing the Heiress

SHERRY THOMAS

BERKLEY SENSATION, NEW YORK

THE BERKLEY PUBLISHING GROUP
Published by the Penguin Group
Penguin Group (USA) Inc.
375 Hudson Street, New York, New York 10014, USA

Penguin Group (Canada), 90 Eglinton Avenue East, Suite 700, Toronto, Ontario M4P 2Y3, Canada
(a division of Pearson Penguin Canada Inc.) • Penguin Books Ltd., 80 Strand, London WC2R 0RL,
England • Penguin Group Ireland, 25 St. Stephen's Green, Dublin 2, Ireland (a division of Penguin
Books Ltd.) • Penguin Group (Australia), 250 Camberwell Road, Camberwell, Victoria 3124, Australia
(a division of Pearson Australia Group Pty. Ltd.) • Penguin Books India Pvt. Ltd., 11 Community
Centre, Panchsheel Park, New Delhi—110 017, India • Penguin Group (NZ), 67 Apollo Drive,
Rosedale, Auckland 0632, New Zealand (a division of Pearson New Zealand Ltd.) • Penguin Books
(South Africa) (Pty.) Ltd., 24 Sturdee Avenue, Rosebank, Johannesburg 2196, South Africa

Penguin Books Ltd., Registered Offices: 80 Strand, London WC2R 0RL, England

This is a work of fiction. Names, characters, places, and incidents either are the product of the author's
imagination or are used fictitiously, and any resemblance to actual persons, living or dead, business
establishments, events, or locales is entirely coincidental. The publisher does not have any control over
and does not assume any responsibility for author or third-party websites or their content.

RAVISHING THE HEIRESS

A Berkley Sensation Book / published by arrangement with the author

PUBLISHING HISTORY
Berkley Sensation mass-market edition / July 2012

Copyright © 2012 by Sherry Thomas.
Excerpt from *Tempting the Bride* by Sherry Thomas copyright © 2012 by Sherry Thomas.
Cover art by Gregg Gulbronson. Hand lettering by Ron Zinn.
Cover design by George Long.
Interior text design by Laura K. Corless.

ISBN: 978-0-425-25087-7

BERKLEY SENSATION®
Berkley Sensation Books are published by The Berkley Publishing Group,
a division of Penguin Group (USA) Inc.,
375 Hudson Street, New York, New York 10014.
BERKLEY SENSATION® is a registered trademark of Penguin Group (USA) Inc.
The "B" design is a trademark of Penguin Group (USA) Inc.

PRINTED IN THE UNITED STATES OF AMERICA

10 9 8 7 6 5 4 3

ALWAYS LEARNING   PEARSON

PRAISE FOR

Ravishing the Heiress

"I'M IN AWE. Only Sherry Thomas can write a romance that is both heartrending and heartwarming. An absolutely ravishing love story!"

—Courtney Milan, author of *Unraveled*

PRAISE FOR THE NOVELS OF SHERRY THOMAS

"Tender, discerning, and lushly romantic, [*Beguiling the Beauty*] drills down into the characters' emotional depths to produce a devastating love story that may appeal to fans of Mary Jo Putney and Laura Kinsale."

—*Library Journal* (starred review)

"Superb . . . Will win readers over with its elegant writing, exceptional characterization . . . and exquisitely romantic love story." —*Chicago Tribune*

"Ravishingly sinful, intelligent, and addictive. An amazing debut." —Eloisa James, *New York Times* bestselling author

"Enchanting . . . An extraordinary, unputdownable love story." —Jane Feather, *New York Times* bestselling author

"Thomas makes a dazzling debut with a beautifully written, sizzling, captivating love story . . . Her compelling tale of love betrayed and then reborn will make you sigh with pleasure." —*RT Book Reviews*

"Deft plotting and sparkling characters . . . Steamy and smart." —*Publishers Weekly* (starred review)

"Historical romance the way I love it."

—*All About Romance*

"Big, dramatic, and romantic." —*Dear Author*

To my husband,
the one with whom I have built my life

ACKNOWLEDGMENTS

To everyone who helped me in the writing of this book and everyone who helped me in arriving at this moment in my life.

CHAPTER 1

Fate

1888 ～

It was love at first sight.

Not that there was anything wrong with love at first sight, but Millicent Graves had not been raised to fall in love at all, let alone hard and fast.

She was the only surviving child of a very prosperous man who manufactured tinned goods and other preserved edibles. It had been decided, long before she could comprehend such things, that she was going to Marry Well—that via her person, the family's fortune would be united with an ancient and illustrious title.

Millie's childhood had therefore consisted of endless lessons: music, drawing, penmanship, elocution, deportment, and, when there was time left, modern languages. At ten, she successfully floated down a long flight of stairs with three books on her head. By twelve, she could exchange hours of pleasantries in French, Italian,

1

and German. And on the day of her fourteenth birthday, Millie, not at all a natural musician, at last conquered Listz's *Douze Grandes Études*, by dint of sheer effort and determination.

That same year, with her father coming to the conclusion that she would never be a great beauty, nor indeed a beauty of any kind, the search began for a highborn groom desperate enough to marry a girl whose family wealth derived from—heaven forbid—sardines.

The search came to an end twenty months later. Mr. Graves was not particularly thrilled with the choice, as the earl who agreed to take his daughter in exchange for his money had a title that was neither particularly ancient nor particularly illustrious. But the stigma attached to tinned sardines was such that even this earl demanded Mr. Graves's last penny.

And then, after months of haggling, after all the agreements had finally been drawn up and signed, the earl had the inconsideration to drop dead at the age of thirty-three. Or rather, Mr. Graves viewed his death a thoughtless affront. Millie, in the privacy of her room, wept.

She'd seen the earl only twice and had not been overjoyed with either his anemic looks or his dour temperament. But he, in his way, had had as little choice as she. The estate had come to him in terrible disrepair. His schemes of improvement had made little to no difference. And when he'd tried to land an heiress of a more exalted background, he'd failed resoundingly, likely because he'd been so unimpressive in both appearance and demeanor.

A more spirited girl might have rebelled against such

an unprepossessing groom, seventeen years her elder. A more enterprising girl might have persuaded her parents to let her take her chances on the matrimonial mart. Millie was not either of those girls.

She was a quiet, serious child who understood instinctively that much was expected of her. And while it was desirable that she could play all twelve of the *Grandes Études* rather than just eleven, in the end her training was not about music—or languages, or deportment—but about discipline, control, and self-denial.

Love was never a consideration. Her opinions were never a consideration. Best that she remained detached from the process, for she was but a cog in the great machinery of Marrying Well.

That night, however, she sobbed for this man, who, like her, had no say in the direction of his own life.

But the great machinery of Marrying Well ground on. Two weeks after the late Earl Fitzhugh's funeral, the Graves hosted his distant cousin the new Earl Fitzhugh for dinner.

Millie knew very little of the late earl. She knew even less of the new one, except that he was only nineteen, still in his last year at Eton. His youth disturbed her somewhat— she'd been prepared to marry an older man, not someone close to her own age. But other than that, she dwelled on him not at all: Her marriage was a business transaction; the less personal involvement from her, the more smoothly things would run.

Unfortunately, her indifference—and her peace of mind—came to an abrupt end the moment the new earl walked in the door.

* * *

*M*illie was not without thoughts of her own. She very carefully watched what she said and did, but seldom censored her mind: It was the only freedom she had.

Sometimes, as she lay in bed at night, she thought of falling in love, in the ways of a Jane Austen novel—her mother did not allow her to read the Brontës. Love, it seemed to her, was a result born of careful, shrewd observation. Miss Elizabeth Bennet, for example, did not truly consider Mr. Darcy to have the makings of a fine husband until she had seen the majesty of Pemberley, which stood for Mr. Darcy's equally majestic character.

Millie imagined herself a wealthy, independent widow, inspecting the gentlemen available to her with wry but humane wit. And if she were fortunate enough, finding that one gentleman of character, sense, and good humor.

That seemed to her the epitome of romantic love: the quiet satisfaction of two kindred souls brought together in gentle harmony.

She was, therefore, entirely unprepared for her internal upheaval, when the new Earl Fitzhugh was shown into the family drawing room. Like a visitation of angels, there flared a bright white light in the center of her vision. Haloed by this supernatural radiance stood a young man who must have folded his wings just that moment so as to bear a passing resemblance to a mortal.

An instinctive sense of self-preservation made her lower her face before she'd quite comprehended the geography of his features. But she was all agitation inside, a sensation that was equal parts glee and misery.

Surely a mistake had been made. The late earl could not possibly have a cousin who looked like this. Any moment now he'd be introduced as the new earl's schoolmate, or perhaps the guardian Colonel Clements's son.

"Millie," said her mother, "let me present Lord Fitzhugh. Lord Fitzhugh, my daughter."

Dear God, it was him. This mind-bogglingly handsome young man was the new Lord Fitzhugh.

She had to lift her eyes. Lord Fitzhugh returned a steady, blue gaze. They shook hands.

"Miss Graves," he said.

Her heart thrashed drunkenly. She was not accustomed to such complete and undiluted masculine attention. Her mother was attentive and solicitous. But her father only ever spoke to her with one eye still on his newspaper.

Lord Fitzhugh, however, was focused entirely on her, as if she were the most important person he'd ever met.

"My lord," she murmured, acutely aware of the warmth on her face and the old-master perfection of his cheekbones.

Dinner was announced on the heels of the introductions. The earl offered his arm to Mrs. Graves and it was with great envy that Millie took Colonel Clements's arm.

She glanced at the earl. He happened to be looking her way. Their eyes held for a moment.

Heat pumped through her veins. She was jittery, stunned almost.

What was the matter with her? Millicent Graves, milquetoast extraordinaire, through whose veins dripped the *lack* of passion, did not experience such strange flashes and flutters. She'd never even read a Brontë novel, for goodness' sake. Why did she suddenly feel like one of the

5

younger Bennet girls, the ones who giggled and shrieked and had absolutely no control over themselves?

Distantly she realized that she knew nothing of the earl's character, sense, or temperament. That she was behaving in a shallow and foolish manner, putting the cart before the horse. But the chaos inside her had a life and a will of its own.

As they entered the dining room, Mrs. Clements said, "What a lovely table. Don't you agree, Fitz?"

"I do," said the earl.

His name was George Edward Arthur Granville Fitzhugh—the family name and the title were the same. But apparently those who knew him well called him Fitz.

Fitz, her lips and teeth played with the syllable. *Fitz*.

At dinner, the earl let Colonel Clements and Mrs. Graves carry the majority of the conversation. Was he shy? Did he still obey the tenet that children should be seen and not heard? Or was he using the opportunity to assess his possible future in-laws—and his possible future wife?

Except he didn't appear to be studying her. Not that he could do so easily: A three-tier, seven-branch silver epergne, sprouting orchids, lilies, and tulips from every appendage, blocked the direct line of sight between them.

Through petals and stalks, she could make out his occasional smiles—each of which made her ears hot—directed at Mrs. Graves to his left. But he looked more often in her father's direction.

Her grandfather and her uncle had built the Graves fortune. Her father had been young enough, when the family coffer began to fill, to be sent to Harrow. He'd acquired the expected accent, but his natural temperament was too lackluster to quite emanate the gloss of sophistication his family had hoped for.

There he sat, at the head of the table, neither a ruthless risk taker like his late father, nor a charismatic, calculating entrepreneur like his late brother, but a bureaucrat, a caretaker of the riches and assets thrust upon him. Hardly the most exciting of men.

Yet he commanded the earl's attention this night.

Behind him on the wall hung a large mirror in an ornate frame, which faithfully reflected the company at table. Millie sometimes looked into that mirror and pretended she was an outside observer documenting the intimate particulars of a private meal. But tonight she had yet to give the mirror a glance, since the earl sat at the opposite end of the table, next to her mother.

She found him in the mirror. Their eyes met.

He had not been looking at her father. Via the mirror, he'd been looking at *her*.

Mrs. Graves had been forthcoming on the mysteries of marriage—she did not want Millie ambushed by the facts of life. The reality of what happened between a man and a woman behind closed doors usually had Millie regard members of the opposite sex with wariness. But his attention caused only fireworks inside her—detonations of thrill, blasts of full-fledged happiness.

If they were married, and if they were alone . . .

She flushed.

But she already knew: She would not mind it.

Not with him.

The gentlemen had barely rejoined the ladies in the drawing room when Mrs. Graves announced that Millie would play for the gathering.

"Millicent is splendidly accomplished at the piano-forte," she said.

For once, Millie was excited about the prospect of displaying her skills—she might lack true musicality, but she did possess an ironclad technique.

As Millie settled herself before the piano, Mrs. Graves turned to Lord Fitzhugh. "Do you enjoy music, sir?"

"I do, most assuredly," he answered. "May I be of some use to Miss Graves? Turn the pages for her perhaps?"

Millie braced her hand on the music rack. The bench was not very long. He'd be sitting right next to her.

"Please do," said Mrs. Graves.

And just like that, Lord Fitzhugh was at Millie's side, so close that his trousers brushed the flounces of her skirts. He smelled fresh and brisk, like an afternoon in the country. And the smile on his face as he murmured his gratitude distracted her so much that she forgot that she should be the one to thank him.

He looked away from her to the score on the music rack. "*Moonlight Sonata*. Do you have something lengthier?"

The question rattled—and pleased—her. "Usually one only hears the first movement of the sonata, the adagio sostenuto. But there are two additional movements. I can keep playing, if you'd like."

"I'd be much obliged."

A good thing she played mechanically and largely from memory, for she could not concentrate on the notes at all. The tips of his fingers rested lightly against a corner of the score sheet. He had lovely looking hands, strong and elegant. She imagined one of his hands gripped around a cricket ball—it had been mentioned at dinner that he played for the school team. The ball he bowled would be fast as lightning. It would knock over a wicket directly and dismiss the batsman, to the roar of the crowd's appreciation.

"I have a request, Miss Graves," he spoke very quietly. With her playing, no one could hear him but her.

"Yes, my lord?"

"I'd like you to keep playing no matter what I say."

Her heart skipped a beat. Now it was beginning to make sense. He wanted to sit next to her so that they could hold a private conversation in a room full of their elders.

"All right. I'll keep going," she answered. "What is it that you want to say, sir?"

"I'd like to know, Miss Graves, are you being forced into marriage?"

Ten thousand hours before the pianoforte was the only thing that kept Millie from coming to an abrupt halt. Her fingers continued to pressure the correct keys; notes of various descriptions kept on sprouting. But it could have been someone in the next house playing, so dimly did the music register.

"Do I—do I give the impression of being forced, sir?" Even her voice didn't quite sound her own.

He hesitated slightly. "No, you do not."

"Why do you ask, then?"

"You are sixteen."

"It is far from unheard of for a girl to marry at sixteen."

"To a man more than twice her age?"

"You make the late earl sound decrepit. He was a man in his prime."

"I am sure there are thirty-three-year-old men who make sixteen-year-olds tremble in romantic yearning, but my cousin was not one of them."

They were coming to the end of the page; he turned it

just in time. She chanced a quick glance at him. He did not look at her.

"May I ask you a question, my lord?" she heard herself say.

"Please."

"Are *you* being forced to marry me?"

The words left her in a spurt, like arterial bleeding. She was afraid of his answer. Only a man who was himself being forced would wonder whether she, too, was under the same duress.

He was silent for some time. "Do you not find this kind of arrangement exceptionally distasteful?"

Glee and misery—she'd been bouncing between the two wildly divergent emotions. But now there was only misery left, a sodden mass of it. His tone was courteous. Yet his question was an accusation of complicity: He would not be here if she hadn't agreed.

"I—" She was playing the adagio sostenuto much too fast—no moonlight in her sonata, only storm-driven branches whacking at shutters. "I suppose I've had time to become inured to it: I've known my whole life that I'd have no say in the matter."

"My cousin held out for years," said the earl. "He should have done it sooner: begotten an heir and left everything to his own son. We are barely related."

He did not want to marry her, she thought dazedly, not in the very least.

This was nothing new. His predecessor had not wanted to marry her, either; she had accepted his reluctance as par for the course. Had never expected anything else, in fact. But the unwillingness of the young man next to her on the piano bench—it was as if she'd been forced to hold a block

10

of ice in her bare hands, the chill turning into a black, burning pain.

And the mortification of it, to be so eager for someone who reciprocated none of her sentiments, who was revolted by the mere thought of taking her as a wife.

He turned the next page. "Do you never think to yourself, *I won't do it*?"

"Of course I've *thought* of it," she said, suddenly bitter after all these years of placid obedience. But she kept her voice smooth and uninflected. "And then I think a little further. Do I run away? My skills as a lady are not exactly valuable beyond the walls of this house. Do I advertise my services as a governess? I know nothing of children— nothing at all. Do I simply refuse and see whether my father loves me enough to not disown me? I'm not sure I have the courage to find out."

He rubbed the corner of a page between his fingers. "How do you stand it?"

This time there was no undertone of accusation to his question. If she wanted to, she might even detect a bleak sympathy. Which only fed her misery, that foul beast with teeth like knives.

"I keep myself busy and do not think too deeply about it," she said, in as harsh a tone as she'd ever allowed herself.

There, she was a mindless automaton who did as others instructed: getting up, going to sleep, and earning heaps of disdain from prospective husbands in between.

They said nothing more to each other, except to exchange the usual civilities at the end of her performance. Everyone applauded. Mrs. Clements said very nice things about Millie's musicianship—which Millie barely heard.

The rest of the evening lasted the length of Elizabeth's reign.

Mr. Graves, usually so phlegmatic and taciturn, engaged the earl in a lively discussion of cricket. Millie and Mrs. Graves gave their attention to Colonel Clements's army stories. Had someone looked in from the window, the company in the drawing room would have appeared perfectly normal, jovial even.

And yet there was enough misery present to wilt flowers and curl wallpaper. Nobody noticed the earl's distress. And nobody—except Mrs. Graves, who stole anxious looks at Millie—noticed Millie's. Was unhappiness really so invisible? Or did people simply prefer to turn away, as if from lepers?

After the guests took their leave, Mr. Graves pronounced the dinner a *succès énorme*. And he, who'd remained skeptical on the previous earl throughout, gave his ringing endorsement to the young successor. "I shall be pleased to have Lord Fitzhugh for a son-in-law."

"He hasn't proposed yet," Millie reminded him, "and he might not."

Or so she hoped. Let them find someone else for her. Anyone else.

"Oh, he will most assuredly propose," said Mr. Graves. "He has no choice."

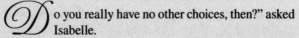 o you really have no other choices, then?" asked Isabelle.

Her eyes were bright with unshed tears. Futility burned inside Fitz. He could do nothing to halt this future that hurtled toward him like a derailed train, and even less to alleviate the pain of the girl he loved.

"If I do, it is only in the sense that I am free to go to London and see if a different heiress will have me."

She turned her face away and wiped her eyes with the heel of her hand. "What is she like, this Miss Graves?"

What did it matter? He could not recall her face. Nor did he want to. "Unobjectionable."

"Is she pretty?"

He shook his head. "I don't know—and I don't care."

She was not Isabelle—she could never be pretty enough.

It was unbearable to think of Miss Graves as a permanent fixture in his life. He felt violated. He raised the shotgun in his hands and pulled the trigger. Fifty feet away, a clay pigeon exploded. The ground was littered with shards: It had been an excruciating conversation.

"So, this time next year, you could have a child," said Isabelle, her voice breaking. "The Graveses would want their money's worth—and soon."

God, they would expect that of him, wouldn't they? Another clay pigeon burst apart; he scarcely felt the recoil in his shoulder.

It hadn't seemed quite so terrible at first, becoming an earl out of the blue. He realized almost immediately he'd have to give up his plan of a career in the military: An earl, even a poor one, was too valuable for the front line. The blow, although harsh, was far from fatal. He'd chosen the military for the demands it would place on him. Returning an estate from the brink of ruin was just as demanding and honorable an occupation. And he did not think Isabelle would at all mind becoming a ladyship: She would cut a dashing figure in Society.

But as he stepped into Henley Park, his new seat, his blood began to congeal. At nineteen, he had not become a poor earl, but a desperately destitute one.

The manor's decline was frightful. The oriental carpets were moth-eaten, the velvet curtains similarly so. Many of the flues drew not at all; walls and paintings were grimy with soot. And in every last upper-story room, the ceiling was green and grey with growth of mold, spreading like the contours of a distorted map.

Such a large house demanded fifty indoor servants and could limp by with thirty. But at Henley Park, the indoor staff had been reduced to fifteen, roughly divided between the too young—several of the maids were barely twelve—and the too old, retainers who had been with the family for their entire lives and had nowhere else to go.

Everything in his room creaked: the floor, the bed, the doors of the wardrobe. The plumbing was medieval—the long decline of the family's fortune had precluded any meaningful modernization of the interior. And for the three nights of his stay, he'd gone to sleep shivering with cold, listening to the congregation of rats in the walls.

It was a step above outright dilapidation, but only a very small step.

Isabelle's family was thoroughly respectable. The Pelhams, like the Fitzhughs, were related to several noble lineages and in general considered just the sort of solid, upstanding, God-fearing country gentry that did the squirearchy proud. But neither the Fitzhughs nor the Pelhams were wealthy; what funds they could scrape together would not keep Henley Park's roof from leaking, or her foundation from rotting.

But if it were only the house, they might still have

somehow managed with various economies. Unfortunately, Fitz also inherited eighty thousand pounds in debt. And from that, there was no escape.

Were he ten years younger, he could bury his head in the sand and let Colonel Clements worry about his problems. But he was only two years short of majority, a man nearly grown. He could not run away from his troubles, which assuredly would only worsen during any period of inattention.

The only viable solution was the sale of his person, to exchange his cursed title for an heiress with a fortune large enough to pay his debts and repair his house.

But to do that, he would have to give up Isabelle.

"Please, let's not speak of it," he said, his teeth clenched.

He didn't want much in life. The path he'd delineated for himself had been simple and straightforward: officer training at Sandhurst, a commission to follow, and when he'd received his first promotion, Isabelle's hand in marriage. She was not only beautiful, but intelligent, hardy, and adventurous. They would have been deliriously happy together.

Tears rolled down her face. "But whether we speak of it or not, it's going to happen, isn't it?"

She raised her shotgun and blasted the last remaining clay pigeon to pieces. His heart was similarly shattered.

"No matter what happens . . ."

He could not continue. He was no longer in a position to declare his love for her. Whatever he said would only make things worse.

"Don't marry her," she implored, her voice hoarse, her eyes fervent. "Forget Henley Park. Let's run away together."

If only they could. "Neither of us is of age. Our marriage wouldn't be valid without the consent of your father and my guardian. I don't know about your father, but Colonel Clements is dead set on my doing my duty. He'd rather see you ruined than allow our marriage to stand."

Overhead thunder rolled. "Isabelle, Lord Fitzhugh," cried her mother's voice from inside the house, "better come back. It's going to rain soon!"

Neither of them moved.

Drops of rain fell on his head, each as heavy as a pebble.

Isabelle gazed at him. "Do you remember the first time you came to visit?"

"Of course."

He'd been sixteen, she fifteen. It had been at the end of Michaelmas Half. And he'd arrived with Pelham, Hastings, and two other mates from Eton. She'd sprinted down the stairs to hug Pelham. Fitz had met her before, when she'd come to see Pelham at Eton. But on that day, suddenly, she was no longer the little girl she'd been, but a lovely young lady, full of life and verve. The afternoon sun, slanting into the hall, had lit her like a flame. And when she'd turned around and said, "Ah, Mr. Fitzhugh, I remember you," he was already in love.

"Do you remember the fight scene from *Romeo and Juliet*?" she asked softly.

He nodded. Would that time flowed backward, so he could leave the present behind and head toward those older, more joyous days instead.

"I remember everything so clearly: Gerry was Tybalt and you Mercutio. You had one of my father's walking sticks in one hand and a tea sandwich in the other. You took a bite of the sandwich, and sneered, 'Tybalt, you rat-catcher, will you walk?'" She smiled through her tears. "Then you laughed. My heart caught and I knew then and there that I wanted to spend my life with you."

His face was wet. "You'll find someone better," he forced himself to say.

"I don't want anyone else. I want only you."

And he wanted only her. But it was not to be. They were not to be.

Rain came down in sheets. It had been a miserable spring. Already he despaired of ever again walking under an unclouded sky.

"Isabelle, Lord Fitzhugh, you must come inside now," repeated Mrs. Pelham.

They ran. But as they reached the side of the house, she gripped his arm and pulled him toward her. "Kiss me."

"I mustn't. Even if I don't marry Miss Graves, I'm to marry someone else."

"Have you ever kissed anyone?"

"No." He'd been waiting for her.

"All the more reason you must kiss me now. So that no matter what happens, we will always be each other's first."

Lightning split the sky. He stared at the beautiful girl who would never be his. Was it so wrong?

It must not be, because the next moment he was kissing her, lost to everything else but this one last moment of freedom and joy.

And when they could no longer delay their return to the house, he held her tight and whispered what he'd promised himself he would not say.

"No matter what happens, I will always, always love you."

CHAPTER 2

Eight years later, 1896

"I hear Mrs. Englewood has arrived in London," said Millicent, Lady Fitzhugh, at breakfast.

Fitz looked up from his paper. The strangest thing: His wife never gossiped, yet she seemed to know everything the moment it happened.

She wore a morning gown of cornflower blue. The morning gown, worn strictly indoors among intimates, was looser of form and construction than its more tightly corseted cousins the promenade gown and the visiting gown. But there was something about his wife that was highly—almost excessively—neat, so that even the slouchier morning gown looked prim and precise on her.

Her light brown hair was pulled back into a tight bun, not a strand loose—never a strand loose, except when she'd smashed a brick fireplace wielding a sledgehammer. Her eyes, a similar shade to her hair, busily scanned one invitation after another. Sweet eyes—she never looked upon anyone in anger, seldom even in displeasure.

Sometimes it surprised him how young she still looked. How young she still *was*. They'd been married almost eight years and she was not even twenty-five.

"Yes," he answered, "your information is correct, as usual."

She reached for the salt cellar. "When did *you* learn?"

"Yesterday evening," he said, his heart skipping a beat with anticipation.

Isabelle. Seven years it had been since his last glimpse of her on her wedding day. Eight, since they last spoke.

And now she was coming back into his life, a free woman.

Lady Fitz sliced open another envelope and glanced at its content. "She will be eager to see you, I'm sure."

He had known, since he first met the former Millicent Graves, that she was unusually self-possessed. Still, sometimes her even-keeledness surprised him. He knew of no other wife who combined this sincere interest in a husband's welfare with such a lack of possessiveness—at least none who didn't have a lover of her own.

"One hopes," he said.

"Would you like me to rearrange your schedule in any way?" she asked without looking at him. "If I'm not mistaken, we are expected tomorrow at the bottling plant to taste the champagne cider and the new lemon-flavor soda water. And the day after tomorrow, the biscuit factory for cream wafers and chocolate croquette."

Isabelle's return had coincided with the semiannual taste test of new product ideas at Cresswell & Graves.

"Thank you, but it won't be necessary: I am invited to call on her today itself."

"Oh," said his wife.

Her countenance often reminded him of blancmange, smooth, mild, and perfectly set. But this moment, an unnamed emotion flickered across her features. And suddenly she resembled not so much a bland dish of pudding as the surface of a well-known, yet never explored lake, and he, standing on the banks, had just seen a movement underwater, an enigmatic shadow that disappeared so quickly he wasn't sure he hadn't imagined the whole thing.

"Then you must convey my regards," she said, reaching again for the salt cellar.

"I shall."

She inspected the rest of the post in her pile, finished her tea, and rose—she always arrived to and left from breakfast before he did. "Don't forget we are expected to dinner at the Queensberrys'."

"I won't."

"Good day, then, sir."

"Good day, Lady Fitz."

Her gait was as neat as her person, her blue skirts barely swishing as she turned down the corridor. By habit he listened as her footsteps receded, the cadence and lightness of her footfalls almost as familiar to him as the rhythm of his own breaths.

When he could hear her no more, he pulled Isabelle's note out of the inside pocket of his day coat and read it again.

My Dearest Fitz,

(Am I too forward in the salutation itself? No matter, I have never been the least reticent and I certainly won't change now.)

Thank you for the lovely house you have arranged for myself and the children. They adore the garden, tucked away from sight. I am particularly fond of the bright, cheerful parlor, which overlooks the green square just across the street.

Such a long time it has been since I last saw you, a few more days ought not to matter very much. Yet I find myself extraordinarily impatient to meet again, even though the house is clearly not yet ready to receive callers. Will you come tomorrow?

Yours,
Isabelle

The letter was most cordial, and her signature the warmest element of all. He had thought of her as Isabelle for many years, but had only ever addressed her as Miss Pelham or—in his recent correspondence—Mrs. Englewood. For her to close her letter with her given name was an unmistakable invitation to further intimacy.

Isabelle. The first girl he'd kissed. The only one he'd ever loved.

He tucked away the note and opened his newspaper again. A maid came to take away Lady Fitz's plate.

A thought occurred to him. "Bring me the plate."

The maid looked at him uncomprehendingly.

"The plate in your hand."

His wife had left behind some scrambled eggs, which was most unlike her: One served oneself at breakfast and she never took more than she could eat. To the maid's surprise, he picked up a piece of the scrambled eggs with his fork.

And would not have been able to swallow it without the help of his coffee. He knew she liked her eggs salted, but this was less scrambled egg than scrambled salt. He'd have to speak to her about it next time he saw her: This much salt in the diet must be injurious to the health.

As unthinkable as it had been eight years ago, they'd become good friends. And friends watched out for one another.

*M*illie met Helena, Fitz's twin, as the latter came out of her room. The twins did not look alike. Fitz, with his black hair and blue eyes, bore a much greater resemblance to their elder sister Venetia. Helena, on the other hand, had inherited their maternal grandmother's auburn hair and green eyes.

This morning Helena was in a hunter green velvet jacket and a matching skirt. Between the lapels of the jacket, the front pleats of her white shirtwaist were as crisp as morning air. A cameo brooch at her throat, featuring not a woman's profile in ivory, but an onyx Roman eagle, completed her ensemble.

Venetia was considered the great beauty of the family, but Helena was lovely in her own right, not to mention confident, capable—and more devious than any of them had suspected.

At the beginning of the year, Fitz's best friend, Lord Hastings, had found out that Helena was having a clandestine affair with Mr. Andrew Martin. Mr. Martin was a nice young man and Millie did not doubt he adored Helena as much as she adored him. The problem was that he'd adored Helena since they first met years ago, but never had the courage to defy his mother and the long-standing family expectation to marry his third cousin.

Millie understood the force of first love—she herself firmly remained in the grip of her own. But Mr. Martin was a married man and Helena, by taking up with him, had placed her reputation in grave peril. Millie and Venetia had whisked Helena to the other side of the Atlantic as soon as they could, in the hope that by distancing Helena from Mr. Martin, she might come to her senses.

The American trip had not been entirely wasted—a series of events begun there had culminated in Venetia's unexpected but deliriously happy marriage to the Duke of Lexington. But unfortunately, in Helena's case, absence only made her heart grow fonder of Mr. Martin.

Helena was both of age and financially independent; her family could not coerce her to give up Mr. Martin. But since January, they'd kept a constant eye on her. Helena never went anywhere without either Venetia, Millie, or her new maid Susie, hired expressly for this purpose, keeping her company.

Susie had already left earlier, so that when the Fitzhugh carriage dropped off Helena at her small publishing firm on Fleet Street, she'd be there, waiting. Then she would sit outside the door of Helena's office, to make sure Helena did not slip out in the middle of the day for an illicit rendezvous with Mr. Martin.

This incessant surveillance was taking a toll on Helena. She looked restless and just shy of miserable. Millie hated having to be one of her jailors, but she had no choice. If Helena wouldn't think of her future, then her family must do the thinking for her.

"Helena, just the person I want to see," she said brightly. "Remember you are to attend Lady Margaret Dearborn's at-home tea this afternoon."

An affair was no reason to stop appearing at functions designed to introduce her to eligible young men—or it would look like her family had given up all hopes of marrying her off. And that would never do.

Helena was not pleased at the prospect of the at-home tea. "Lady Margaret Dearborn runs with the horse-and-hound set. Her guests never talk about anything but the fox hunt."

"You've published a memoir on fox hunting, if I recall."

"Published on commission at no risk to me, or I'd never have taken it on."

"Still, that gives you something to talk about with the horse-and-hound set." Millie raised herself to her toes and kissed Helena on her cheek. "Your carriage awaits, my love. I will see you in the afternoon."

"Wait," said Helena. "Is it true what I hear? That Mrs. Englewood is back in England?"

Mille ignored the pang in her chest and nodded. "Fitz will be calling on her this afternoon. Quite a momentous day for them, isn't it?"

"I imagine." The question in Helena's eyes, however, was not about Fitz, but about Millie.

Millie was never possessive, never effusive, and never demonstrative. Her even-tempered approach to her marriage should have been enough to convince everyone that she admired, but did not love, her husband. Yet for years now, his sisters had suspected something else.

Perhaps unrequited love was like a specter in the house,

a presence that brushed at the edge of senses, a heat in the dark, a shadow under the sun.

She patted Helena on the arm and walked away.

*T*he garden had come to life.

The grass was as green as a river bank, the trees tall and shady. Birds sang in the branches; the fountain trickled and murmured. In a corner of the garden, purple hydrangeas were in bloom, each flower head as big and bright as a nosegay.

Have a garden, Mrs. Graves had counseled Millie on her wedding. *A garden and a bench.*

Millie spread her fingers on the slats of the bench. It was simple but handsome, made of oak and varnished a light, warm brown. The bench did not belong to her; it had been here for as long as she'd been Fitz's wife. But at Henley Park, there was an almost exact replica, which Fitz had given her a few years ago, as a token of his regard.

And she'd seen it as such a sign of hope—more fool she.

"I thought you might be here," said her husband.

Surprised, she looked over her shoulder. He stood behind the bench, his hands lightly resting on its back—the same elegant hands that had turned music for her while his words had turned her inside out.

Now on his right index finger, he wore a signet ring the crest of which bore an intaglio engraving of the Fitzhugh coat of arms. The ring had been a present from her. The sight of it on his hand had stirred her then and stirred her still.

She wanted to touch it. Lick it. Feel its metallic caress everywhere on her body.

"I thought you'd already left."

From her perch upstairs, she'd watched him stroll away. It was early yet, hours from his meeting with Mrs. Englewood. But as he'd turned the corner, he'd swung his walking stick a full circle in the air. That, coming from him, was the equivalent of another man dancing in the streets.

"I realized I will be going past Hatchard's today," he said. "Would you like me to check whether your order of books has come in?"

"That's very kind of you, but surely, you have a busy day ahead and—"

"It's settled, then: I'll have a quick word with the bookseller."

"Thank you," she murmured.

He smiled. "My pleasure."

She'd mentioned the special order she'd put in at Hatchard's once, days ago. That he'd remembered and offered to check for her would have thrilled her another time—she'd have taken it as yet another sign that they were growing ever closer.

Today his consideration only signified that he himself was gloriously happy at the prospect of seeing his beloved. He was summertime itself, young, luminous, lit from within by rekindled hopes and reawakened dreams. And every beggar along his path—herself included—could expect redoubled generosity and kindness.

He turned to leave but stopped. "I almost forgot, you ought to be more mindful of your intake of salt—you put enough into your scrambled eggs to preserve them for the next decade."

And then he was gone, leaving her alone in the garden.

* * *

$\mathcal{F}$itz stood outside Isabelle's house.

He thought he'd learned to be levelheaded, but every emotion that tumbled through him was unrestrained, heart-stopping. Second chances—not many received such graces, and even fewer were in a position to seize them with both hands.

Dread and hope pulsed in his blood with equal intensity. So many years had passed. He'd changed. She, too, must have changed. Would they even have anything to say to each other when they came face-to-face?

He rang the bell. A maid in a large white cap and a long white bib opened the door, took his card, and asked him to follow her into the house. He stopped, however, in the vestibule, empty except for a rectangular mirror and a narrow console table underneath. A silver tray for calling cards sat on the table. Beside it, an instantly recognizable photograph.

He had a copy of the same photograph somewhere in the depths of his dressing room. It had been taken near the end of his first stay at the Pelham house, the ladies in their Sunday finery seated in the front row, the gentlemen, a solemn-looking lot, standing behind them. He himself looked impossibly young; Isabelle was uncharacteristically demure, her hands folded chastely in her lap.

But those hands concealed a secret. Directly after the photographer pronounced himself satisfied, she'd pulled Fitz aside and given him what she'd been stowing in her pocket: a tiny dormouse she'd named Alice. Alice had been the perfect pet for a busy student: She hibernated for much of Michaelmas Half and all of Lent Half, emerging only in April to live in his pocket on a delicate diet of berries, nuts, and an occasional caterpillar.

"I always keep that photograph close to me," said a familiar voice. "It's the only one I have of you."

He set down the photograph and carefully, slowly, turned toward her.

Isabelle.

She was both taller and leaner than he remembered—and not eighteen anymore. Her face had settled into a somewhat harsher shape. There was tension to the contour of her jaw. Her skin seemed to require a greater effort to stretch over her features.

But those features were as chiseled and proud as ever. Her hair was the same blue black. The fire in her eyes remained undiminished. And in the intensity of her gaze he recognized the Isabelle Pelham of yesteryear.

And at the sight of her, long-lost memories, recollections that had become as faded as pages in an ancient manuscript, suddenly reacquired color, brightness, and focus. Isabelle in spring, holding an armful of hyacinths. Isabelle in her white tennis dress, waving her racquet at him, her smile brighter than the sun shining on the deep green lawn. Isabelle crunching fallen leaves underfoot, turning occasionally to say something to her governess, who trailed several steps behind them, and whom he barely noticed, because he had eyes only for his girl.

"Mrs. Englewood," he said. "How do you do?"

"Fitz, my goodness," she murmured. "You are exactly as I remember you. *Exactly.*"

He smiled. "I still look nineteen?"

"No, of course not. You are a man full grown. But the essence of you has not changed at all." She shook her head slightly, as if in wonder. "Come, we can't hold a conversation in a passage. Let's sit down."

The tea things had already been laid out in readiness. Isabelle poured for them both.

"Tell me everything," she said.

"Tell me about India," he said at the same time.

They both smiled. He insisted that she regale him first with her stories, so she did. Delhi was unbearably hot in the month of April. Kashmir was very likely the most beautiful place on earth, especially Srinagar on the shores of Dal Lake. And she enjoyed the food of Hyderabad the best. He, in turn, gave her the latest on their mutual friends and acquaintances: courtships, marriages, children, and scandals minor and major.

An hour flew by.

Eventually she lifted her teacup and looked at him. "You haven't said a thing about yourself, Fitz. How have you been?"

How *had* he been? "I can't complain," he said.

Isabelle's gaze was fluid and just slight mocking. A smile played at the corners of her lips. How well he recalled this particular expression on her—she was about to say something naughty. "I hear you have been very successful with the ladies."

He lowered his gaze. Between the two of them, he'd always been the shyer one. "It's a way to pass time."

A way to cope—and to forget.

"Lady Fitzhugh is very understanding, then."

"She's always been very sensible."

"When I was still in India I'd heard it said that the two of you got on very well. I hadn't quite believed it—but I guess it's true."

At last they came to it, the subject of his marriage. Her face turned somber, her gaze that of one regarding a friend's tombstone.

"For someone who had no say in the matter," he said, "I've been fortunate in the wife I've been allotted."

"So . . . you are glad you married her?"

He did not look away this time. "I didn't say that. You know I'd have crawled over broken glass to marry you, had the circumstances been different."

"Yes," she said, her voice unsteady. "Yes, I know that."

The front door of the house opened and in wafted the sounds of children at lively chatter, followed by a quick "shhh" from their minder.

"Excuse me a moment," said Isabelle. She left the parlor and came back with a boy and a girl. "May I present Hyacinth and Alexander Englewood. Children, this is Lord Fitzhugh, an old friend of Uncle Pelly's and Mama's."

Hyacinth was six, Alexander a year younger, both beautiful, both with their mother's coloring. Suddenly, Fitz couldn't speak. Had things been different, they would have been *his* children, and would not regard him with solemn, curious wariness, but run to him with open arms and wide grins.

They stayed only a minute before leaving for the recesses of the house with their governess. Isabelle lingered a moment at the door, her eyes following them. "They grow up so fast."

Fitz swallowed a lump in his throat. "You always did like the names Hyacinth and Alexander."

"I did. Hyacinth and Alexander Fitzhugh," she murmured, a sheen of tears in her eyes.

She retook her seat. The sun streaming in from the open

curtains sparkled on the gold trim of the saucers. She turned her cup round and round on its saucer—she was never one for staying still.

And then she looked at him, bold, resolute, Isabelle as he'd always remembered. "Is it too late to reclaim some of what we could have had?"

As if she had to ask. As if he hadn't been thinking of the very same in the weeks since her first letter arrived. As if he wouldn't hold on to this rare, priceless second chance with both arms and never again let go.

"No," he said. "It's not too late."

CHAPTER 3

The Pact

1888 ～

A fortnight after the dinner, lawyers from both sides sat down once more at the negotiating table. But while the new earl had capitulated to the demands of his estate, the price he asked for his surrender was as steep as the Matterhorn.

Such was the influence of youth and beauty that Mr. Graves barely grumbled over having to pay nearly twice as much for *this* earl. The negotiations concluded quickly and Millie once again found herself engaged to marry.

Throughout it all, she never once heard from Lord Fitzhugh himself. There were no notes, no flowers, and no engagement ring. Citing his studies, he declined a second dinner with the Graves. For the Fourth of June, the biggest holiday at Eton, a time when friends and family flocked to the school, the Graves received not a single invitation to participate in the festivities.

And why should he act differently? Were Millie Lord Fitzhugh, she, too, would furiously enjoy the final days of her freedom and waste not a precious second on those to whom she'd soon be shackled for the rest of her life.

But understanding why he was so distant only made things worse. When she wasn't buffeted by misery, she was overcome with shame. To him, she would always symbolize everything that was *un*appealing about coming of age: the crushing pressures of duty, the paucity of choices, and the appalling necessity to forgo dreams to pay creditors.

No aloofness on Lord Fitzhugh's part, however, could dissuade Mrs. Graves from dragging Millie to Lord's Cricket Ground on the day of the Eton and Harrow game.

Cricket was popular, a pastime enjoyed by young and old, gentlemen and laborers. More easygoing parsons sometimes joined their parishioners for a Sunday afternoon match. And certainly it was *the* dominant game in the lives of schoolboys.

The Eton and Harrow game at Lord's, however, was not a sporting event. Or rather, the sporting event was but an excuse for all of Society to gather for a merry daylong picnic under a fair summer sun. And since no invitations were needed at Lord's, it was also one of the few opportunities for the merely rich to rub elbows with the blue-blooded.

For that reason, Mrs. Graves always began planning for what she and her daughter would wear to the grand event months in advance. But two years in a row, they'd had to abstain, first because of the passing of Millie's maternal grandfather, then due to severe abdominal troubles that had left Mr. Graves in need of his wife's and daughter's tender attention.

This year, with no one expiring and no one remotely under the weather, Millie could only watch helplessly as Mrs. Graves, in a burst of energy, orchestrated the outing.

On the first day of the match, their beautiful landau, its boot laden with picnic baskets, was dispatched to St. John's Wood before the crack of dawn, to secure a place for the ladies at the side of the cricket ground. The ladies themselves, however, did not leave the house until eleven o'clock, arrayed in the latest gowns from Worth's Paris atelier.

Cricket was not the point. The point was to see and be seen—and that was best done during the luncheon hour.

They arrived just as the players were walking off the field. With an alacrity that belied her complaints of arthritic joints, Mrs. Graves leaped down from the second-best carriage that had conveyed them to the outskirts of the cricket ground, which was now ringed by carriages three, sometimes, five deep. Pulling Millie along, she joined the great stampede of spectators making for the playing field that the two teams had just vacated.

The sky was a flawless blue, the clipped lawn a lively green. Thousands of ladies in their spring best milled about, splashes of pastels everywhere one looked, set off all the better against the somber black of the gentlemen's day coats, like gems upon the dark velvet of a jewelry box.

It was a marvelous sight, if one were of the mind to enjoy the day. Millie was not. She'd never been one to relish public attention, especially not the kind of sidelong glances she gathered in her extravagant clothes that were beyond the means of many wellborn ladies. Worse, Mrs. Graves had turned into Parvenu Mother.

Mrs. Graves was not normally Parvenu Mother: She was proud of the haute bourgeoisie respectability from which she came. Social climbing was never foremost on her mind. She did it out of duty to her husband's kin, especially his dead father and brother, both of whom had longed fiercely to ally the family with noble blood.

But this particular occasion seemed to turn her head. She informed everyone who would stand still that her daughter, paired with the winsome Lord Fitzhugh, was going to take Society by storm. *Oh, my Millie has the most charming figure on the dance floor. Oh, my Millie has the most captivating way with conversation. Oh, the worst snobs among them will admire my Millie and she will be invited everywhere.*

Millie's protestation of her mediocre appeal only made Mrs. Graves scale ever greater heights of hyperbole.

Finally Mrs. Graves ran into an old friend who knew all about Millie's imminent ascension as the Countess Fitzhugh and who was already convinced that Millie would set a new standard of popularity as a Society hostess. As a result, their conversation revolved around Millie's trousseau, her wedding breakfast, and her honeymoon.

As Mrs. Graves waxed poetic about a honeymoon in Rome, which she herself would have enjoyed, were it not for Mr. Graves's virulent objection to eating nothing but macaroni for two continuous weeks, the crowd shifted, revealing Lord Fitzhugh.

He stood amidst a flock of uniformed Eton students and their butterfly-bright sisters. There were at least five girls, but he had eyes only for one, a beautiful young lady with jet-black hair and lips of the loveliest pink Millie had ever seen, the color of Mrs. Graves's prize peonies.

Millie was envious, but not overly alarmed at first: It was only too normal for a young man's attention to be drawn to a beautiful young woman. Then she saw that the earl's gaze was not one of mere interest, but of desperate yearning, as if he were a prisoner in his cell, staring at the tiny square of sky allotted him.

It shattered Millie. For all her hair-rending over his reluctance to marry her, she'd yet to consider that he might be in love with someone else. But he was, wasn't he, desperately in love? And desperately unhappy for the loss of his beloved.

She was frantic to hide herself. He must not see her. He must not think that she'd come to be near him. And he must never, never know that she felt anything for him besides a polite obligation.

God heard her prayers: The warning gong sounded. Millie tapped Mrs. Graves on the sleeve. "The game is to resume soon, Mother. Shall we return to our carriage?"

Mrs. Graves scoffed at her suggestion. "No one gets off the field until at least the second gong."

A look around showed that, unfortunately, Mrs. Graves was right. The happy crowd remained firmly affixed. Laughter boomed like artillery shots all around her, each one leaving a new dent on her heart.

She glanced toward the earl, hoping he hadn't seen her. But just then he looked in her direction. Their eyes met. And the expression on his face—a recoil of the soul—told her everything she already knew and could no longer deny.

She wrenched her gaze away, crushed beyond all endurance.

* * *

*T*he second warning gong rang, louder and more strident. And with it came the police, ready to enforce the resumption of the game, if need be. But of course the elegant crowd who attended the Eton and Harrow game would never be mixed up with the police. Ladies and gentlemen melted from the playing ground, back to the stands, the benches, and the carriages.

Mrs. Graves's visiting, however, continued for another hour. Millie was glad for the excuse to turn her back on the game. But everywhere they went, there seemed to be a young boy nearby, a cricket fanatic who pestered his mother and sisters to watch the goings-on. The earl's name came up all too often.

Did you see that? Fitzhugh just sent one clear over the boundary. That's six runs! shouted an Eton enthusiast.

No, not another one out of bounds! At least it touched ground, so only four runs, grumbled a Harrow supporter. *Fitzhugh already scored ninety. When is he going to be dismissed?*

At last they returned to their landau and ate their picnic luncheon.

"Shall we go now?" Millie asked Mrs. Graves.

"Of course not," answered Mrs. Graves. "When the match breaks for tea, we will go to the Eton pavilion and have your fiancé present his friends to you."

His mates had to know how he truly felt. They'd probably already commiserated with him. Should Mrs. Graves begin to express her great delight, oblivious to the earl's

distaste for his imminent trip to the altar—Millie could
well imagine the snickering.

"But we have not been invited to approach the Eton
pavilion and we—"

Mrs. Graves placed her gloved hand over Millie's. "My
dear, you must not feel apologetic about this marriage.
Never forget all that you are bringing to the marriage and
never consider yourself inferior simply because he is young
and handsome. He is getting the better bargain here. Do
you understand?"

The real question was, did *he* understand?

He did not. And he would not.

Mrs. Graves touched Millie's cheek. "I love your father
dearly, but how I wish he were not so needlessly stubborn
on the matter of your marriage. You should have a husband
who treasures you, for no man can possibly be more fortunate than the one who has your hand.

"But reality being what it is, I have brought you here
today. Do not hide, my love. And do not retreat. I know it
will not be easy for you. But it will only be worse if you lock
yourself in a cupboard. Hold your head high. Stake out your
ground. So he hasn't invited us when he should have. That
means it is up to you to make your presence felt, to compel
him to publicly acknowledge your position in his life."

She couldn't. She had nothing in her to compel anyone.
She only wanted to disappear.

"Yes, Mother," she said.

"Good." Mrs. Graves patted Millie on her shoulder.
"Now let me close my eyes for a moment. Then we will
show our magnificent selves to Lord Fitzhugh. And he'd
better be properly awed and pleased."

* * *

*M*rs. Graves napped. Millie wrestled with her handkerchief. The boy in the next-over carriage narrated the general goings-on, thankfully not bothering with the names of the individual players.

Abruptly the boy fell silent—midsentence. Millie glanced his way, wondering whether he'd choked on something he was eating. But the boy only stared ahead, his jaw halfway to the ground.

He was not alone. The other occupants of his carriage—parents, a sister, and a brother—wore similar expressions of frozen astonishment. Around them, other people in other carriages also stopped what they were doing to stare in the same general direction.

Millie turned around and beheld the most beautiful woman on God's green earth. A mythological creature, surely, Helen of Troy reincarnated or Aphrodite herself, down from Mount Olympus to rendezvous with her Adonis.

She probably did not walk, but glided over the ground. Her cream lace parasol shielded a face that was at once flawless in its symmetry and unsettling in some indescribable way that separated the beautiful from the merely pretty. Millie could swear that the clouds, which had shielded the crowd from the sun for the past half hour, allowed one brilliant ray to fall on the woman, to illuminate her singular beauty, because it would have been a discourtesy for such loveliness to not also be perfectly lit.

Impossibly enough, she approached the Graves carriage.

"Miss Graves, is it not?" she asked, smiling.

Her smile was so stunning that Millie nearly tumbled backward. She had to fish around for her voice. And was she Miss Graves?

"Ah . . . yes?"

"I know it is rude to introduce oneself, but seeing as we are going to be family soon, I hoped you wouldn't mind terribly."

Millie had no idea what the stranger was talking about. In fact, she barely heard any words, her attention entirely taken by the movements of the woman's lips. But she was sure of one thing: No matter what the woman wanted, no one would ever, ever mind.

"No, no, of course not."

"I am Mrs. Townsend. And this lovely young lady is my sister, Miss Fitzhugh."

Until Mrs. Townsend introduced her companion, Millie hadn't even noticed that there was anyone with her. Indeed there was, a tall, slender redhead who was quite pretty in her own right.

"Very pleased to meet you both, I'm sure," said Millie, still agog at Mrs. Townsend's beauty.

"You are engaged to marry my twin," said Miss Fitzhugh, who had noticed that Millie had lost all powers of reasoning.

"Oh, of course."

He had sisters. Millie knew that. And now that she'd been jolted out of her daze, she even remembered that the sisters had been abroad, Miss Fitzhugh at school in Switzerland, and the incomparable Mrs. Townsend in the Himalayas, on safari with her husband.

"Mr. Townsend and I started back as soon as we learned of the previous earl's passing. We traveled as fast as we could, but we crossed the channel only yesterday," explained Mrs. Townsend, "after retrieving Miss Fitzhugh from Geneva."

At first Millie had thought Mrs. Townsend as ageless as a goddess, but the latter was actually quite young, barely over the cusp of twenty.

"And I am glad we hurried," continued Mrs. Townsend. "It was not until we landed that we learned the date of the wedding had already been set."

Mr. Graves, not wanting to lose another potential son-in-law to the vagaries of fortune, had demanded that the wedding take place as soon as the financial agreements had been reached. But Lord Fitzhugh refused absolutely: He would not marry while he was still at school. The ceremony had therefore been scheduled the day after the end of summer term, a little more than two weeks away.

"Our brother is a very fine young man—the finest there is," Mrs. Townsend went on. "But he *is* a man and as such can be relied upon to know nothing of what needs to be done in case of an engagement and a wedding. Besides, he can't orchestrate anything from Eton. But now that I am back, we shall proceed apace, beginning with a garden party to introduce you to our friends, a dinner to celebrate the engagement, and of course, when you have returned from your honeymoon, a ball in your honor—a country ball, that is, since London will have emptied by then."

Millie had thought herself completely disillusioned. It was not true; there had been one last barrier of hope around her heart: A belief that at least some of Lord Fitzhugh's disdain had not been his own, but a reflection of his family's aversion at the kind of marriage he must contract to keep their fortunes afloat.

Now that his sisters had shown themselves to be kind and helpful, Mrs. Townsend offering to throw her weight behind Millie's entry into Society, Millie had no more excuses to turn to.

This marriage would crush her.

She could not run. She could not hide. And the wedding was in two weeks.

 hen the idea came, it was as fully formed as Athena, leaping out of Zeus's forehead. Millie only wondered that she hadn't thought of it earlier.

Or perhaps she had, in all the days and nights since it became clear that she was going to become Lord Fitzhugh's wife. Beneath her trying not to imagine the worst, perhaps she had been planning for just that.

Mrs. Graves woke up shortly after Mrs. Townsend announced her plans for the party, the dinner, and the ball. Millie's participation was no longer needed, leaving her free to examine and refine her plan, while pretending to listen to the discussion.

At teatime, the walk to the Eton players' pavilion was very long—and all too short.

The introductions to Lord Fitzhugh's friends were a blur. Millie was grateful for Mrs. Townsend, in whose presence the young men could barely form coherent sentences, let alone remember that Lord Fitzhugh did not want to marry this mousy girl to whom they were being presented.

Then, quietly, she made the request to Lord Fitzhugh for a word. Thanks to the magnetic pull of Mrs. Townsend, all Lord Fitzhugh had to do was lead Millie a few paces

43

away from the eager cricket players trying to impress his sister. The noise of the crowd milling about gave Millie and her fiancé all the privacy they needed.

He was leaner than she remembered, warier, his tone quiet. "What may I do for you, Miss Graves?"

Was this how he would always speak to her, with this meticulous, distant politeness? "I have been thinking about what you said the other day. You made me realize that yes, I *have* been forced into this. I was never given any other choice, never told that there was any other way to justify my existence on this earth but to be the conduit that united the Graves name with a lineage nobler and more ancient.

"It is a stupid goal. But such are the circumstances of our lives that we must hold our noses and proceed, or we shall both be far worse off. With your predecessor, there was no question that I would be expected to produce an heir as soon as possible. But—dare I assume you are not in as much of a hurry to rush headlong into fatherhood?"

He glanced to his left. She did not follow the direction of his gaze but she had no doubt that if she did, she would find the young lady he loved. "You would be correct," he said. "I have no desire to fill nurseries anytime soon."

"Neither do I. I do not want to become a mother in the immediate future. And perhaps not even in the intermediate future."

"So what do you propose? A nonprocreation covenant?" There was a grim humor to his voice, but none in his eyes.

"Something a little more comprehensive: a covenant of freedom."

He tilted his head; for the first time he appeared interested in the conversation. "What is it?"

"We say our vows and then, until the time comes for the matter of heirs, we live unencumbered—as if we'd never married. Notice I do not say as if you'd never been left the title. I cannot help you there: Unless you find a general willing to tolerate a lord in his ranks, you will not have a career in the army. But in everything else you should do as you wish: travel, enjoy your friends, woo all the ladies you care to. Go to university if it's what you'd like. There will be no nagging wife to answer to when you come home. No responsibilities; no consequences."

"And you? What will you do?"

"The same, except for the obvious differences, of course: There are certain things an unmarried girl does not do and I will hold myself to that standard. That aside, I will enjoy being the mistress of my own household. And I will not have to worry about how I will get on with my husband—at least for some years."

He was silent. In the afternoon sun, his cricket kit was brilliantly white, his person sensationally beautiful.

"Well, what do you think?"

"Sounds tempting. Any catches?"

"None whatsoever."

"All good things come to an end." He didn't sound as if he believed her entirely. "When does this covenant expire?"

She hadn't thought of a specific time limit, except that it should be long. "How about in six years?"

Six years was outrageous. Even if he halved the length, she should still have enough time to put herself back together again.

"Eight," said her fiancé.

He'd never touch you if he had the choice.

By now she should have become numb to the humiliation of this marriage, but her heart choked with pain. She squared her shoulders and offered him her hand to shake. "We are agreed, then."

He glanced down at her outstretched hand. For a moment his impassiveness foundered. His expression turned harsh with rebellion—but only for a moment. The deal was done, the contract signed. He had no choice; what he wanted was besides the point.

When his eyes met hers again, they were quite blank—the gaze of the dead.

"Agreed," he said, shaking her hand. His voice was equally blank, a wall that concealed his fury. "Thank you."

She trembled inside. "No need to thank me: I did it for myself."

A truer word she never spoke.

CHAPTER 4

1896

*T*hanks to a traffic logjam, by the time Helena and Millie returned from Lady Margaret Dearborn's at-home tea, there was barely enough time to change before heading out for dinner.

Fitz was waiting for them as they came down the stairs. "You both look lovely."

Helena could not see anything immediately different about her twin, who must have spoken to his Isabelle for the first time in eight years, but his gaze did linger on his wife longer than usual.

"Thank you, sir," said Millie. "We must hurry or we will surely be late."

Her tone was that of an ordinary wife in an ordinary marriage on an ordinary day. Strange that Fitz never seemed to notice how odd it was. Such perpetually neutral responses were unnatural—at least to Helena.

The conversation in the brougham on the way to the Queensberrys' was also largely ordinary: Society was still curious about their sister Venetia's elopement with the Duke of Lexington; people bought tinned goods in ever greater quantities; Helena reached an agreement with Miss Evangeline South, whose charming picture books she'd sought hard to publish.

It was only as they turned onto the Queensberrys' street that Millie asked, as if it were an afterthought, "And how is Mrs. Englewood?"

"She seems well—glad to be back," said Fitz. Then, after a small pause, "She introduced me to her children."

At last Helena detected a catch in his voice. Her chest constricted. She remembered his numb despair when he'd given them the news of his imminent wedding. She remembered the tears rolling down Venetia's cheeks—and her own. She remembered how difficult it had been not to cry in public the next time she'd run into Isabelle.

"They must be good-looking children," murmured Millie.

Fitz looked out the window. "Yes, they are. Exceptionally so."

Millie had timed her question perfectly: That precise moment, the brougham stopped before the Queensberry residence and no more was said of Isabelle Pelham Englewood or her children, as they entered the house and greeted the gathered friends and acquaintances.

Much to Helena's displeasure, Viscount Hastings was also present. Hastings was Fitz's best friend and the one who had informed her family of Helena's affair—*after* he'd swindled a kiss from Helena on the pretense of keeping her secret. His cheeky rationale was that he'd only promised to conceal the identity of her lover, not to hold silent on the affair itself.

Fortunately he had not been seated next to her at dinner—she was not to be trusted with implements that could stab him in the eye when she was exposed to his presence for more than a quarter hour at a time. But after dinner, when the gentlemen rejoined the ladies in the drawing room, he did not wait long before approaching her.

She'd been sharing a chaise longue with Millie and Mrs. Queensberry, who greeted Hastings with great cordiality, then, as if by conspiracy, both rose to mingle elsewhere in the room.

Hastings sat down and braced his arm along the back of the chaise, quite effectively letting it be known he did not want anyone else to join them.

"You look frustrated, Miss Fitzhugh." He lowered his voice. "Has your bed been empty of late?"

He knew very well she'd been watched more closely than prices on the stock exchange. She couldn't smuggle a hamster into her bed, let alone a man.

"You look anemic, Hastings," she said. "Have you been leaving the belles of England breathlessly unsatisfied again?"

He grinned. "Ah, so you know what it is like to be breathlessly unsatisfied. I expected as little from Andrew Martin."

Her tone was pointed. "As little as you expect from yourself, no doubt."

He sighed exaggeratedly. "Miss Fitzhugh, you disparage me so, when I've only ever sung your praises."

"Well, we all do what we must," she said with sweet venom.

He didn't reply—not in words, at least.

The vast majority of the time, she dismissed him without a second thought. But then he'd gaze upon her with that slight smile about his lips and a hundred dirty thoughts on his mind, and she'd find herself fighting something that came close to being butterflies in her stomach.

He'd rowed for Eton and Oxford and still possessed that powerful rower's physique. The night he'd confronted her about her affair, when she'd allowed him to press her into a wall and kiss her, she'd felt his strength and muscularity all too clearly.

"I'm looking for a publisher," he said abruptly.

She had to yank herself out of the memory of their midnight kiss. "I didn't know you were literate."

He *tsked*. "My dear Miss Fitzhugh, were Byron to come back to life today, he'd take a club to his good foot, out of jealousy of my brilliance."

She had a horrible thought. "Please don't tell me you write verse."

"Good gracious, no. I'm a novelist."

She breathed a sigh of relief. "I do not publish fiction."

He was undeterred. "Then consider it a memoir."

"I fail to see what you have done in your life that is worth setting down in print."

"Did I not mention that it is an erotic novel—or an erotic memoir, as it may be?"

"And you think that's something suitable for me to publish?"

"Why not? You need books that sell, to subsidize Mr. Martin's histories."

"That does not mean I am willing to stamp the name of my firm on pornography."

He leaned back, a look of mock consternation on his face. "My dear Miss Fitzhugh, everything that arouses you is not pornography."

Something hot swept over her. Ire, yes—but perhaps not entirely. She leaned in toward him, making sure she dipped her chest enough to give him a straight line of sight down her décolletage, and whispered, "You are wrong, Hastings. It is *only* pornography that arouses me."

As his eyes widened in surprise, she rose, swept aside the skirts of her dress, and left him on the chaise longue by himself.

*M*ay I have a moment of your time?" asked Fitz. Helena had gone to her room the moment they'd returned. Fitz's wife, after speaking to their housekeeper, had also started up the stairs.

She turned around. "Certainly, my lord."

He liked her slightly arch tone. When they first married, he'd thought her as bland as water, whereas Isabelle had been more intoxicating than the finest whisky. But he'd since come to realize that his wife possessed a dry wit, a quick mind, and an ironic view of the world.

"Do you suppose it has ever occurred to Hastings," she asked, as she descended the steps, "that cynical mockery might not be the best way to court our Helena?"

Pearls and diamonds gleamed in her hair: His countess was not at all averse to some glamour in the evening. "I dare say it occurs to him daily, but he is too proud to alter his approach."

She ran the house from her sitting room one floor above. But when they received callers on matters of business, or when they had something to discuss, they always used his study.

She sat down in her customary chair on the opposite side of his desk and opened her fan, a confection of black lace over tortoise shell slats. Her taste in personal adornment sometimes surprised him—the fan was more than a little seductive. But he could hardly fault her for enlivening her usually prim wardrobe with an unexpected accessory or two.

She ran a gloved finger across the slats. "You want to see me about Mrs. Englewood?"

Of course she'd have guessed. "Yes."

Did her fan tremble? He couldn't tell, for she closed it in a crisp motion and laid it across her lap. "So you plan to reestablish old ties?"

He must have been quite transparent. "We would like to."

She tilted her face toward him and smiled slightly. "I am glad for you. It was terrible that the two of you had to be apart for so long."

"About our pact—" he began.

"Don't worry about it. The last thing I want is to come between you and Mrs. Englewood."

"You misunderstood what I was about to say: I am not embarking on an affair with Mrs. Englewood—not *merely* an affair, in any case. It will be a permanent arrangement and I intend to be her faithful companion."

"I did not misunderstand anything," she said quietly. "I expected no less of you. And I wish the two of you all the best."

Something in her sympathetic agreement made him

ache to hold her. She rarely came across as lonely, but now she did.

"Before Mrs. Englewood and I begin our arrangement, I intend to honor our pact first."

The fan slid from her fingers and hit the floor with a hard thud. "What do you mean by honoring it first?"

He retrieved the fan and handed it back to her. "It would be a dereliction of duty on my part otherwise. It also wouldn't be fair to you and your family—for me to accept this great fortune and then not even try to give you a son to inherit the title."

Her usual keenness seemed to have deserted her. "You want to give me a son," she echoed slowly.

"It's only fair."

"But we don't know how long it would take for me to produce an heir. You might have to wait for an indefinite period of time." She came to her feet. Her voice rose two octaves. "What if I am infertile? What if I am one of those women meant only to have daughters? What if—"

She broke off in midsentence, as if realizing that she was reacting in a most uncharacteristic manner. He was transfixed: He hadn't seen her display this much emotion since their honeymoon—and then it had been because he'd been in danger of ruining both his health and his mind.

She swallowed. "My assessment of the matter differs from yours." Her voice was once again modulated—under control. "I understand perfectly that your arrangement is to be a lasting one and I applaud it. And I think that after all the years that have gone by, you should not waste any more time."

An appalling realization stole upon him: She didn't

want him to touch her. Even with their marriage transformed by friendship and affection, the thought of sleeping with him still upset her as much as it had when she'd first proposed their pact.

"It won't be very long," he said. "Six months. It doesn't matter whether you conceive or not and it doesn't matter whether the child is a boy or a girl: six months and the rest is the will of God."

"Six months," she repeated faintly, as if he'd said sixty years in Siberia.

On any given day, he could recite her schedule by the minute. Yet her heart was like a walled garden, invisible to one not granted entrance.

"I know the real reason you'd prefer our pact never come to pass," he heard himself say. "You wanted to postpone it several months ago, before we even learned of Mrs. Englewood's plans to return."

She stared at him, as if afraid of what he was about to say.

"You don't mention him but I haven't forgotten. There was someone you had to give up to marry me."

She gave a queer little laugh. "Oh, him."

He closed the distance between them. She never wore perfume, but her soap smelled of the lavender from their estate—along with a hint of something softer, sweeter. So that when combined with the warmth of her body, the otherwise austere scent of lavender became subtle. Interesting. Sultry, even.

He placed one hand on her shoulder. She trembled almost imperceptibly at his touch—he hoped it was surprise and not revulsion.

"Millie—I think I may safely call you Millie, no?"

She nodded.

"We are friends, Millie—good friends, furthermore. We'll get through this together. And when it is all said and done, I won't be the only one free to pursue old dreams. You will be able to go after yours with all my best wishes."

She looked away. "I scarcely know what to say."

"Say yes, then."

"You won't—you won't require that we begin tonight, will you?"

His pulse raced. Of course not, but the very thought of it made him hot everywhere.

Then he realized why she would think him capable of such an abrupt, indelicate demand: His fingers hadn't been content to remain in one place, but had roamed up the column of her neck to explore the tender place just beneath her ear.

In a motion that might be called a caress.

He hastily withdrew his hand. "No, not tonight."

"When, then?" Her voice was barely audible.

He stared where his hand had been, her smooth, bare shoulder, her slender throat, her dainty earlobe. "A week from tonight."

She said nothing.

"Listen to me: It will be fine. And who knows? You might conceive right away."

She averted her face, but even from this oblique angle, for him, who'd studied the subtle gradation of her expression for years, it was easy to see she was trying very hard not to grimace.

He was hesitant to touch her again so soon, but it was unthinkable that he should not comfort her.

"It will be all right," he said, pulling her into a loose embrace, "I promise."

It would be all right for him, not for her.

Could he not understand what he was asking of her? To become his lover knowing that she would be set aside at a specific date, knowing that even as he lay with her, his heart and mind were already contemplating his blissful future with Mrs. Englewood?

Tell him. It's nobody's fault but your own if you don't tell him.

He kissed her hair.

Stop. Don't touch me.

But she loved their rare instances of physical contact. When he'd lifted her and spun her around, when he'd danced four waltzes in a row with her, when he'd wrapped his arm around her shoulder upon the airship. And of course, that night in Italy. Those were the memories she savored over and over again, every detail polished to a high sheen, each sensation savored to the full.

Even now her body yearned to be closer to him. She wanted to press her nose into his skin and inhale hungrily— he always smelled as if he'd just taken a walk across a sunny meadow. She wanted to rub her palm against his jaw to feel the beginning of stubbles. She wanted to slide her hands underneath his shirt and learn every single shape and texture, with the fierce dedication she'd once put into mastering the *Grandes Études*.

There is no one else. I love you. I have loved only you. For pity's sake don't make me do this.

He kissed her on her ear, a close-lipped, chaste peck.

Desire charred her all the same. She was burned to the ground, reduced to rubble.

"It will be over soon," he murmured. "It will be over before you know it."

And for the rest of her life, she would be only an after-thought in his and Mrs. Englewood's radiant happiness.

I can't. I can't. *Leave me alone.*

"I will be the most considerate lover. I promise."

A small sob escaped her despite her best efforts to the contrary.

He embraced her more tightly. She could scarcely breathe. She wanted him to never let go.

"All right," she said. "Six months, a week from tonight."

"Thank you," he whispered.

It was the beginning of the end.

Or perhaps, it was only the end of something that was never meant to begin.

CHAPTER 5

The Honeymoon

1888 ∽

There was a giant in Fitz's head, tirelessly wielding a sledgehammer the size of Mount Olympus. He twitched, the floor hard and cold against his aching body.

"Get up!" shouted the giant, his bellow like a nail driven through Fitz's skull. "For the love of God, get *up*!"

It wasn't the giant who yelled, but Hastings. Fitz wanted to tell him to shut up and leave him alone—if he could get up he wouldn't be on the floor like a common drunk. But his throat seemed coated in sand and grit; he couldn't push a word past.

Hastings swore and gripped Fitz by the back of his shirt. They were of a similar height but Hastings was brawnier. He dragged Fitz along the floor, the motion making Fitz's stomach queasy and his head hurt, as if it were being batted against a wall.

"Stop. Goddamn it, stop."

Hastings didn't care. He hauled Fitz into something resembling a vertical position then dunked him, fully dressed, into a bathtub full of scalding water.

"Jesus!"

"Get clean, get sober," growled Hastings. "I can only keep Colonel Clements waiting for so long."

Colonel Clements can go fuck himself.

Then Fitz remembered, as the sledgehammer came down again, that it was his wedding day. Time stopped for no one, least of all a young man who only wanted to hold on to what he had.

He wiped a wet hand over his face and opened his eyes at last. He was in a bath with peeling brown wallpaper, straggly scum-green curtains, and a dented mirror frame that was missing the mirror inside. His town house, he realized, cringing.

Hastings had no sympathy for him. "Hurry up!"

"Colonel Clements—" He sucked in a breath. It felt as if someone had stuck a fork into his right eye. "He isn't supposed to be here until half past ten."

The wedding was at half past eleven.

"It is quarter to eleven," Hastings said grimly. "We have been trying to get you ready for the past two hours. The first footman couldn't even make you stir. The second you threw across the room. I managed to get you into your morning coat and you had to eject your ill-digested supper all over it."

"You are joking." He had no recollection.

"I wish I were. That was an hour ago. Your morning coat is ruined; you'll need to wear mine. And if you ruin mine, I swear I will set my dogs on you."

Fitz pressed damp fingers into his temple. It was quite

the wrong thing to do: Barbed wires of agony dragged through his brain. He hissed with pain. "Why did you let me get so drunk?"

"I tried to stop you—you nearly broke my nose."

"What are you talking about?"

"Your behavior last night, Lord Fitzhugh. One of the girls Copley hired ran off, by the way, screaming that she could not possibly perform the unnatural acts you wanted of her."

Fitz would have laughed if he could. Twenty-four hours ago he'd been a virgin—he might still be one, for all he knew. "That's impossible," he muttered weakly.

"It happened," said Hastings, his expression a mix of impatience, sorrow, and futility. "Enough, you need to pull yourself together. The carriage leaves at eleven—we should have *reached* the church at eleven."

Fitz covered his eyes. "Why is this happening to me?"

"I don't know. I don't know." Hastings's voice caught. His hand clamped hard over Fitz's shoulder. "What can I do?"

What could he do? What could anyone do?

"Just—leave me alone for now."

"All right. You have ten minutes."

Ten minutes.

Fitz buried his face in his hands. How could he pull himself together, when his entire life had fallen apart? Not in ten minutes, that was for certain. Not in a hundred and ten years.

*M*iraculously the groom's party arrived before the bride's party, but only by mere seconds. Hastings tried to get Fitz to run into the church, so that he wouldn't be seen still outside when the bridal carriage drew up. But Fitz could not have broken into a sprint had someone held a knife at his back.

He pushed away Hastings's hand. "I'm here. What more do they want?"

The church was only ten minutes by carriage from his new town house. He should have been at the church at least an hour ago, cooling his heels in the vestry until it was time to stand before the altar.

And he would have been, God, he would have been, were he marrying Isabelle. He'd have risen with the sun and made ready before any of the ushers. He'd have been the one knocking on their doors to make sure they got up on time and dressed properly. And had there been loose women at the party to commemorate the end of his bachelorhood, he'd have steered them to his classmates—it was not for him to sully his body the night before his wedding.

But here he was, sullied, ill groomed, and late—and for all that, more than good enough for the ceremony that would seal the sale of his name and, eventually, his person.

A relentlessly bright sun made his head pound harder. The air in London was nearly perpetually dirty—sometimes one could taste the grit. But all the torrential rains from his dreary final week of freedom had washed it clean. The sky was a wide-open, cloudless blue, stupidly lovely, perfect for any wedding except his own.

Miles of white organza had been jammed into the interior of the church. Thousands of lilies of the valley, too, their smell thick as incense. His still-fragile stomach shuddered.

The pews were seated to capacity. As he started down the aisle, a sea of faces turned toward him, accompanied by a roar of whispers—no doubt comments on his almost unforgivable tardiness.

Yet as he progressed toward the altar, row by row, they fell silent. What did they see on his face? Revulsion? Grief? Wretchedness?

He could see nothing before him.

Then all he could see was Isabelle, rising from her seat in the pews and turning toward him.

He stopped and stared. Her eyes were red and puffy, her cheeks sharp, her skin pale as ice—and she was beautiful beyond measure.

She gazed back at him. Her lips parted and formed the words *Run away with me*.

Why not? Let Henley Park rot. Let his creditors stew. And let the Graveses find someone else to shackle to their daughter. This was *his* life. And he would live it as *he* pleased.

All he had to do was stretch out his hand. They'd find their own place and forge their own destiny, take life by the horns and wrestle it to the ground.

He lifted his hand an inch, then another. Forget honor, forget duty, forget everything he'd been brought up to be. All they needed was love.

Love would make a pariah of her. She would lose her family, her friends, and all her prospects. And should something happen to him before they both came of age— he'd have condemned her for life.

He dropped his hand.

Hastings gripped his arm. He yanked free. He *was* the man he had been brought up to be. He needed no one else to drag him to the altar.

His eyes still locked on Isabelle, he mouthed, *I love you*.

Then, head held high, he marched the rest of the way to his doom.

*N*ot once did Millie look at her bridegroom during the wedding ceremony.

At appropriate times she would turn her face toward him, but behind the veil, she stared only at the hem of her wildly extravagant gown—the beading as heavy as her heart. And when he lifted the veil to kiss her chastely on the cheek, she concentrated on his waistcoat, mist grey with the subtlest weaving of checks.

Now they were man and wife, and would be for as long as they both drew breath.

The congregation rose as they began their walk toward the church door. None of the groom's friends extended a congratulatory hand to him. No one even smiled at the new couple. A clump of ladies, their heads bent together, whispered and pointed.

Suddenly Millie saw her, Miss Isabelle Pelham, wan, defeated, yet at the same time almost majestic in her pride and stillness. With infinite slowness and clarity, a teardrop rolled down her face.

Shock whipped Millie. Such a public display of emotion was alien to her—wanton, almost.

She could not stop herself: She looked at Lord Fitzhugh. He did not shed any tears. But in everything else—his ashen complexion, his dimmed eyes, his despair of a soldier who'd lost the war—he and Miss Pelham were exact matches, their beauty only made more so by their anguish.

It didn't matter that Millie had no say in the matter; it did not matter that the devil's own claws were in her heart.

She read the verdict on the guests' faces: *She* was the usurper here. The Graveses, with their vulgar fortune and even more vulgar ambition, had rent asunder a perfect, passionate pair of lovers, and destroyed any possibility either had at happiness in life.

She did not need guilt in addition to her misery. But guilt, all the same, wedged itself hard into her soul.

*M*rs. Graves attended to Millie's toilette herself, lifting the leaden wedding gown and laying it aside. Millie felt no lighter; the weight on her heart could not be dislodged.

Her body moved obediently, pushing her arms through the sleeves of a white blouse, stepping into a navy blue skirt of worsted wool. Mrs. Graves held out the matching jacket; she put that on, too.

"You should have a garden, my dear," said her mother as she unfastened the circlet of orange blossoms from Millie's hair. "A garden and a bench."

What for? A prettier place in which to relive the ignominy of her wedding? The wedding breakfast, marked by Miss Pelham's conspicuous absence, had been no better. And now, instead of changing into her traveling clothes at her new home, she was back in the Graves residence because her husband had claimed that his town house was too dilapidated to host a refined young lady such as herself.

"A garden makes everything better," said Mrs. Graves softly. "And it will keep you busy, when you need something to do. You'll be glad of it, Millie."

Millie kept her head bent. Would a garden make her

forget that her husband loved another? Or that she'd fallen in love with the last man who would love her in return?

Mrs. Graves had advocated for a honeymoon in Rome, but Lord Fitzhugh, at the engagement dinner given by his sister, had asked, "Aren't the marshes around Rome a malarial hazard in summer?" The Lake District, where there was never the risk of malaria, was chosen instead.

Millie met her new husband at the rail station. He was quiet, impassive, but unfailingly civil. With one last hug from her mother, she was entrusted into the care of this boy who had yet to come of age himself.

The rail journey took most of the rest of the day. Millie brought two books to read. The earl stared out of the window. She studiously turned the pages every three minutes, but in the end, she could not have said whether she'd read a chronicle of the Napoleonic Wars or a handbook on housekeeping.

They arrived at their destination late in the evening.

"Lady Fitzhugh will take her supper in her room," Lord Fitzhugh instructed the innkeeper.

It was what Millie would have asked for: a quick meal in complete privacy. But she sensed that he hadn't made the request out of consideration for her fatigue, but only to have her out of his way.

"And you, my lord?" asked the innkeeper.

"The same—and a bottle of your best whisky."

She looked sharply at him—his deathly pallor, had it been the result of too much drink? He stared flatly back at her. She glanced away in haste.

Her supper, she barely touched. She rang for the tray to be taken away and undressed herself—she'd given her maid a holiday coinciding with the duration of the Lake District sojourn, so as not to leak the truth of the "honeymoon."

In her nightgown, she sat down before the vanity to brush her hair. Her face in the mirror gazed unhappily back at her. Not that she was unsightly: With the right dress and the right coiffure, she passed for pretty. But it was a bland, unmemorable prettiness. Some of her mother's acquaintances kept forgetting that they'd already met her; even within the family the more elderly aunts routinely mistook her for her various cousins.

Nor did she possess the kind of forceful personality that could animate otherwise unremarkable features and make them compelling. No, she was a quiet, sensible, self-contained girl who would rather die than shed tears in public. How could she ever compete with Miss Pelham's magnetic passions?

She turned off the lamps in the room. With the dark came a profound quiet. She listened for sounds from Lord Fitzhugh's room, but could detect nothing, no footsteps, no creaking of bed, no whisky bottle scudding across the surface of a table.

Her window overlooked the inn's garden, beds and clumps of shadows in the night. A match flared, illuminating a man standing against a sundial: Lord Fitzhugh. He lit a cigarette and tossed the match aside. She did not realize, until several minutes later, when the moon emerged from behind the clouds, that he had not been smoking, but only holding the cigarette loosely between the index and middle fingers of his right hand.

When the cigarette had turned to ashes, he lit another. And that, too, burned by itself.

* * *

*S*he was awake for a long time. When she finally drifted into a troubled slumber, it seemed she'd slept for only a minute before bolting up straight in bed. An eerie silence greeted her. But she could swear that she'd been startled by a loud crash.

It came again, an awful racket of glass on glass.

She scrambled off the bed, pulled on her dressing gown, and flung open the connecting door. In the dim light, porcelain shards and food scraps were strewn all over the floor—the earl's supper. The mirror on the wall had cracked hideously, as if Medusa had stood before it. A whisky bottle, now in pieces, lay beneath the mirror frame.

Lord Fitzhugh stood in the middle of the wreckage, his back to her, still in his travel clothes.

"Go back to bed," he ordered, before she could say anything.

She bit her lip and did as he asked.

In the morning the connecting door was locked from his side. She tried the door that led to the passage, and that, too, was locked. She picked at her breakfast, then spent a fitful two hours sitting in the garden, pretending to read.

Eventually his window opened. She could not see him. After a few minutes, the window closed again.

*T*o her surprise, he appeared when she was halfway through her luncheon.

He looked awful, rumpled and unshaven. Unhappily she realized that as unwell as he'd appeared at the wedding, he—or someone else, most likely—had gone to some effort to make him presentable. No such effort had been made today.

"My lord," she said—and didn't know what else to say.

"My lady," he said, sitting down across from her, his face utterly expressionless. "You needn't worry about the state of my room. I've already settled it with the inn-keeper."

"I see."

She was glad he had taken responsibility for it; she'd have found the occasion too humiliating. What did one say? *I am terribly sorry, but it appears that my husband has destroyed part of your property?*

"I have also arranged to remove to an establishment twenty miles north where I will have more privacy."

He would have more privacy. What of her?

"I will be execrable company," he continued, his gaze focused somewhere behind her. "I'm sure you will enjoy yourself better here."

One day married and already he couldn't wait to be rid of her. "I will come with you."

"You don't need to do such wifely things. We have an agreement in place."

"I am not doing anything wifely," she said, finding that it required great effort to keep her voice low and even. "If I stay here, after my husband demolished his room and left, I dare say I will not enjoy the pity and idle curiosity from the inn's owners and staff."

He looked at her a minute, his otherwise beautiful blue eyes entirely bloodshot. "Suit yourself, then. I leave in half an hour."

* * *

The place twenty miles north was beautiful. They were halfway up a steep, densely wooded slope that overlooked a mirror-bright lake. The colors of the hills changed constantly, grey and misty in morning, a brilliant blue-green at noon, almost violet at sunset.

But an *establishment* it was not. Millie had expected a country estate of some description. Or, failing that, a hunting lodge. What she found was a cottage little larger than a cabin and only two steps removed from primitiveness.

The nearest village was six miles away. They had no carriages, no maids, and no cook. The earl expected them to survive on bread, butter, potted meat, and fruits that were delivered every three days. Or rather, he expected *her* to live on those. He himself needed only whisky, which came in crates.

Nightly he retired with several bottles. Nightly he brutalized something in his room: plates on the wall, the washstand, the solid oak desk. She cowered in her bed during his bursts of violence. Even though he'd never said a harsh word to her—or even so much as looked at her—every crash shattered her.

Sometimes she left her bed, put on her heaviest coat, and went outside, as far away as she dared in the pitch dark, to look at the stars. To remind herself that she was but a speck of dust mote in this vast universe—and her heartache just as insignificant. Then he would destroy something else, fracturing the silence of the night, and her entire universe would again shrink to a singular point of despair.

He slept during the day. She walked for hours in the

hills, not returning until she was exhausted. She missed her mother, her kind, wise, and unwaveringly loving mother. She missed the peace and tranquility of her old house, where no one drank himself into a stupor day after day. She even missed the relentless piano practices—she had nothing to do, no goals to achieve, no standard of excellence to which she could aspire.

She rarely saw him. One day, after the washbasin in his room had departed for the rubbish bin in fragments, she came upon him bathing in the stream behind the cottage, stripped to the waist. He'd lost a shocking amount of weight, his entire torso but skin over skeleton.

Another time, he hissed as she lit the oil lamp in the parlor. He was sprawled on the long sofa, his arm thrown over his face. She extinguished the lamp with an apology and left to her room. On the way she passed his: The wardrobe had been overturned, the chair was now firewood, and, over everything else, razor-sharp shards of God knew how many whisky bottles.

She couldn't breathe. His misery rose all about her, a dark tide full of undertows of rage. She hated him then: Nothing and no one had ever made her feel so *wrong*, as if her entire existence served only to tear apart soul mates and turn perfectly promising young men into destructive shadows of their former selves.

All the same, her heart broke for him, into a thousand pieces.

*T*he isolation of the cabin, no doubt excellent for keeping private pains private, was unhelpful in every other respect. Lord Fitzhugh had no duties to perform, no obligations that required him to adhere to a proper schedule, and no friends or family before whom he needed to keep up an appearance of sobriety and normalcy.

There was nothing left to smash in his room—having axed his bedstead to kindling the previous week, he now slept on a pallet on the floor. Millie feared he'd start on the parlor. Instead, he plunged into a deep lethargy. The whisky, at first only a nocturnal friend, was now his constant companion.

Millie was inexperienced in such darker aspects of life. But she had no doubt that he was sliding faster and faster down a dangerous path. He needed help, badly—and soon. Yet when she sat down to compose an appeal, she had no idea to whom she ought to address the letter.

Could Mrs. Townsend persuade her brother to stop drinking? Could Colonel Clements? Certainly no one in the Graves family could be of any assistance. And even if Millie were to swallow what remained of her pride and beg Miss Pelham for help, would Miss Pelham's family allow her to become involved again in the earl's affairs?

Via Mrs. Graves's pragmatic advice, Millie had been equipped to deal with a remote husband, disdainful servants, and a Society wary of yet another heiress breaching its defenses. No one, however, had ever thought to teach her what to do when her husband was determined to shove his youth and vitality down the throat of a whisky bottle and throw it all away.

She abandoned her letter and grabbed her hat. The swollen clouds that blanketed the sky promised rain, but she didn't care. She had to get out of the cabin. And if she returned a drowned rat, developed pneumonia, and expired before the end of the month, well, so much the better for—

She stopped dead.

Her husband, who had not been outside in days, sat on the front steps of the cabin, staring into the barrel of a rifle.

"What—what are you doing?" she heard herself ask, her voice high and reedy.

"Nothing," he said, without turning around, even as his hand caressed the barrel.

Slowly, not daring to make a sound, she shrank back into the cabin. And there, for the first time in her life, she clutched her heart. Her throat closed; her head spun.

He was contemplating suicide.

itz had lost track of time and he minded not at all. The past was infinitely preferable to the present, or the future. And even better when the boundary of reality and fantasy blurred.

He was no longer anywhere near the Lake District, but at the Pelham home, engaged in an animated conversation with Isabelle, while her mother embroidered at the far end of the room.

She was so interesting, Isabelle, and so interested. Her eyes shone like stars, but her beauty was the winsomeness of morning, bright and glorious, full of heat and verve. And when he looked upon her his heart was weightless with joy, rising to the sky like a balloon.

"I need to speak to you, Lord Fitzhugh," she said.

Lord Fitzhugh? Lord Fitzhugh was his third cousin twice removed.

"What is it?"

"You cannot go on like this."

"Why not?" He was bewildered. This was exactly how

he'd like to go on, a carefree young man, with the girl he loved by his side.

"If you won't think of yourself, then please think of your family. Your sisters will be devastated."

He opened his eyes. Strange, had he been holding a conversation with his eyes closed all the while? And when had the room become so dark, so full of shadow and gloom?

He was lying down. And she, above him, was as close as the reach of his hand. He lifted his arm and touched her face. She shivered. Her skin was softer than the memory of spring. He'd missed her so. It was her. It was always, always her.

Very gently, so as not to startle her, he pulled her down and kissed her. God, she tasted so sweet, like spring water at the source. He slid his fingers into her hair and kissed her again.

It was as he undid the top button of her dress that she began to struggle.

"Shh. Shh. It's all right," he murmured. "I will take care of you."

"You are delusional, Lord Fitzhugh! I am not Miss Pelham. I am your wife. Kindly unhand me."

Shock spiked through him. He scrambled into an upright position—Christ, his *head*. "What the—why are you talking to me in the dark?"

"Last time I lit a lamp your eyes hurt."

"Well, light one now."

The light came, stinging his eyes, but he needed the prickling, burning sensation. His wife had fled to a far corner of the room. How in hell had he mistaken her for

Isabelle? They could not be more different, in height, in build, in voice—in every aspect.

"Perhaps it is time to rethink being so inebriated that you mistake your wife for your beloved," she said coldly.

He lay down again. The light of the lamp flickered in circles of diminishing brightness upon the ceiling. "It helps me forget."

"What good is that when you must remember everything anew the next day?"

Of course it was no good. The drink was a weakness—his father would never have countenanced such a show of unmanliness. But then again, his father, at nineteen, had everything to live for. The rest of Fitz's life stretched endless and barren before him. Only pain was a certainty: His classmates from Eton would receive their commissions as officers; Isabel would marry another man and bear his children.

What did he have to look forward to? Roof repairs at Henley Park? An intimate knowledge of the preservation of sardines? Lady Fitzhugh, with her primly disapproving face, sitting across the table from him at ten thousand breakfasts?

"Continual sobriety is unappetizing," he said.

Sometimes he was amazed he could even withstand an hour of it.

"You don't always remember to close your door. I have seen you clutch your head in agony; I have heard you retch. Is it not enough that your heart aches? Must you ruin your health while you are at it?"

"I will stop when I am inclined to do so."

His hand, by habit, reached for the fresh bottle of

whisky by his side, only to encounter nothing at all. Strange, even if he'd poured its contents down his throat, the bottle should still be here.

"I'm afraid you'll have to stop sooner," said his wife. "I disposed of the whisky."

Damned interfering woman. He'd been somewhat thankful that she hadn't tried to cheer him up or censor his drinking—guess that was too good to last. No matter, she'd emptied one bottle; he still had half a crate left.

Using the arm of the sofa for support, he struggled to his feet. Walking had become hazardous. He'd stumbled and bruised his shoulder the other day—the perils of being a sot. A sot, a lush, a man who drowned his troubles in his cup—or tried damn hard, at least.

He usually had ten or fifteen bottles stocked in the cupboard next to his room. The cupboard was empty. He swore. Now he had to take himself all the way outside.

He lurched and staggered to the shed behind the cabin. He wouldn't have kept the whisky so far away, but one night, as he smashed things in his room, he'd damaged several unopened bottles. The next day he'd moved the whisky for its own protection.

The crates were neatly stacked in the shed, the bottles dully glistening. His heart trilled with relief. He grabbed one bottle by the neck and yanked it toward his parched lips. Something was wrong—it was too light. The bottle was empty. He threw it aside and pulled up another bottle. Again, empty.

Empty. Empty. Empty.

I disposed of the whisky.

She'd been thorough.

He kicked the stack of crates and almost lost his

balance completely, banging heavily into the wall of the shed.

"Are you all right?" said her bloodless voice somewhere behind him.

Was he all right? Could she not see with her own eyes that he'd never be all right again?

He tottered out of the shed. "I'm going to the village."

He was going to have his drink if it killed him.

"It's going to be completely dark in half an hour. And you have no idea where the village is."

He hated her reasonableness, her do-good ways, and her stupid assumption that she was *helping* him.

"I can't stop you from leaving tomorrow. And I most certainly can't stop you from falling on the next delivery of liquor. But for tonight I strongly advise that you stay put."

He swore. Turning—his heart thumping unpleasantly— he went back into the shed and pulled out an empty bottle, hoping that there might be a drop or two at the bottom. But the only thing left was the sweet, alcoholic fume.

Her voice came again, flat, inexorable. "I know the sky has fallen for you, my lord. But life goes on and so must you."

He threw the bottle against the back of the shed. It didn't break, but only thudded against the wall and fell with a plop onto a mound of burlap sacks. He stormed out to face her.

"What the hell do you know about the sky falling? This is the life for which you've been preparing for years."

She raised her eyes to him. It was stunning, the intensity of her gaze set against her practically nondescript face.

"Do you think you are the only one who has lost some-one you love because of this marriage?"

She did not bother to explain her cryptic statement, but pivoted on her heels and returned to the cabin.

It seemed all right at first, no worse than the bad heads he'd become accustomed to when he woke up. But as the evening ground on, his headache turned ugly, doubling, then doubling again in viciousness. His hands trembled. Perspiration soaked his nightshirt. Waves after waves of nausea twisted his innards.

He'd never ailed so badly. For the first time in his life, pure physical misery drove everything else from his thoughts—except the lovely amber-hued nectar for which he yearned so desperately. He prayed to be given a glass of it, an inch, a sip. It didn't need to be top quality whisky: brandy would do, as would rum, vodka, absinthe, or even a dram of common gin, the kind adulterated with turpen-tine for flavor.

Not a drop of distilled spirit sallied forth to his aid. But from time to time he'd vaguely realize that he was not alone. Someone gave him water to drink, wiped away the beads of sweat from his face, and might have even spread open clean sheets beneath him.

At some point he fell into a trouble sleep, his dreams full of thrashing monsters and forced good-byes. Sev-eral times he jerked awake, his heart pounding, convinced he'd just fallen from a great height. Each time there would come soothing murmurs at his ear, lulling him back to sleep.

He opened his eyes again to a dim room, feeling as if

he'd just recovered from a raging fever: His tongue was bitter, his muscles feeble, and his head annihilated. Sheets had been tacked to the window, making it difficult to judge the time of day. A kerosene lamp cast a dark orange glow on the walls. And was that—he blinked his sore, crusted eyes—a large bouquet of daisies in an earthenware pitcher? Yes, it was, small daisies, with crisp white petals and yellow centers as vivid as the sun.

Behind the daisies dozed his wife on a footstool, her sandy hair in a simple braid that hung over her shoulder.

Pushing himself up to a sitting position, he saw that next to his pallet on the floor was a tray with a fat-bellied teapot, slices of buttered toast, a bowl of grapes, and two boiled eggs, already peeled, covered under a pristine, white handkerchief.

"I'm afraid the tea is quite cold," came her voice as he reached for the teapot.

The tea was quite cold. But he was so thirsty it barely mattered. And he was hungry enough that his queasiness didn't prevent him from eating everything in sight.

"How did you manage to make tea?" A lady might pour tea in her drawing room for her callers, but she never boiled the water herself. And certainly she would not know how to build a fire for her kettle.

"There is a spirit lamp and I've learned to use it." She came forward, lifted the empty tray from his lap, and looked at him a moment, as if he were a shipwrecked stranger who'd washed up before her. "I'll let you rest."

She was on her way out when he remembered to ask, "What are the daisies doing here?"

"The chamomiles?" She glanced back at the riotous bunch. "I've heard chamomile tea helps one fall asleep.

I've no idea how to make chamomile tea, so I hope you like looking at them."

The chamomiles were so bright they hurt his eyes. "I can't say I do, but thank you."

She nodded and left him alone.

*N*ight was falling—without quite knowing it, Fitz had slept most of the day away. It was too late to set out, find the village, and secure himself a new supply of whisky. But even if he had plenty of daylight left, he was still far too depleted to make the trip on foot.

Although, had he known that his second night would be as wretched as the night before, he might have made an attempt. The headaches roared back; tremors, palpitations, and roiling nausea, too, returned en masse. An eternity passed before exhaustion overtook him. He slept, holding on to someone's hand.

His third night was far better, his slumber deep and dreamless. And when he awakened, more or less clear-headed, it was morning, not afternoon or evening as it had been lately.

The sheet still blocked the window. With one hand shielding his eyes, he yanked it off and let light stream into the room. What the sun illuminated was not pretty. All the walls were splattered with gouge marks, some large, some larger, as if a rabid beast with spikes and yard-long tusks had been penned in, desperate to get out. He rubbed his fingers against some of the rougher gouge marks, vaguely surprised that he'd been capable of such violence.

The chamomiles, droopy but no less cheerful, were still there; his wife was not. She had, however, left behind another pot of tea that had gone cold. Since he was well enough to move about on his own, he went out of his self-made prison cell to look for the spirit lamp that she'd mentioned.

He found it, but it had run out of the methylated spirits used as fuel. So he started a fire in the grate, pumped water into the kettle from the pump outside, and put it to boil—the first thing a junior boy learned at Eton was how to make tea, scramble eggs, and fry sausages for his seniors. While the water heated, he set chunks of bread on a toasting fork.

When he had tea and toast both ready, Lady Fitzhugh was still nowhere to be seen.

He found her in bed, fully dressed—walking boots included—sleeping facedown on top of the covers, her arms at her side, as if she'd reached the edge of the bed and simply pitched forward into it.

He hadn't meant to spy, but as he turned to leave, his gaze fell on an unfinished letter on her desk. It was addressed to his sisters.

Dear Mrs. Townsend and Miss Fitzhugh,

Thank you for your warm missive of last week. I apologize for our late reply: Your letter reached us only three days ago, along with our other semiweekly supplies from the village of Woodsmere.

The weather here remains delightful. And of course the lakes are ever so blue and lucid. I find myself constantly astonished by the beauty of my surroundings, even though it has been weeks since we first arrived.

Lord Fitzhugh had every intention of writing himself but alas, in the last few days, he has been under the weather—due to something he'd ingested, most probably. But he has bravely faced the rigors of his ailment and is now very much on the mend.

To answer Miss Fitzhugh's question, I do plan to drive out and see Mr. Wordsworth's house in Grasmere, as soon as Lord Fitzhugh is fully recovered.

With the exception of his intention to write—he hadn't even known they'd been receiving letters—she'd managed not to lie, no mean feat when this honeymoon must have been some of the grimmest days she'd ever known.

He glanced back at her and noticed that her left hand bore several deep scratches. Alarmed, he approached the bed and lifted her hand for a closer look.

She stirred and opened her eyes.

"What happened to your hand? I hope I didn't—" He couldn't imagine he'd harm a woman, drunk or not. But there were some gaps in his memory.

"No, not at all. I cut myself a few times when I was learning how to use the tin opener."

He'd opened tins for her in the beginning, when he opened tins for himself. But lately, bedridden, he'd forgotten that task altogether.

"I'm sorry," he said, ashamed.

"It was nothing at all." She pushed herself off the bed. "Are you better?"

He was still tired and sore, but it was a cleansing fatigue. "I'm all right. I came to tell you breakfast is ready if you want it."

She nodded, this girl who'd seen him at his very worst,

who'd remained a rock of sanity and good sense when he'd nearly given in to a self-indulgent wretchedness. "Good. I'm hungry."

Over breakfast, he read the accumulated letters, three from his sisters, two from Colonel Clements, two from Hastings, and a half dozen from other classmates. "You replied to all of them?"

"I'm not quite finished with the latest letter to your sisters, but the other ones, yes." She glanced at him. "Don't worry, I didn't say you were deliriously happy."

There was a mutable quality to her face. Every time he looked at her he was disconcerted: She never quite looked like what he thought she looked like.

"They wouldn't have believed you anyway."

"Yes, I know," she said, her tone calm, matter-of-fact.

Something about her composure defused tension, even when the subject was highly flammable.

"Are *you* all right?" he asked.

"Me?" His question surprised her. "Yes, I'm well—well enough at least."

"Why aren't you crying over your fellow?"

"My what?"

"The one you had to give up to marry me."

She added another spoonful of milk powder to her tea—they were out of fresh cream. "It's different for me. We did not have any history—it was largely wishful thinking on my part."

"But you love him?"

She looked down into her cup. "Yes, I love him."

The pain that had been dulled by an excess of whisky came roaring back. "We are in the same boat, then— neither of us can have the one we want."

"It would seem so," she said, blinking rapidly.

It was a shock to realize she was holding back tears, even as he adjusted his opinion of her from bland deference to quiet strength: When he'd lost all his bearings, she'd been the one to guide him back from the wilderness.

"You've conducted yourself far better than I have," he said, his words awkward and tentative, at least in his own ears. "I don't know how you do it, putting up with me when it has been just as difficult for you."

She bit her lip. "Don't tell anyone else, but I am secretly a laudanum fiend behind your back."

It took him a moment to realize she spoke in jest. He felt himself smiling faintly. The sensation was strange: He couldn't remember the last time he'd smiled.

She rose. "I'd better finish the letter before Mr. Holt from the village arrives. He will be"—she hesitated—"he will be coming with whisky."

*M*illie would have liked to decline the whisky for her husband. But she had told him the day she poured out every bottle—the aggressiveness of her action still astonished her—that the choice was his.

So it must be.

She took delivery of milk, bread, eggs, butter, fruit, and salading. There was a box of tinned sardines, potted meat, and tinned plum pudding—everything manufactured by Cresswell & Graves. And there was the whisky.

"The spirits are no longer needed," said Lord Fitzhugh.

Millie had become accustomed to the bearded, wild-haired, slovenly drunkard. The young man who stood before the cabin was clean-shaven and sharply dressed.

He was still too gaunt and too pale—behind his eyes was a grief as old as love itself. But Millie had to force herself to tear her gaze away: He had never been more striking, more magnetic.

"Very good, sir," said Mr. Holt. "I'll carry the rest inside. And—I almost forgot—there is a cable for you."

Lord Fitzhugh took the cable and opened it. His expression changed instantly. "There is no need to unload anything. If you could wait half an hour or so and take us down to Woodsmere, I'd be grateful."

Mr. Holt touched the brim of his hat. "Anything, milord."

Millie followed him back into the house. "What's the matter? Who sent the cable?"

"Helena. Venetia's husband has passed away."

"Of what?" Millie was incredulous. Surely her kind, beautiful sister-in-law could not have been made a widow so young. Mr. Townsend had been in perfect health at the wedding. And in Mrs. Townsend's recent letters there had been no mention of any illnesses on his part.

"Helena didn't give the cause of death, only that Venetia is devastated. We must go back and help with the arrangements."

We. It was the first time he'd referred to the two of them as one unit. She couldn't help a leap of her heart. "Of course. I'll start packing right now."

Twenty minutes later, they were on their way. The lurching and swaying of the cart couldn't be easy on his still fragile person, but he endured the discomforts without complaint.

In some ways, they were not too unalike. They both put duty first. They were both reserved by nature. And they both had a greater capacity to bear private pain than either had suspected.

"Thank you," he said when they were still a mile from the village. "If you hadn't disposed of the whisky when you did, I'd be in no shape to be of any use to my sister. I'm glad you had the resolve and the fortitude."

The pleasure she derived at his compliment was frightful. She looked down at her hands, so as to not betray her emotions. "I was afraid you might do mortal harm to yourself."

"That would probably need more than a few weeks of drinking."

She almost could not bring herself to speak of it. "I was talking about the rifle."

He looked genuinely puzzled. "What rifle?"

"You were staring into the barrel of a shotgun."

"You mean the dummy rifle I found in the shed?"

Her jaw dropped. "It was a *dummy*?"

"Very much. A child's toy." He laughed. "Perhaps we should introduce you to some proper firearms, so you can tell the difference next time."

Her face heated. "This is terribly embarrassing, isn't it?"

Now that he was sober, his eyes were an unearthly blue. "It is, for *me*: that I should have behaved in such a way as to cause anyone to doubt my will to live."

"You'd endured a terrible loss."

"Nothing others—including yourself—haven't endured."

He was inclined to gloss over heartbreak and affliction—again, like her.

The road turned. A gorgeous vista opened before them: a wide, oval lake, as green as the emerald peaks that framed it. All along the banks, late summer flowers bloomed, their reflections, white and mauve, like a string of pearls around the lake. On the distant shore stood a pretty village with ivy-covered cottages, their window boxes still aflame with geraniums and cyclamens.

"Well," she said, "at least the honeymoon is over."

"Yes." He tilted his face to the sky, as if marveling at the sensation of sunlight on his skin. "Thank God."

CHAPTER 6

1896

*F*itz stood outside Isabelle's house.

The day before, he'd hesitated in front of her door because he'd needed to cope with both an exorbitant hope and an equally strong fear of disappointment. But that was yesterday, before they'd committed themselves to a future together, a future once thought to be lost. Today he should enter her home with a spring in his step and no uncertainties whatsoever.

But last night he had discussed the matter with Millie. And sixteen hours later, he remained unsettled by her burst of panic, her horror at what he'd proposed. She'd agreed in the end, but the sense of rejection had lingered, as if all their years of mutual affection and common purpose counted for nothing.

He rang the bell and was duly admitted. In Isabelle's sunny parlor, they embraced a long time before taking their seats. She was well; the children were well. She'd taken them for a tour of the British Museum in the morning. Alexander couldn't get enough of the suits of armor. Hyacinth had been fascinated by the mummies, especially those of animals—and was already plotting to preserve General, their elderly cat, for all eternity, when the latter gave up the ghost.

"I can guess where she might have come by her mischief," said Fitz.

Isabelle chortled. "I dare say she will quite surpass me as a miscreant."

The tea tray was brought in. She rose and went to a side cabinet. "Tea is such a silly drink for a man. Can I offer you something stronger?"

He had not touched a drop of "something stronger" since the Lake District. "No, thank you. Tea is fine."

She looked a little disappointed. There was much she did not know about him—or he her. But they had time for catching up on the past later.

She sat down again and poured tea. "Yesterday you said you needed to speak to your wife. Did the conversation go well?"

If the conversation had gone well, then he ought not feel this strange hollowness inside. Yet he could not report that it had gone ill, since he did obtain what he wanted.

"Well enough," he said, and gave Isabelle a highly abbreviated version of what he and Millie had agreed between them.

"Six months!" Isabelle exclaimed. "I thought speaking to your wife would be a mere formality."

"It's never quite so simple when you are married." Or so he'd begun to realize.

"But you've been married almost eight years. If you haven't managed to procreate in that much time, how will six more months help?"

He'd anticipated this question. "We have seldom attempted to procreate. I had my needs met elsewhere and Lady Fitzhugh, as far as I could tell, was pleased to be left alone."

"How seldom?"

"We spent a few nights together during the honeymoon."

Technically, he was not lying, but he *was* deliberately creating the wrong impression. He did not want anyone, especially Isabelle, to think that there was anything irregular or incomplete about his marriage. Millie would be mortified.

It surprised him how easily he thought of her as Millie—perhaps he'd done so for a while now, without quite realizing it.

Isabelle's reaction was ambiguous: Disappointment dragged across her face, followed by a flitter of relief. For him to have never bedded his wife would have been a terrific statement of faithfulness to her; but it would also mean that in trying for an heir, he'd be taking on a new lover, which Isabelle could not possibly want.

"I know you don't care for the arrangement, Isabelle, but you understand that Lady Fitzhugh and I must do our duty at some point. I believe you'd prefer to have this out of the way, rather than for me to go back to her periodically, once we are together."

"This is mind-boggling," said Isabelle unhappily. "You should have taken care of the matter of your heirs much sooner. It was a complete dereliction of duty on your part."

"It was," he admitted. "But then I never imagined you'd come back into my life and change everything."

"I don't like this."

He took hold of her hand. "We must still be fair. Lady Fitzhugh deserves the same freedom that she has given me. However, without an heir, she will never pursue that freedom. It will bother me to think of her alone and untended—and it will taint our happiness."

"But six months is such a long time. Anything could happen."

"Six months is not so long compared to how much time we've spent apart, or the number of years that await us."

Isabelle gripped his fingers. "Remember what I'd told you in my letter? Captain Englewood and I caught the same fever. He was as hardy as a mountain goat. Yet in the end, I lived and he did not.

Her eyes dimmed. "You should not be so trusting of fate, Fitz. Life turned against you before and it could turn against you again. Don't wait. Seize the moment. Live as if there is no tomorrow."

He'd already tried that, in the Lake District. But tomorrows had an inexorable persistence about them: They always arrived. "I'd dearly love to, but I'm not temperamentally suited to living that way."

Isabelle sighed. "Now I remember: I could never change your mind once you'd made it up, especially when you are set on being dreadfully responsible."

"I apologize for being such a stick-in-the-mud."

"Don't," said Isabelle. She pressed his hand into her cheek, her eyes tender again. "It's what I've always liked about you—that you can be counted upon to do the right thing. Now enough of this high-mindedness. Let's talk about the future."

He was relieved. "Yes, let's."

She rose and retrieved a folded newspaper from a writing desk. "I've been looking at advertisements of properties for let—a home in the country for us. At the moment, they all sound terribly idyllic. Let me read you a few that I find particularly enticing."

Her animation was remarkable. When her face lit with excitement, the entire room grew incandescent. Her zest, her keenness, her appetite for life—all the qualities that had once dazzled him had remained amazingly intact. To listen to her was to be transported to a different age altogether, a time before life first humbled them.

But part of him could not help feeling uneasy. His situation was complicated, but hers was no less so with young children under her roof. It would be years before Alexander was old enough to be sent to school. And Hyacinth was not going anywhere until the day she married.

Their cohabitation must be conducted with care and a great deal of decorum, so that they neither gave the children the wrong impression of acceptable conduct, nor mortified them before their peers.

That would have been the first hurdle Fitz chose to tackle, not houses, which were easy to come by. But after Isabelle had run down the list of properties that had caught her interest, she launched into a discussion of ponies instead. For Christmas she wished to present her children each with a pony, what did Fitz think of the different breeds?

It was still early, he reasoned with himself. And hadn't they dealt with enough of reality for a while? Let her dream unimpeded for a little longer. There was time later to consider the practical ramifications of their new life together.

"I had a Welsh pony when I was a child," he said. "I liked it very well."

$\mathcal{H}$elena paced in her office. She had to find a way to see Andrew. But Susie, her new maid, adhered to her like flypaper. Come Susie's half days, Millie always managed to fill the afternoons with engagements for Helena, so there was no opportunity to slip away.

She might be less agitated if she could catch a glimpse of Andrew at some of the functions she was obliged to attend—it was how they'd maintained their friendship over the years, via running into each other regularly. Or if he would resume writing to her. But neither happened.

A knock came at her door. "Miss Fitzhugh," said her secretary, "there is a courier for you."

"You may take the delivery."

"He insists that he must hand his parcel to you in person."

Authors and their precious manuscripts. Helena opened her door and took the sizable package. "Who is the sender?"

"Lord Hastings, mum," said the courier.

Good gracious. As satisfying as it had been to knock him off his perch, had she somehow given him permission to send her items from his no doubt vast collection of smut?

She returned to her desk and tossed the package in a corner. But five minutes later, she found herself opening it, out of a frankly prurient curiosity. And he certainly knew how to keep her in suspense—the package was like a Russian babushka doll, one layer of wrapping after another.

A fabric outer cover, a pasteboard box, an oilcloth, and at last, a large envelope. She tilted the contents of the envelope onto her desk: a stack of papers wrapped with twine, with a handwritten note on top.

My Dear Miss Fitzhugh,

What a delightful chat we enjoyed last night at the Queensberrys'. I am gratified by your overwhelming interest in reading my novel—or memoir, as it may be—on the human condition in its most sensual manifestations.

Your servant in all things, particularly those of the flesh,
Hastings

She snorted. Degenerates would be degenerates.

However, Hastings degeneracy didn't affect only himself. He had a natural daughter who lived with him in the country. He'd already inflicted the stigma of illegitimacy upon the poor child, and now he'd further shame her by becoming a pornographer?

Beneath the letter, the first page of the manuscript gave its title, *The Bride of Larkspear*, and Hastings's pseudonym, A Gentleman of Indiscretion—at least he had that correct. The dedication on the next page was to "The pleasure seekers of the world, for they shall inherit the earth."

The man's cheekiness knew no bounds.

She turned the page.

Chapter 1

I shall begin with a description of my bed, for one must make the setting of a book clear from the first line. It is a bed with a pedigree. Kings have slept on it, noblemen have gone to their deaths, and brides beyond count have learned, at last, why their mothers ask them to "Think of England."

The bedstead is of oak, heavy, stout, almost indestructible. Pillars rise from the four corners to support a frame on which hang heavy curtains in winter. But it is not winter; the heavy beddings remain in their cedar chests. Upon the feather mattresses are spread only sheets of French linen, as decadent as Baudelaire's verses.

But fine French linen is not so difficult to come by these days. And beds with pedigrees are still only furniture. What distinguishes this bed is the woman attached to it—her wrists tied behind her to one of the excessively sturdy bedposts.

And this being a work of Eros, she is, of course, naked.

My bride does not look at me. She is determined, as ever, to shunt me to the periphery of her existence, even on this, our wedding night.

I touch her. Her skin is as cool as marble, the flesh beneath firm and young. I turn her face to look into her eyes, haughty eyes that have scorned me for as long as I remember.

"Why are my hands tied?" she murmurs. "Are you afraid of them?"

*"Of course," I reply. "A man who stalks a lioness
should ever be wary."*

On the next page was a charcoal illustration of a nude
woman, her body lanky rather than lush, her breasts thrust
high thanks to the position of her arms. Her face was
turned to the side and hidden by her long, loose hair, but
there was nothing retiring or fearful in her stance. The
way she stood, it was as if she *wanted* to be seen precisely
so, her charms displayed to taunt the man who beheld
them.

Helena was breathing fast—and it irked her. So Hastings could string a few words together and draw an obscene
picture. That he put his talents to such ignoble purposes
was no cause to revise any of her prior opinions and certainly no cause for her to feel . . .

Naked herself.

She slammed the pages she'd moved aside back on top
of the manuscript and shoved the entire thing back into its
envelope. The envelope she pushed deep into a drawer and
locked it.

Only after she'd left her office for the day did she realize that she'd put Hastings's smutty novel on top of Andrew's
love letters.

*Y*ou had some tough questions for poor Mr. Cochran
today, Millie," said Fitz.

His comment broke the silence inside the brougham.
They were on their way home from a tasting at Cresswell &
Graves's offices. Or rather, Millie would go home when
the carriage stopped before their town house, but he would

go on elsewhere, no doubt to call on Mrs. Englewood again.

"I asked very few questions. You, on the other hand, were much too undemanding today." Her voice was testy. *She* was testy—eight years and still a distant second best. "Usually you do not approve of a product until you've sent it back to be refined and improved upon three times. The new champagne cider has never undergone such rigors and yet you approved it right away."

"It tasted charming. Effervescent without being too gushy. Sweet with just the right amount of tartness."

He could have been speaking of Isabelle Englewood.

"I thought it was passable, nothing to be excited about."

"That's odd," he said quietly. "Our tastes tend to converge, not diverge."

She'd been looking stubbornly out of the window. Now she glanced at him. A mistake—he gave the impression of a man deeply content with his lot.

The signet ring she'd given him glistened on his hand. She wanted to rip it off and throw it out of the carriage. But then she'd also need to throw away his gold-and-onyx watch fob and his walking stick, the porcelain handle of which was glazed a deep, luminous blue. Like his eyes.

So many Christmas and birthday presents. So many practically transparent attempts to stake her claim on his person, as if pieces of metal or ceramic could somehow change a man's heart.

"I trust your judgment more when you aren't so—buoyant," she said.

"Buoyant, that's a weighty charge." He smiled. "No one has accused me of being buoyant in years."

His smiles—she used to think them signposts pointing

the way to a hidden paradise, when all along they were but notices that said, "Property of Isabelle Pelham Englewood. Trespassers will have their hearts broken."

"Well, things have changed recently."

"Yes, they have."

"I'm sure you've been to see Mrs. Englewood again. What does she think of the six-month wait? I dare say she hates being made to wait."

"You are my wife, Millie, and you step aside for no one. Mrs. Englewood understands this."

Something in his tone made her heart skip two beats. She looked away. "I will gladly step aside for her."

He rose from the opposite seat and sat down next to her. As spouses, it was perfectly proper for them to share a carriage seat. But when they were alone in a conveyance, he always took the backward-facing seat, an acknowledgment that he was not truly her husband.

He draped an arm over her shoulder. His nearness, which she had never become accustomed to, was now almost impossible to endure. She wanted to throw open the door of the carriage and leap out. Her agreeing to honor their pact did not give him the right to touch her before it was time.

"Don't look so put out, Millie. Something wonderful might come of this: We can have a child." His other hand settled on her arm, the warmth of his palm branding her across the thin fabric of her sleeve. "I've never asked you, would you like a boy or a girl?"

"I don't know."

"You'd make a wonderful mother, kind but firm, attentive but not smothering. Any child of yours would be a fortunate child indeed."

There had been a part of her, however small, however circumspect, that had always hoped perhaps when they at last consummated their marriage, their lovemaking would be the final alchemical ingredient to give wings to their friendship. But now it would serve only a biological function. Their friendship would remain earthbound—never to take flight.

The carriage came to a stop before the Fitzhugh town house. She pushed him away and leaped out.

CHAPTER 7

Alice

1888 ～

The death of Fitz's brother-in-law, Mr. Townsend,
turned out to be quite a messy business.

Millie had met him only twice, at her engagement dinner and at the wedding breakfast. Both times her insides
had been in turmoil and she'd gleaned only the most superficial impressions of the handsome, proud man.

It was a shock to learn of his death, but a greater one
to find out the manner of it: He'd killed himself with an
overdose of chloral. Even worse, unbeknownst to his wife,
he had become bankrupt. It had necessitated the sale of
his entire estate, along with the liquidation of a plot of land
Mrs. Townsend had inherited from her parents, to appease
his creditors.

Millie had believed that beauty like her sister-in-law's
must act as a powerful talisman, protecting one so blessed
against storms and monsters, so that she sailed smoothly

through life upon the twin currents of love and laughter. But it was not true. Misfortune hesitated for no one, not even a woman as lovely as Aphrodite herself.

As Mrs. Townsend drifted through the aftermath of her husband's death, staggered and dazed, Millie, alongside Miss Fitzhugh, did her best to be useful. They made sure Mrs. Townsend ate enough, took her for drives so she wasn't always sitting in a sunless parlor, and sometimes, sat in that sunless parlor with her, Miss Fitzhugh holding her sister's hand, Millie in a nearby chair, finishing frames upon frames of embroidery.

Throughout the ordeal, Lord Fitzhugh was a rock. Gone was the disconsolate drunk. Daily he was at his sister's side as they settled Mr. Townsend's affairs, the epitome of consideration and sense—and forcefulness, when needed. An inquest had very nearly taken place, which would have turned a private death into a public spectacle. His uncompromising stance before a police inspector made the difference; in the end the police accepted the explanation that Mr. Townsend must have suffered from an unexpected hemorrhaging of the brain.

They stayed in London for six weeks before matters relating to Mr. Townsend's estate were resolved. It was a largely somber time, but there were moments Millie treasured. Miss Fitzhugh imitating Lord Hastings and making her sister laugh, however briefly. Lord Fitzhugh and Mrs. Townsend sitting together, his arm around her, her head on her shoulder. Mrs. Townsend taking hold of Millie's hand one day and telling her, "You are a wonderful girl, my dear."

The day before they left London, the women took tea together. Miss Fitzhugh was to begin her classes at Lady

Margaret Hall. Mrs. Townsend, after accompanying her sister to the women's college at Oxford, would go to Hampton House, their childhood home in the same shire, which Lord Fitzhugh had put at her disposal.

"Are you sure you wouldn't wish to come to Henley Park with us, Mrs. Townsend?" Millie asked one last time. She and Lord Fitzhugh had been trying to persuade Mrs. Townsend to stay with them at the estate he'd inherited alongside his title—to no avail.

"I have troubled you and Fitz enough," said Mrs. Townsend. "But thank you, Millie—may I call you Millie?"

"Yes, of course." Millie was aflutter that Mrs. Townsend wished to use the more familiar address of her given name.

"You will call me Venetia, won't you?"

"And call me Helena," said Miss Fitzhugh. "We are sisters now."

Millie looked down at her hands to compose herself. She'd been brought up not to expect such intimacy from her in-laws, who were sure to sniff at being related to the Sardine Heiress. But Mrs. Townsend and Miss Fitzhugh—Venetia and Helena—had been helpful and accepting from the very beginning.

"I've . . . never had sisters," she said, afraid she sounded too gauche. "Or any siblings."

"Ha, lucky you. This means you never had anyone tell you that you were actually found in a bassinet under an apple tree when your parents went for a walk in the country." Helena raised an eyebrow at Venetia. "Or that if you ate black-colored food, you'd have black hair like everyone else."

Venetia shook her head. "No, that was Fitz. He wanted you to eat the blackberries so he'd have more raspberries to himself. It never occurred to any of us that you'd try squid ink."

Millie listened with a sense of wonder at the oddity and camaraderie of children growing up in the same household. The warmth of that conversation still lingered as she and Lord Fitzhugh traveled in her parents' private rail coach to Henley Park.

This time it was he who read—Edward Gibbon's *The History of the Decline and Fall of the Roman Empire*, Volume IV—and she who stared out of the window. Most of the time. The rest of the time she studied him surreptitiously.

He had not regained all the weight he'd lost during his three weeks of strenuous inebriation—his clothes still hung slightly loose, his eyes were set deeper, and his cheekbones more prominent. But he no longer looked unwell, only lean and grave. His hair, cut short, lent a further austerity to his aspect, a solemnity beyond his years.

He set down his book, dug his hand into his pocket, and pulled out a—

"Is that a dormouse?"

He nodded. "This is Alice."

Alice was tiny, with lovely golden brown fur and curious black eyes. He gave her a piece of hazelnut, which she nibbled with great enthusiasm.

"She's getting chubby," he said. "Probably will start hibernating within the week."

"Is she yours? I haven't seen her before."

"I've had her for three years. Hastings has been taking care of her recently. I just got her back."

Millie was enchanted. "Did you find her yourself?"

"No, she was a present from Miss Pelham."

Isabelle Pelham. Millie's smile froze. Fortunately he was not looking at her, his attention wholly occupied by Alice.

No wonder he had not brought Alice on their honeymoon.

"She looks darling," Millie managed.

He stroked the fur atop Alice's head. "She's perfect."

He did not offer Alice for Millie to hold. And she did not ask.

It was not easy, remaining sober.

Some nights, when he could not sleep, when he missed Isabelle so much he could scarcely breathe, Fitz thought of things that might help him: whisky, laudanum, morphia. He thought especially hard of morphia, of the lovely torpor it would bring, the long forgetfulness.

The house had such things—he'd seen them when he'd first inspected Henley Park. So he left the house, to walk and run—mostly run—until he was overcome with exhaustion.

He also, once he put his mind to it, realized that there was an easier way of alleviating his loneliness: naked women. He took up with one of his new neighbors, a widow five or six years older than him, who was more than glad to have him service her repeatedly.

Alice began her hibernation. He kept her in a padded, ventilated box and checked on her twice a day. Everything had changed. Alice remained the one familiar touchstone, a link to life as he'd known it.

Two weeks after they arrived at Henley Park, his wife sent him a message, wishing to see him in the library.

Except at dinner each night, he hardly saw her at all, though he knew she kept herself busy during the day, as he did, with matters concerning the house and the estate.

The library, dour and smelly, was in the north wing, the worst part of the house. She was examining books for damage. He was surprised to see her in a day dress of russet silk. Since Mr. Townsend's death, she'd worn mourning colors, a silent, somber ghost at the periphery of his awareness. But today the vibrant, autumnal hue of her dress made her the brightest object in the room.

"Good morning," he said.

She turned around. "Good morning."

For a moment he was struck by how young she looked without a dark, drab garment to age her. Had he passed her on the street, he might have thought her fifteen.

Had the Graves lied about her age? "Excuse me, but how old are you again?"

"Seventeen."

"*Seventeen*? Since when?"

She lowered her gaze, as if embarrassed. "Since today."

Now he was equally embarrassed. He'd had no idea. "Happy birthday."

"Thank you."

An awkward silence fell. He cleared his throat. "I don't have a present for you. Is there anything you'd like—and can be found in the village?"

She waved a dismissive hand. "A birthday is just another day. I think it's terribly silly that people make such a to-do about it. Besides, your sisters have already sent books and a pretty box of new handkerchiefs."

"If Venetia, with all her troubles, can remember, then I have no excuse—except that I didn't know the date at all."

"Please don't worry about it—there's always next year. Now, would you mind looking at some of the rooms with me?"

He'd already seen all the rooms, but since it was her birthday . . . "Lead the way," he said.

She'd obviously examined each room multiple times, and had taken copious notes of all the damages. It was a guided tour of the north wing's failings. As they walked on, she reported an ever rising estimate of how much it would cost to repair everything.

They were only on the third room of the next floor when he said, "We should dynamite this entire house."

"That would be rather an extreme course of action," said his wife. "But I would have no objection to getting rid of this wing."

He stopped cold. "What did you say?"

"According to the ledgers and the plans, this wing was an addition undertaken at the beginning of the century— the original house's wall, if I'm not mistaken, would have been right there. From what I can tell, there was no particular reason for the addition, except that the then-earl was jealous of his cousin's newer, better house and wished to compete."

And the family had been in debt ever since.

"I know you were jesting when you said to dynamite the house, but I'd like to submit for your sober consideration the idea of not renovating the north wing. It was poorly conceived and even more poorly built. Even if we patch everything today, we'd still need to be constantly vigilant against new leaks, rots, and cracks."

The north wing was two-fifths of the manor. He stared at her a moment—she was perfectly serious. The girl had audacity. But of course she did: She'd singlehandedly pulled him back from the brink of a precipice.

"All right. Let's do it."

At his assent, she was the one who was taken aback. "Do you think we might need to petition parliament for something like this?"

He thought for a moment. "One doesn't petition parliament before an accident takes place, does one?"

She smiled. "No, indeed one doesn't. And our discussion never happened."

He smiled back.

She dipped her head. "Now if you will excuse me, I must decide whether any of the books are worth keeping."

It was only later in his room, gazing at a peacefully slumbering Alice, that Fitz realized he and his wife had just made their first joint decision as a married couple.

*T*hat evening Millie dined alone. Lord Fitzhugh sent a note saying he would take his supper at the village pub. Supper was probably a euphemism for a woman. Not that she begrudged him a little pleasurable distraction, but she wished—

No, she did not wish that he'd come to her instead. She did not want to be used for only that purpose. But she could not help envying his lovers. She, too, would like to know what it was like to be touched and kissed by him—when he was sober. There was a physical grace to him, a manner of movement that was swift and easy. She could not help imagining what it would be like, someday, for him to suddenly notice her not merely as his wife, but as a woman, a desirable one.

But she always cut those reveries short, whenever she

discovered herself in the middle of one. Perhaps there was nothing she could do about hope springing eternal, but she would not water or tend it. She would prune it harshly, ruthlessly, the way she would a weed in the garden.

After dinner, she sat in the drawing room, studying. She'd decided to take her mother's advice and create a beautiful garden. But the pleasure garden would have to wait until she had first restored the more utilitarian kitchen garden. The estate had one such, but with the departure of the head gardener nearly a decade ago, it had grown wild.

She pored over an old diagram for the walled garden, consulting her handbook on horticulture. Salsify she'd eaten. Celeriac she hadn't, but had at least heard of. But what in the world was a scorzonera? Or a skirret? Or a cardoon, for that matter?

She was searching for *couve tronchuda* in an encyclopedia when her husband surprised her by striding into the drawing room—she'd thought he'd remain out until long after she was abed.

"Good evening," she said.

Perhaps it was the light, but he looked . . . strapping. Her heart stuttered.

"Evening," he answered, standing with his hands behind his back. "I was at the village pub tonight. We'll have twenty able-bodied men here tomorrow to dismantle the north wing—or at least to begin the work."

"So soon!"

Her father took forever on his decisions. Even when he agreed to a change in principle, he'd still dither for years over the specifics of its implementation. She had not remotely anticipated that Lord Fitzhugh would set about the overhaul of Henley Park this quickly.

He looked about the drawing room. She'd had make-shift new curtains and carpets brought in, but it was still a dismal place—there was no point in replacing the curling, water- and soot-stained toile wallpaper until they had a new roof and better chimneys. "Not soon enough," he said. "At least fifty years too late."

When they'd first arrived in the country, she'd worried that he might re-embrace whisky. But it was sobriety that he clasped tight and did not let go. During the day he, like she, threw himself into his duties. At night, instead of turning to the bottle, he turned to the outdoors. Sometimes she, waiting beside her window in the dark, would see him return, hunched over before the manor, his hands on his knees, breathing hard with exertion.

All because of this cursed house, half of which someone should have demolished fifty years ago.

But his voice was calm. What had been done had been done. There was no use pointing fingers at the dead or at forces beyond his control that had sent agricultural prices stumbling in their lifetime.

"And this is for you." He handed her a brown-paper package that he'd hid behind his person. "I stopped by the general merchandiser's. But the selection was paltry. I chose the least terrible of the lot."

She was astonished. "You didn't need to."

Inside the package was a rather plain music box that must have sat on the shop's shelves for the better half of a decade. Even with the obvious signs of recent cleaning, its corners and creases were still encrusted with dust. When she opened it, it played a few tinny, scratchy bars from "Für Elise."

"As I said, it's not much good."

"No, it's fine. Thank you." It took a great effort for her to not hug the music box to her chest. "I will keep it well."

"I'll do better next year." He smiled. "Good night."

"Good night," she answered.

Some hopes were weeds, easy to eradicate with a yank and a pull. Some, however, were vines, fast growing, tenacious, and impossible to clear. As she played the music box again, alone in the drawing room, she began to realize that hers were of the latter kind.

She would never stop hoping.

*T*he last thing Millie expected to see was her husband on the roof of the house, stripping the slate tiles alongside the men he'd hired. He was in old tweeds and a woolen cap. She'd nearly mistaken him for a village lad until someone addressed him as "milord."

"What are you doing, Lord Fitzhugh?"

"I'm supervising the men."

"You seem to be working with the men, if my eyes don't deceive me."

He tossed a tile at an older man, who passed it to another, who in turn slid it down a long chute set at forty-five degrees. The tile was caught on the bottom by one of two waiting men and, after passing through a few more hands, carefully placed in stacks.

"Your eyes do deceive you!"

"So they must," she shouted back and left him to it.

It was quite ungentlemanly of him to be performing manual labor. But come to think of it, his days at Eton had been heavily driven by sports—association football in the Michaelmas Half, field game during the Easter

Half, and come the Summer Half, cricket. The sedentary nature of married life must contribute to the ennui of it. And the demolition of the north wing, besides the satisfaction of literally destroying the house that had derailed his life, provided an outlet for a young man's pent-up energy.

It also gave them something to talk about at dinner, the only time of the day they spent in each other's company and not much time at that, as he had no use for protracted dinners—in fact he still ate like a student, with a speed she found difficult to match.

So it was during the taking down of the north wing that she learned about the nest of bats in the attic, the mold that had been growing inside the plaster, the fact that the oldest man in the demolition party had fought in the Crimean War in his youth. She told him of her plans to build an electrical plant on-site, wire the house with electricity, and modernize the plumbing.

"You would not believe the flush commodes that the man in London tried to sell me. They had the queen's face painted in the bowl."

Lord Fitzhugh choked on his lamb. "You are making this up."

"I am not. I was aghast, while the man tried to reassure me that it was all perfectly proper."

"I hope you did not buy any. I don't think I can—" They stared at each other for a moment and both burst out laughing.

"No, neither can I—ever!" she declared emphatically, still laughing. "No, our new commodes will be blue enamel, with white daisies."

He choked again. "Daisies?"

"Believe me, I tried to find a more masculine commode—something with maybe a hunt scene or a dragon painted inside—but such a thing apparently does not exist."

"Daisies," he still sounded dazed. "My friends will never stop laughing."

It was the first time he ever alluded to the possible presence of his friends at his home. For a moment her imagination ran away and she saw a crowded drawing room, full of laughter and high spirits. And she saw the two of them at the center of all that cheerful goodwill, Lord and Lady Fitzhugh. And someone raising his glass, crying, "To our delightful hosts."

"Good thing I'm not inviting anyone here," said the real-life Lord Fitzhugh.

She bent her face to her plate, so he would not see her disappointment.

She accepted this marriage for the alliance of convenience it was. But when they worked toward a common purpose, when they conspired to keep the secret of the house's "repairs" from the rest of the world, and when he sat across from the table from her and laughed, it was nearly impossible to believe that they were not building something together.

They were: a better house.

And nothing else.

*L*ord Fitzhugh left Henley Park frequently. Most of the time he left in the morning and returned at night—he'd stop by Oxford to see both Helena and Lord

Hastings, and then call on Venetia, whose house was not too far from the university. But occasionally, he stayed away for longer.

When he told Millie he'd be gone a week, she issued an invitation to her mother to come stay with her—her father would be indignant about the north wing, but Mrs. Graves would understand their choice to not burden themselves and their heirs with a house that could never be adequately maintained.

Mrs. Graves, when she came, was more than a little shocked at the architectural skeleton of what had once been the north wing. "Whose decision was this?" she asked, her jaw slack.

"It was a joint decision," answered Millie. She could not help the note of pride seeping into her voice. "Our thoughts are exactly aligned on this matter."

Mrs. Graves considered the remnants of the north wing for another minute. Then, she smiled and gave Millie's hand a squeeze. "Very good, my love. Keep on making these joint decisions. They will give you a foundation upon which to build a life."

It was late November, the days cold and damp. Millie and Mrs. Graves spent most of their time inside, drinking hot cocoa and discussing the manor's many pressing needs. But on the day of Mrs. Graves's departure, the sky cleared to a glorious blue and they took a walk on the grounds of Henley Park.

Millie showed Mrs. Graves the walled kitchen garden. She'd been busy hiring more staff for the estate. They were still shorthanded, but work had begun on clearing the kitchen garden.

She gestured at a row of apple, pear, and quince trees

espaliered to the southern wall of the garden. "Mr. Johnson, our new head gardener, believes that these fruit trees may yet be saved. He and his apprentices pruned back years of overgrowth just last week. Mrs. Gibson is waiting for them to bear fruit to make jams and preserves."

"Will the fruit trees be the only ones bearing fruit in Henley Park next year?" asked Mrs. Graves. "Your father is eager to know."

"We'll also be putting in beds of strawberries—they will bear fruits. But if Father is referring to a grandchild, then I'm afraid he'll have to wait quite a while longer."

"Does Lord Fitzhugh not visit your chamber?"

Embarrassment singed Millie's cheeks but she kept her voice detached. "That is another one of our joint decisions. I know Father would prefer a grandson as soon as possible, but neither Lord Fitzhugh nor I want children now and our wishes should count in this matter. More than Father's."

Mrs. Graves was silent. They walked past beds of dormant weeds that had yet to be cleared and an old wooden beehive, the residents of which had long ago left for better blossoms elsewhere.

"Your own garden, my dear, have you given any thoughts to it?"

Millie exhaled in relief—and gratitude—at her mother's acceptance. "Yes, I've thought about it. But I've yet to set anything into motion."

Mrs. Graves twined her arm with Millie's. "Don't forget it come spring."

Millie looked toward her empty house. "Will it make me happy?"

"That I cannot answer, my love. But it will give you something to do and something to look forward to—as well as a place of your own." Mrs. Graves set her gloved hand briefly against Millie's cheek. "It may not equal happiness, but it is not a bad place to start."

*F*itz returned on a Sunday afternoon.

The servants had the day off; the house was silent. He went through the correspondence that had accumulated for him. A letter from Colonel Clements caught his attention: The Clementses planned to visit him after Christmas.

He immediately went in search of his wife.

She was not in the house. He looked in the gardens, the stables, and near the badly choked trout stream—no sign of her. Finally, as he approached the house from the north side, he heard the sounds of demolition.

But it was Sunday. The village men were at their pub; no one worked.

He rounded a wall. His wife, hatless, in a sack of a dress and a brown cloak, stood in a room that had now become detached from the rest of the house, wielding one of the smaller sledgehammers, going after a fireplace. She'd broken through the facade of the mantel and now swung the sledgehammer at the bricks underneath.

The door was already gone. He knocked on the window frame.

She spun around. "Oh, you came back."

"What are you doing?"

"Well, when you did it, you seemed to enjoy yourself. So I thought I'd have a go at it."

Sometimes he forgot that he was not the only unhappy

spouse in this marriage. That she too wanted to smash things.

"You are going to give yourself blisters."

"Not yet."

She swung the sledgehammer again and dislodged several bricks. She also managed to dislodge a lock of hair from her chignon, which was too old a style on a seventeen-year-old girl, even if she was a married ladyship.

He took off his overcoat and picked up a bigger sledgehammer. "Need some help?"

She glanced at him, surprised. "Why not?"

They settled into a steady rhythm. For a girl who'd never done anything more strenuous than lifting a teacup, she was quite handy with her sledgehammer—and strong. They each swung in turn at the fireplace, and she kept up with him strike for strike.

When all that remained of the fireplace was a pile of bricks, they were both panting. She placed her hand over her heart, her cheeks brightly flushed. "Well, that was good."

He tossed aside his sledgehammer. "Is there anything to eat?"

"We've a sponge cake and a beef pie in the larder."

They made their way together to the kitchen, where several stock pots sat simmering. He filled a pot with water, stoked the fire, and set it to boil. She, meanwhile, found some plates and silverware, and located the sponge cake and the beef pie.

"Missing your fellow?" he asked after he'd finished his portion of the beef pie.

She raised an eyebrow in question.

"That was why you were wrecking the fireplace, wasn't it?"

She shrugged. "Maybe."

He felt a pang of sympathy for her. He could always find someone willing to give him a few hours of oblivion. How did *she* cope?

"How was London?" she asked. "Did you enjoy it?"

He caught an undertone in her words. Goodness, she knew precisely what he'd been up to in London. The girl was not as prim as he'd made her out to be. "It was all right."

"Good," she said. "I'm glad."

He caught something else to her tone. "Are you?"

She looked directly at him, all maidenly innocence again. "Why wouldn't I want you to have a good time?"

He had no answer for that. So he gave her Colonel Clements's letter. "The colonel is coming to visit."

She scanned the letter. To her credit, she didn't turn a hair. "Well, we'd better annihilate some more of the north wing after tea, ought we not?"

"Ready?" Fitz asked, as the brougham carrying Colonel and Mrs. Clements pulled into view.

Lady Fitzhugh nodded. She had on her most somber dress, her hair in a chignon again—this time Fitz approved. They were two minors going up against a formidable man and this was no time for her to look her age.

"Are *you* ready?" she murmured.

"I must confess: I'm rather looking forward to this."

"I came, I saw, I smashed," she said drily.

"Precisely."

The carriage came to a stop before the house. As the drive had been repaved after the building of the north wing to show it off during the approach, the colonel would have already seen its absence.

And indeed, before they could utter a welcome, the colonel barked, "What happened to the manor, Fitz?"

"Colonel," said Fitz, "Mrs. Clements, so delighted you could join us."

"What a lovely brooch, Mrs. Clements," chirped his wife. "Please, come in."

Colonel Clements was not so easily distracted. "You will answer my question. What happened to the manor?" he bellowed as they entered the manor.

Fitz felt himself perspiring. "We are in the midst of repairs still, sir. Please excuse the state of the house."

"Repairs? Half of the manor is gone."

"Sometimes repairs involve unanticipated results."

"Such results are unacceptable. You will rebuild the north wing."

"Of course we will put the manor to rights. But that is not what we are about to do tonight," said Lady Fitzhugh, with a confidence and a skill that belied her years. "Tea, Mrs. Clements?"

Colonel Clements would not let the subject drop. "I cannot believe you countenanced this destruction of your home, Lady Fitzhugh."

Fitz sucked in a breath. To pretend Colonel Clements was overreacting was one thing, to be subject to his direct ire, quite another. Lady Fitzhugh, however, was not the least bit intimidated. "Countenanced it, sir? No, I encouraged it. It was my idea."

She didn't just have audacity. She had *enormous* balls.

Colonel Clements sputtered. "Explain yourself, young lady."

"Had the north wing been better built, Lord Fitzhugh and I would have endeavored to rehabilitate it. However, it was ill conceived and badly executed. Even if we restored it today, we still must keep restoring it forevermore, committing infinite outlays of funds so that it does not once again fall into disrepair. And since no one is possessed of infinite funds, we chose to have a more modest house that is within our means of upkeep.

"The other choice is to someday sell my future firstborn son on the marriage mart. And that I absolutely refuse to even contemplate. Lord Fitzhugh had to submit to such a fate; that was enough. It will not happen again, not while I have a breath left."

Her tone was eminently reasonable and she maintained a friendly smile throughout. But there was no mistaking the underlying vehemence of her words. Colonel Clements was rendered momentarily speechless. And Fitz—it began to dawn on him that he had married no ordinary girl.

Tea was brought in. Lady Fitzhugh poured for everyone.

"This is excellent tea, Lady Fitzhugh," said Mrs. Clements.

"This is utter heresy." Colonel Clements found his voice. "The house is entailed. You cannot—"

"Colonel, you will not upset our hosts. Why don't you have some of this lovely sandwich?" said Mrs. Clements firmly. "Now, Lady Fitzhugh, tell me how you are finding Somerset."

And that was that.

At the end of tea, with the Clementses shown up to their

room to change for dinner, Fitz approached his wife and squeezed her hand. "Well done, old girl."

She looked at him, surprised by his gesture. Then she smiled—she was a pretty girl after all, with nice, even teeth. "You did very well yourself. Now make sure you are amenable to everything the colonel says for the rest of their visit."

He nodded, understanding her perfectly. "I will be most abjectly agreeable."

*N*ot all the north wing was smashed. Much of it was carefully preserved: The glass panes of the conservatory were earmarked for the rebuilding of the greenhouses, the stones of the wall for a later restoration of the kitchen, and the roof tiles for the chicken coop, the dovecote, and the mushroom house.

More curiously, however, Lord Fitzhugh had left a fifteen-foot-long section of wall standing. When Millie asked him why the wall had not been knocked down along with everything else, he'd said lightly, "For those days when we are again in the mood to smash something."

The first of such days came a week after the first anniversary of their marriage, which passed unremarked.

She heard the sound of the sledgehammer from her sitting room, early in the morning. The answer to her question was found in the *Times*. Miss Pelham's mother had announced the betrothal of her daughter to a Captain Englewood. The name was somewhat familiar. She dug up the guest list from her wedding and there was a clan of Englewoods. Captain Englewood, it seemed, was either an Eton classmate of Lord Fitzhugh's or the elder brother of a classmate.

At noon she took a sandwich and a flask of tea to him. In his shirtsleeves, he sat on an empty windowsill, his head resting against the frame of the wall, Alice in his hand.

"I'm sorry," she said. It hurt her to see him in pain.

He shrugged. "It was always going to happen."

"But you would have preferred that it happened later—or not at all."

"I won't deny there is a part of me that never wants to let go of her. But I don't wish her to go through life alone; it would be far better for her to marry. If only the thought of it didn't make me so—"

He looked up at the sky. "I haven't kept up with her news—when we married, I resolved to remove myself from her life entirely. So I don't know the circumstances surrounding her engagement. On the one hand, I'm worried—terrified—that she said yes to Captain Englewood simply because she could no longer stand to be alone. On the other hand, she could be in love with him and he could very well turn out to be a wonderful husband to her. And does this thought make me glad? Not at all. If she is miserable, I am miserable. If she's happy, I'll still be here, taking a sledgehammer to a wall."

Millie didn't know what to do. Or what to say. Tears welled in her eyes and she let them fall. What was the point of not crying? His pain and her own seemed one strangely whole entity: a longing for what could not be regained, or gained in the first place.

She wiped away her tears before he could see them.

"Anyway," he said, "thank you for my lunch. I'm sure you have much to do around the house."

In other words, he wished to be alone now.

"I can—I can do those things tomorrow," she ventured.

He shook his head slightly. "It's very kind of you, but it's hot and dusty out here."

"Right," she said. "I'll go back inside, then, where it's much nicer."

He did not look at her. He had eyes only for Alice, his beloved Alice.

When would she remember that their pain was not the same? That while she would welcome any opportunity to be close to him, even if it was to hear of his love for another woman, he, on the other hand, sometimes simply could not bear the sight of her.

That although occasionally she proved herself an ally, always she was—and always she would be—the personification of all the forces that had kept him from the happiness that should have been his.

*M*illie resolved to fall out of love with her husband.

She didn't know why she didn't think of it earlier. Somehow, when she'd fallen in love, she'd accepted it as a chronic condition, something that must be endured for as long as she lived.

Such could not be true. She must recognize this: There was nothing special about her love. She was simply an ordinary young girl, dazzled by the good looks of an equally young man. What was her love but a desire to possess him? What was his love but a similar drive to own Miss Pelham body and soul?

Some things in life were truly difficult. Finding the source of the Nile, for example. Or exploring the South Pole. But falling out of love with a man who never looked at her twice, why should that prove an insurmountable challenge?

*A*lice was not quite right. It was September. She should be gorging herself, putting on weight in readiness for her long hibernation, but her appetite was poor. Fitz tempted her with seeds, berries, nuts of all descriptions. He took her on long walks and searched for aphids and other small insects she might find interesting. He had the gardeners germinate various plants so she might have fresh leaf buds, a delicacy she hadn't enjoyed since spring.

Nothing had any effect. She ate poorly and spent the rest of her waking hours in varying degrees of listlessness, her eyes dim, her breathing labored.

She was getting old. But he'd counted on her to have at least another year in her, twelve more months of gentle snoozing and happy snacking, three hundred sixty-five more days for him to grow accustomed to the fact that she could not live forever.

Not so soon, not with Isabelle's wedding breathing down his neck. There was no long engagement, as he'd secretly hoped; the nuptials would take place before the end of Captain Englewood's home leave. The honeymoon would be spent in France and Italy, en route to India, where Captain Englewood was posted.

Fitz would have married her when he was Captain Fitzhugh, on home leave from his regiment in India. And they would have passed through France and Italy on their way to their new life together, completely wrapped in each other, completely thrilled to be married at last.

She was doing her level best to claim the life for which they'd planned—without him.

He still had her letters, the photograph with the entire gang, and the various small presents she'd pressed into his hands over the years. But those were static things, representing only certain moments of the past, whereas Alice was a living, breathing embodiment of all that they were and all that they'd hoped to be. As long as Alice lived, a part of their connection remained unbroken, time and distance be damned.

But without Alice, beautiful Alice . . .

All around him, life went on. The finishing touches were being put to the restored manor: new floors laid, new wallpapers hung, and shiny, blue enamel commodes installed one by one. His wife seemed to have terribly ambitious plans for the flower garden: Thickets and brambles were cleared; Peruvian guano arrived by the railcarful, along with enormous sacks of bulbs, for those first splashes of color in spring.

Sometimes he'd see her in a wide-brimmed hat, conferring with the gardeners, consulting the master plan in her hand as they measured out new flower beds to be built and new paths laid.

And despite his panic, he would gather up Alice and head down to his study, to meet with his steward, his architect, and his foreman; receive his tenants and mediate their problems; and write his weekly report to Colonel Clements on the discharge of his numerous responsibilities.

He was becoming like his wife in some ways: the stoicism, the determination to carry on no matter what.

Alice, however, could no longer carry on.

"I always thought you'd pass away in your sleep," he told her, adjusting the bed of soft cotton batting he'd made for her. "And it would be so easy you wouldn't even know it."

She wheezed another arduous breath. Her eyes were closed. One of her little feet twitched from time to time, but otherwise she'd become too weak to move.

"I want to have you in my pocket all of my days. And I'll wager you want the same. I'll wager you wish you were just having a hard time falling asleep, that when you wake up, it will be spring again and you'll be strong and healthy and ready to eat your weight. But we can none of us have everything we want, can we?

"You are going to a beautiful place, where it is always spring. I won't be there, but I'll remember you from here. And I'll think of you surrounded by fresh buds and hazelnuts—hungry again, young again."

She stopped breathing.

He wept, tears falling unchecked. "Good-bye, Alice. Good-bye."

An invitation to Isabelle Pelham's wedding came for the Fitzhughs, but neither Millie nor Lord Fitzhugh attended.

Or rather, Millie assumed her husband did not attend. She was home alone in the country and he off somewhere. She had not asked about his whereabouts. In fact, she did not even keep count of how long he'd been gone—except to know that it had been more than seven days and less than ten.

He came back two days after the wedding. She expected to hear the sledgehammer again. But through her open window came only the sound of the wind, and of the grounds staff as they went about their duties.

Her curiosity outweighed her resolve not to care. She slipped into a room that overlooked the ruined wall. He stood before the wall, still in his traveling clothes, one hand braced against it. Then slowly, he began to walk, his palm sliding across the wall, as if he were a student of archaeology, examining the ruins of Pompeii for the first time.

She went on her afternoon constitutional. When she came back, he was still there, leaning against the stonework, a cigarette dangling between his fingertips.

He raised his chin in acknowledgment of her approach. Somehow the pensive, wistful expression on his face told her everything.

"You went to the wedding," she said, without further preamble.

"No and yes," he said. "I didn't go inside."

"You waited outside the church while she was inside exchanging her vows?"

Such a forlornly and stupidly romantic gesture—another reason to not love him. Yet all she felt was her heart tearing apart.

"I watched them come out from the church, get into the waiting carriage, and drive away."

"Did she see you?"

"No, she didn't," he said softly. "I was but a face in the crowd."

"She must have made a beautiful bride."

"Yes, very beautiful. Her groom was thrilled; she

looked happy." He tilted his head up. "I've been dreading the day of her wedding. But now that it has come and gone, I feel almost . . . relieved. It has happened at last: She has become another man's wife. I need to dread it no more."

"So—you are actually happy for her?"

"I wish I were him: I envy him and I will never not envy him. All the same, when I saw her smile at him, it was as if a load fell from my shoulders."

He looked at Millie. "It is good to know that I'm not as selfish as I thought I might be."

Don't you dare do this to me. This is no time for you to act noble and generous.

He reached into his pocket and drew out a package wrapped in silk and tied with a length of ribbon. "This is for you."

"You already gave me a birthday present."

"We both know that it was Venetia who remembered to give you a birthday present from me. You have been a steadfast friend. I have not expressed my appreciation very well up to this point, but please know that I am grateful to you."

Don't, she almost said. *Don't.*

"You didn't let me drown in whisky. You didn't leave me to face Colonel Clements alone. And you are always, always kind. I hope I can be just as good a friend to you someday."

She bit her lower lip. "What is in the package?"

"A lavender cutting for your garden. I asked your maid and she told me that you are very fond of lavender. After Isabelle's wedding I went to Lady Pryor's place and applied for a few cuttings. I understand it's better to propagate in spring but that it's still doable in autumn."

She opened the package, and indeed, wrapped inside was a sprig of lavender.

"More will come tomorrow, but I thought I'd bring this one in person."

"You shouldn't have." He really ought not have. Six weeks of dogged efforts to fall out of love with him—he would ruin it all with a single gesture.

"All we've done here is take things down and prevent further deterioration," he said. "Let's grow something—something new, something that is ours."

You don't know what you ask. You don't know the terrible hopes this will ignite in me.

"Thank you," she said. "It will be beautiful."

CHAPTER 8

1896

*L*avender honey," read Isabelle from the handwritten label on the glass jar.

"You like honey—if I recall correctly," said Fitz. "We make this honey at Henley Park. Very good stuff."

And very beautiful, glowing golden and clear in the gingham-covered jar.

"My goodness, to make lavender honey you must have a whole field of lavender."

"Acres and acres of it. It's quite a sight to see, especially after three months in London." Fitz felt a surge of pride and warmth at the mere thought. He missed it, his corner of the Earth.

"You never told me about those acres and acres of lavender. I thought Henley Park was nothing but a ruin."

"It was. The lavender fields were started in my

tenure—although most of the credit must go to Lady Fitzhugh. She is an indefatigable gardener."

Isabelle had been holding up the jar of honey, admiring it in the light. She set it down abruptly. "You are giving me something that comes from her garden?"

Her voice was tinged with both suspicion and displeasure—she was reading too much into a simple gift. "*Our* garden," he said firmly. "I got the first cuttings from Lady Pryor."

Isabelle pursed her lips. "That might be even worse, that this comes from something belonging to the both of you."

"You are taking up with a married man, Isabelle. Much of my life is intertwined with my wife's."

"I know that." She sighed, an exasperated sound. "But the reminder does not really help, does it?"

He'd seen the honey at breakfast, remembered that she enjoyed honey on her toast, and asked his housekeeper whether there were any unopened jars on hand—as simple as that. But nothing, alas, was so straightforward.

"If you don't care for it, I'll take it back and find you something you'll like better."

"Of course I like it—I adore anything you give me." Her lips turned down briefly at the corners. "I'm just frustrated that there is so much of your life I do not—and cannot—share."

"It will change now. My wife and I had nothing in common when we married." Realizing he hadn't given the best example, he hastened to add, "It will take time, that's all. We must catch up on all the years we've been apart, and then build something new."

"You make it sound as if there is a distance between us that needs to be bridged."

He was taken aback she'd dispute him on this point. "That's quite inevitable, isn't it? We have changed. It will take us a while to know each other as we once did."

"I have *not* changed." Her voice turned vehement. "Yes, I have experienced marriage and motherhood. But I remain the same person I have always been. If you knew me then, you should know me now."

"I do know you, but not as well as I would like to." He sounded defensive to his own ears.

"Not as well as you know your wife, you mean."

He wasn't sure why the conversation kept circling back to his wife. "Certainly I know her daily itinerary as well as I do my own, and I know her character. But she is an opaque one, Lady Fitzhugh; I'm never sure what she is thinking."

"What about me? Can you tell what I'm thinking?"

He recognized the half-defiant, half-rueful look on her face. She knew she'd overreacted, but wasn't yet ready to admit her error. He smiled—with relief. "I think you, or part of you at least, would rather we talked about something else instead."

"Maybe, if I could be assured that your wife hasn't somehow managed to wedge herself into your heart."

"The very idea of it is silly. If I love her, then what am I doing here with you?"

His reasoning apparently passed muster. She smiled a little sheepishly. "Shall we talk about a honeymoon of our own? A place to go when your six months have ended."

"We'd be in the dead of winter, wouldn't we?"

"Yes," said Isabelle, her eyes lighting up. "So we should head somewhere warm. The weather in Nice would be perfect. But Nice is so crowded in winter; we won't wish to bump into everyone. Majorca would be just as lovely—or Ibiza, or even Casablanca."

An unhappy sensation stole over him. Christmas at Henley Park had become a grand tradition, an extended embrace of family and friends. He did not want to curtail the festivities to head to parts unknown—some of his fondest memories of recent years had come of those gatherings. And he could scarcely stomach the idea of deserting his wife right after Christmas.

Perhaps in his way, he'd become as opaque as his wife. Isabelle chatted avidly on the possibilities—apparently there was a sturdy supply of scenic places on Spain's Mediterranean coast—not once noticing that his enthusiasm didn't quite match hers.

But that was all right, he supposed. He had become too comfortable in his existence. All creatures of habit needed to be shaken out of their habits once in a while, so as not to become too rigidly set in their ways. He only wished Isabelle hadn't thought to make such a major production out of the beginning of their future. He was committing adultery after all, and it seemed that they ought to go about it with more silence and discretion.

Isabelle, however, was Isabelle, exuberant and passionate, full of insuppressible vitality. And why should he begrudge her a little speculation, or a most likely delightful excursion to a place with palm trees and a warm ocean?

If only the thought of Millie spending January alone didn't distress him so, as if he was about to leave the door of the greenhouse open on the coldest day of the year and would return to find all the carefully nurtured plants inside withered from cruelty and neglect.

*H*elena could not believe her eyes: Andrew! He stood on the platform of the rail station, waiting, not twenty feet from her.

She sent her maid Susie to buy a paper, and some roasted nuts from street hawkers outside the station. Once she was sure Susie had been swallowed by the crowd, she made her way to Andrew and tapped him on the shoulder.

The ecstatic surprise on his face was almost—almost— worth their long separation.

"Helena," he said reverently, his quiet voice largely lost in the noise of a busy rail junction.

His coloring was a more diffuse version of hers, his hair ginger, his eyes hazel—it had been one of their earliest topics of conversation, two redheads in families full of raven-haired siblings—hers—and blond cousins—his. He was dimpled, a little rumpled, round-shouldered from all his hours sitting before a desk, and just a hair shorter than her, something he joked about good-naturedly.

Everything he did was good-natured and honest. In a cynical world, he was the rare creature, one of both intelligence and genuine sweetness.

"Andrew." She longed to take his hands in hers, but she dared not in public. They shook hands instead, holding on to each other's fingers a second longer than was completely appropriate. "Are you going somewhere?"

"Yes, to Bodley to read some manuscripts." He'd spent a great deal of time at the Bodleian Library at Oxford even when he'd been a student there. "And you?"

"Venetia is officially returning from her honeymoon today. I thought I'd be on hand to welcome her back to London."

"How terribly exciting. I haven't had the chance to congratulate her in person." He bit the corner of his lips. "But I suppose she wouldn't really wish to see me anymore."

"What are you talking about?"

He'd removed his right glove when he'd shaken hands with her. Now he twisted that glove uneasily. "I thought— your brother—you didn't know?"

"Fitz?" Her heart was already sinking. "What does he have to do with any of this? Please don't tell me he'd called on you."

That was the reason Andrew had written her to cry off their affair, citing the perils to her reputation and whatnot.

"He was very kind about it, but he is right, Helena. What we were doing was terribly dangerous. And I'd never be able to live with myself if I damaged your good name."

So Fitz had known—and Venetia and Millie, too—all this while. If anyone could be said to be the party responsible for the affair, it was her, yet he had chosen to go behind her and speak with Andrew instead. They'd made decisions for her while leaving her in the dark, as if she were a child, when she was barely fifteen minutes younger than Fitz—and to her face they'd pretended nothing was happening, as if one of the most significant choices of her life was but so much rubbish to be swept under the rug.

"My good name, is that all anyone can think of? I thought we'd already agreed that there is more to life than reputation. I thought we'd agreed that happiness was worth a risk or two."

"I do agree still. But that was before we were found out. Thank goodness it was only your brother. Had it been anyone else—I can't even conceive of the consequences."

Damn Hastings. He must have told Fitz after all.

"Do you really not want to see me ever again?"

"Helena." Andrew's voice shook just perceptibly. "You know I would give anything to see you, but I promised your brother—"

"Is your promise to him more important than your promises to me?"

Andrew winced. "I—"

Out of the corner of her eye she saw Susie coming back. "You will meet me again. Because you will not let me down and you will not leave me without hope."

She turned and walked away before Susie could come too close.

*O*nly to see Hastings fifteen feet away, an expression of mild interest on his face. He'd seen her and Andrew together. She did not bother coming up with a task, but only told Susie, when the latter reached her, that she was going for a private word with Lord Hastings.

Before she could excoriate him for breaking his word, however, he said, "I didn't tell Fitz the identity of your lover. In fact, he punched me in the face when he realized that I hadn't told him everything."

"Then, who did?"

"Give members of your family some credit. Do you think they do not remember that you were in love with him? Do you believe they cannot put two and two together? And don't forgot all those love letters that arrived by the bushel from your beloved. They only needed to stumble upon one to learn his identity."

There *had* been the one letter she could not account for after her return from America. "Why didn't they say anything to me?"

"Probably because they knew you wouldn't listen to reason."

"That is pure hog swill."

"Would you have listened to them?"

"They would have tried to persuade me with conventional thinking—not at all the same as *reason*. Not all of us live by the same logic."

"Yet you still have to abide by the same set of rules as the rest of them. The consequences won't be any different for you."

"You say it as if I don't know what the consequences are."

"You know exactly what the consequences are. But you don't believe they could happen to you."

"And why should they? I have been rigorously careful."

"Have you? Three nights at Huntington I observed you come and go from your assignations—you didn't notice a thing. On the last night, another couple on their secret rendezvous was headed right in your direction. I had to divert them. After that I had no choice but to speak to your family."

She had not known this, but still her ire rose. "And bilk a kiss from me besides."

"For someone who deals with writers, you should choose your words with greater care." He smirked. "I came by my kiss honestly."

The lecher.

"And how do you like my book? Does it not astound you with its literary finesse?"

"We are talking about smut with dirty drawings."

"Ah, so you have been reading."

"I glanced through two pages and that was enough for me."

He smiled. "It's that good, eh?"

Her breath caught. "It is a waste of paper. And what are you doing here, anyway?"

"I've come to welcome our duchess back to London. She is practically my sister, too. Now if you'll excuse me."

"Where are you going?" she was not so much curious as suspicious.

"Fitz will be here soon. Martin might know everything that happened in East Anglia before Canute the Great made it a mere fiefdom, but I see he doesn't have the sense to remove himself and avoid giving the impression that he has come to meet you."

"He hasn't. He happens to be on his way to Oxford."

"All the more reason not to give Fitz the wrong ideas. If there is no misconduct, then you shouldn't waste people's suspicion."

He ambled off, took Andrew by the shoulder, and guided him away.

Fitz arrived at the rail station to find Helena and Hastings standing together, speaking in that particular push-pull rhythm of theirs. Fitz listened to their exchange of mildly veiled insults with his usual amusement—and a twinge of melancholy. It was a testament to Hastings's skill and determination that Helena, after all these years, still did not realize he was in love with her. But what good was such love, too proud to make itself known?

He wondered whether the same applied to his wife. Once she had her freedom, would she be too timid to pursue her fellow, to whom she'd remained chastely devoted all these years?

An odd thing, his continued anonymity. She did not make her debut until after she was Lady Fitzhugh, so she could not have been acquainted with many young men before she married. In the intervening years, Fitz had met most of the Graveses' social set and never once had he come across a man who elicited any reaction in her.

"My goodness, Mrs. Englewood!" Hastings cried. "What an adorable coincidence running into you."

Fitz was jolted out of his reverie. Isabelle, in a promenade dress of black velvet, appeared at Fitz's elbow. She shook hands warmly with both Hastings and Helena. "Adorable, yes, coincidence, no. Fitz told me that the duchess is due back this afternoon. I am dying to meet her new husband and see her again—as well as the rest of you. How could I pass the opportunity when I know that everyone will be gathered here?"

Everyone, including Millie.

Had she been anyone else, Fitz would have suspected her of trying to usurp Millie's place. But Isabelle was a creature of impulses, not wiles. There was no malice to her, nor machinations.

All the same, this was ill done of her. Inserting herself openly into a family occasion—she might as well take out a notice in the papers stating their intention to set up a household together. No matter how romantic a reunion of young lovers, he would still be committing adultery and he preferred to do so discreetly, and not give his wife reasons to think she'd been publicly thrown over.

He was not alone in his reaction. Once Helena and Hastings realized that Isabelle had come deliberately and would remain with them, they both glanced toward the gates of the platform: It was only a matter of time before Millie arrived.

And then they both glanced at Fitz with uncertainty—and more than a little anxiety on Helena's part—trying to gauge his reaction, to determine whether he approved of Isabelle's action or whether he shared their unease.

Venetia's train pulled into the station. She and her husband, the Duke of Lexington, stepped down from the duke's private rail coach. The two had supplied the bulk of the gossip for the early part of the Season, culminating in an elopement that had shocked everyone, members of their families included. Fitz had guessed more of the reasons behind their sudden marriage than most, but still he'd worried, until the couple had come for a quick visit to London not long ago and he'd seen for himself how happy and relaxed Venetia was in her new marriage. They had then returned to the duke's estate in the country for the rest of their honeymoon and were only now rejoining Society, beginning with the ball in their honor, hosted by Fitz and Millie—the same night they would consummate their marriage.

Only two days away now.

Helena waved. Venetia waved back, all smiles. The crowd hushed—Venetia was the great beauty of their generation and her appearance often caused awed silences.

But as she walked arm in arm with her husband toward her family, the gawkers gradually returned to their own concerns.

Her smile faltered as she saw Isabelle. Perhaps her hand tightened on her husband's arm also, for the duke bent his head toward her. Fitz could not tell what question he asked, but her answer, judging by the movement of her lips, seemed to be, *Everything is fine. I'll tell you more later.*

She was warm and gracious as she greeted Isabelle and introduced her husband. They were all old friends. Isabelle and Hastings had pulled many a prank together when the boys visited the Pelham house. She and Helena had always got on well. And Fitz had learned, from a remark Helena let stray years ago, that in the days leading up to his wedding, Venetia had spent many hours holding Isabelle's hand as the latter wept and raged against the cruelty of fate.

This, then, should have been a more buoyant reunion. But Isabelle alone brought the delight and the vivacity. She was thrilled for Venetia's match with the duke. She made hearty digs at Hastings for Helena's continued scorn of him. She could not wait to be more settled so that she could throw a dinner for the old gang.

Everyone else was cordial in their manners, but their smiles reminded Fitz of those one put on when faced with an overly chatty vicar.

"Yes," said Isabelle, as they walked toward the exit and the carriages that awaited beyond. "I do enjoy it. And did Fitz tell you? He was the one who arranged for the house."

Swift, inscrutable glances darted Fitz's way.

"Fitz is terribly modest," said Venetia. "Not for him to boast what he has done for his friends."

Isabelle laughed. "Modest, Fitz? When did you become modest? I remember you bragging with the best of them."

He had, hadn't he? He'd strutted, too, as young, athletic boys so often did. One could say having his dreams executed before his eyes killed his swagger outright. But the truth was, he'd always admired quiet confidence better than braggadocio and would have moderated his bluster at some point, even if life hadn't beat him to it.

"Modesty is a more appealing quality in an older gentleman such as myself."

Isabelle laughed. "Oh, how funny."

He had meant to poke fun at himself but what he said was not a joke.

"So, my dear Mrs. Englewood, what are your plans now that you are back?" asked Hastings.

"Oh, so many of them." Isabelle turned her face toward Fitz, her look of anticipation unmistakable.

Hastings tapped his fingers against the handle of his walking stick. Venetia adjusted the angle of her hat. Helena tugged at the brooch at her throat. Isabelle might not recognize the signs but they were uncomfortable, especially his sisters.

"Mrs. Englewood is going to visit her sister in Aberdeen in a day or two," Fitz said.

"Oh, how delightful," said Venetia. "Will you stay for a while? Scotland is lovely this time of the year."

There was hope in her voice.

"No, a week at most. I will visit her for a longer time after the end of the Season but for now I shall miss London too much." She gazed again at Fitz, not caring that she was essentially flirting—possibly even thrilling to it.

Perhaps Fitz had shot well past modesty into outright prudery. But Isabelle had children and he a wife. They ought to be more circumspect in their public conduct, even if they were only before his family and his most trusted friend.

Then he saw her, Millie, descending from her brougham, looking right and left preparing to cross the street. Her eyes landed on him at the same moment. But the pleasure on her face faded away as she took in the sight of Isabelle walking next to him, comfortably ensconced among members of his family.

In *her* place.

She blinked a few times, her sweet, delicate face straining for composure. Lowering her head, she turned around and climbed back into the brougham.

It drove away, inconspicuous, one vehicle in a sea of carriages.

*A*lice was in her usual place on the mantel of Fitz's study, her eyes closed, her tail curled around her plump little body. The clear glass bell jar that protected her from dust and moisture provided a clue that she'd long ago departed for the hereafter, but she remained so lifelike Millie still expected her to stir and wake up.

"I've been looking for you everywhere in the house," came her husband's voice behind her. "Why didn't you join us?"

Millie did not immediately turn around. She needed a minute to pull herself together. The sight of the Fitzhugh party coming out from the rail station was still seared in her mind, Isabelle retaking her place as if the past eight years never happened. "You are back early," she said. "I thought everyone was to take tea at the duke's house."

"Everyone includes *you* and I've come to get you."

He had spoken to her of fairness when she'd have put their pact on a bonfire and burned it. No doubt he was again motivated by his need to restore her to her rightful place. But she wanted to be an inseparable part of his heart, not a consideration for his conscience. "It will be awkward with Mrs. Englewood there."

"She won't be there."

He joined her at the mantel, the shoulder of his day coat speckled with drops of water—it had started to rain as she'd reached home. And then, utterly unexpected: his hand on the small of her back; his lips on her cheek.

The gesture was more familiar than intimate. Still, they did not greet each other this way: nods and smiles, perhaps, but not kisses on the cheek that left an etching of heat upon her skin.

He turned the bell jar a few degrees. "I never asked you, Millie. But why did you have Alice preserved?"

Sometimes Millie forgot that it had been her idea. No, more than her idea: She'd also been the one to engage the services of a taxidermist. "You loved her so much I couldn't bear to put her underground."

He was silent, his thumb rubbing against the small plaque that bore Alice's name.

"Do you miss her still?" she asked.

"Not as much as I used to. And when I do miss her—she was a fixture of my school days, to think of her is to remember what it was like to be seventeen and without a care in the world."

"You miss your old life." It was a given, but still she hurt to be reminded of it.

"Doesn't everyone, from time to time?" He replaced the bell jar and turned toward her. "Ten years from now I'm going to miss my life as it is today, simply because I will never be twenty-seven again. There is always something worth remembering in every stage of the journey."

"Even in the year you married?"

"Yes." His expression was—surely she deluded herself—nostalgic. "Demolishing the north wing, for one—that opportunity will not come again. Mrs. Clements telling the colonel to shut up. Our conversation about the commodes with the queen's portrait inside—still one of the funniest things I've ever heard."

She didn't know why it should be so, but her eyes tingled with tears. It had been a horrible year, but his words carried a great fondness—for this most arduous time of their life together. As if in looking back, the grief and the anguish had been sifted away, and only the gems remained—moments of camaraderie, memories that shone.

"Of course," he said, smiling, "how can I forget, your panic over my determination to kill myself with a dummy rifle."

Her voice caught. "You will never let me live that down, will you?"

"No. I can't believe it: We never did give you any firearm lessons, did we?"

"There were always more pressing concerns."

"We'll do it this year—make you a crack shot in no time."

"I'm sure the grouse will happily disagree as I miss every last one of them."

"Grouse isn't the only thing to shoot. The seasons for partridge and pheasant don't end until first of February. And that's plenty of t . . ."

His voice trailed off.

Understanding came all too swift to Millie, like a tropical sunset that abruptly turned day into night. There was no next year for them. Come January he would go to Mrs. Englewood.

"It's all right," she said gamely. "Not all of us are meant to be crack shots."

He looked at her as if he hadn't seen her in a very long time. Or perhaps, as if he might never see her again, and must memorize her features one by one.

When he finally spoke, he said, "They are still waiting for us for tea, you and me. Shall we go?"

CHAPTER 9

The Partnership

1889 ~

$\mathcal{M}$illie's father died three weeks after Alice. But whereas Alice had given every indication that she was not long for this earth, Mr. Graves's heart failed unexpectedly. He was forty-two.

Millie was stunned. Her mother was incoherent with shock. Thankfully, as he had done after Mr. Townsend's passing, Lord Fitzhugh stepped in and took charge of the arrangements.

Mr. Graves's will was simple enough. He settled a number of trusts on longtime retainers and employees, gave miscellaneous gifts to members of his extended family, provided generously for his widow, and left all of Cresswell & Graves Enterprises to Millie.

After the funeral, Mrs. Hanover, Millie's aunt, suggested that Mrs. Graves, devastated by grief, would do well to spend some time in a bright and cheerful place.

Millie and Mrs. Hanover together accompanied Mrs. Graves to Tuscany, to recuperate in a sun-drenched landscape of cypresses and vineyards.

They'd planned to stay for at least three months. But a month into their sojourn, a letter came for Millie from her husband. He dutifully wrote once a week—short missives that numbered not more than five sentences between greetings and salutations. But this letter was three pages, front and back.

He had performed an audit of the firm, from its accounts and records to its factories and other physical assets. He had also spoken with a number of retailers who sold Cresswell & Graves wares.

Mr. Graves, during his tenure, had been excessively cautious. The plum pudding and the mackerel had been the only new products added to the line during the past decade. His philosophy had been to produce few products and produce them well. With the ever expanding number of companies that daily introduced more varieties to the market, Cresswell & Graves still sold about the same number of products from year to year, but they were becoming a smaller and smaller percentage of the retailers' stock.

Moreover, they could not even boast their wares as the best-made tinned goods anymore. Yes, their ingredients were still carefully sourced and thoroughly inspected, and the manufacturing process was clean and conscientious, but newer technologies and production methods had become available in the past ten years—means to make preserved foods taste fresher and last longer—and Cresswell & Graves had adopted none of them.

The company was stagnating. In Lord Fitzhugh's opinion, they had not yet reached a point of crisis. But should things continue at the same sluggish pace, it might not be long before they were moribund.

Change must happen. If they didn't initiate the change now, it would be forced upon them soon. He meant to convene a meeting of lawyers and managers and discuss a new, more energetic direction for the company. Would Lady Fitzhugh join him?

Millie was dumbfounded—almost more by his request than by the company's declining fortunes. From birth she'd been trained to be a lady. She knew nothing about the business. She'd never set foot in one of Cresswell & Graves's factories. And until her honeymoon, never eaten from a tin.

It seemed almost blasphemous for her to participate in the running of the business in any capacity. Her mother never had. Her father, were he still alive, would be scandalized by any involvement on Millie's part.

"What should I do?" she asked her mother.

"What do you wish to do?" said Mrs. Graves. She still looked pale and fragile in her widow's weeds, but her old strength of mind was returning.

"I'd like to do what I can to help Lord Fitzhugh—and myself. But I'm not sure what my presence will accomplish. I haven't the slightest experience when it comes to matters of business."

"But the firm belongs to you. Without your support, Lord Fitzhugh cannot take over the management of it."

"I'm astonished he wants to." Lordships didn't involve themselves in the nitty-gritty details of how their money was made.

Mrs. Graves tilted her embroidery frame to better examine it in the light. "I approve. A young man should have ambitious tasks with which to occupy himself. Even with all the work that remains to be done at Henley Park, the majority of the improvements will finish sometime in the not-too-distant future. But an ongoing concern such as Cresswell & Graves will always keep the man in charge busy."

Millie remained awake half the night, thinking. In the morning, before breakfast, she sent out her reply.

I will start by the end of the week.

*L*ord Fitzhugh was on the platform, waiting, as Millie's train reached London. She had not expected his presence. When she arrived at a destination behind him, she could always expect that he'd have dispatched a carriage for her, but he'd never before come to collect her in person.

He nodded when he spotted her, her face very nearly pressed to the window. Ever so beautiful, her husband, but there was something different in his aspect today. He was dressed rather formally, gleaming top hat, a black frock coat, a mourning band on his arm—but that was not it.

Then she realized that for the very first time since she'd met him, he looked genuinely excited. Unlike the earldom, which he took on most reluctantly, he relished the prospect of remaking Cresswell & Graves.

He offered her his arm as she disembarked. "How was your trip, Lady Fitzhugh?"

"It was fine. I had to wait overnight in Calais—too much fog on the channel—but other than that, quite smooth."

"And how is Mrs. Graves?"

"Much better. She sends her regards—and she approves of your ambitions."

"Your mother, without a doubt, is the most forward-looking person I've ever met."

"She would have been very gratified to hear of it."

"Then, I will be sure to tell her in person next time we meet. What of you, Lady Fitzhugh, do you also approve of my ambitions?"

She was speaking to a different person. Lord Fitzhugh as she'd known him had been a stoic who carried out his duties because it was expected of him. But this young man next to her had something he wanted to accomplish.

Mrs. Graves had called their joint decisions the foundation upon which to build a life. But after the foundation they'd need a framework. And Cresswell & Graves just might prove to be that framework.

"Yes, I do," she said. "I think taking over the company is exactly what you should do."

He handed her into their waiting carriage and climbed in after her, taking the backward-facing seat. "Thank goodness—I was afraid you'd consider it too distasteful."

"The thought of you managing the tinneries, I'll owe, is a bit shocking. But commerce and manufacturing is where the money is nowadays. Since I am not too ashamed to spend that money, I ought not be too ashamed to make it."

"Excellent." He tapped his walking stick against the top of the carriage. It pulled away from the curb. "When you've had a chance to rest, would you like to look at the summary I've made of the accounts and ledgers?"

"Yes, alongside those accounts and ledgers themselves."

He raised an eyebrow. "Not trusting my mathematical abilities?"

"Far from it. But since our goal is to have you installed at the head of Cresswell & Graves, it is better for me to be as fluent in the condition of the company as you. If I am an ignoramus, then my word will carry very little weight."

He tented his fingers before him. "On the other hand, if you are astonishingly well versed, they might find you too intimidating, and close ranks against us."

"A fine line to walk, isn't it?"

"Moreover, installing me at the head of the company is only a short-term victory. I need the longtime managers to come to my point of view, so I must make them think that my ideas are their own."

"Another tall order."

"We have much work to do, Lady Fitzhugh."

His tone was serious, yet at the same time full of anticipation. She found herself both daunted by what he wanted and fiercely determined to rise to the challenge. Perhaps a garden was not the only thing they'd grow together. Perhaps they could also nurture a successful partnership.

"I'm not afraid of work," she said. "Give me a goal and point me to it."

*Y*ou really aren't afraid of work," Fitz marveled a few days later.

"I used to practice the piano five hours a day," she said. "I hated it. Compared to that, this is nothing."

She might have smiled—her eyes crinkled, but he couldn't see the rest of her face, which was concealed by a black scarf. She was nearly entirely swamped in black, a dress of black silk trimmed with crape, a thick black mantle, a sable muff for her hands. Fitz was dressed just as heavily, three pairs of stockings inside his boots, gloves, two woolen mufflers. A fire burned in the grate and still he was cold.

Since their marriage, most of their energies had been concentrated on Henley Park, not the town residence, which remained dank and drafty. In summer, it was bearable. But now, late in the year, he fancied himself growing arthritic in the frigid temperatures.

At night it was so frosty in his room that he'd given serious consideration to knocking on her door and asking to climb in bed with her—not to break their pact, but for warmth.

"You play beautifully." Sometimes, when his sisters or Hastings visited Henley Park, they asked her to play for them.

"I play well. *Beautifully* is another matter altogether. You need musicality to play beautifully. I can only press the keys and make sounds."

"I can't tell the difference."

"Many people can't—all those hours of practice."

"Good. By the time we are done here with all *our* hours of practice, your father's managers won't be able to tell that we've maneuvered them."

"You really think so?"

"I do," he said. "You are very convincing. And surprisingly wily. You'll have them eating out of your hand."

Her eyes crinkled again. He wondered once more whether she'd let him hold her at night—just for warmth. But of course he'd never ask. A pact was a pact.

She pulled her scarf more snug around her face. "Should we practice some more with you as Mr. Hawkes?"

"No, I think I'll be Mr. Mortimer this time."

"Oh, good, you do a very fine Mr. Mortimer." She looked at him, her eyes bright and clear. "I know the stakes are terribly high, but this is actually fun."

"Yes, it is," he agreed. "It is."

*T*he meeting was set to take place in January, a day after Lord Fitzhugh's twenty-first birthday. It was important that he come into his majority, so that they no longer needed Colonel Clements's permission—or forgiveness—for any decisions. And so that they were not two children dealing with men who'd been in business for decades.

The night before, after dinner, she'd given him his birthday present, a signet ring with the Fitzhugh coat of arms. And inscribed inside, the family motto, *Audentes fortuna iuvat.*

"*Fortune favors the bold*," he translated. "Highly applicable to the occasion. I will wear it tomorrow."

"Oh, good," she said, trying not to sound breathlessly gratified—which she was.

He gauged the size of the ring and put it on the index finger of his right hand. "A perfect fit."

Now she was only breathless. His hand looked different with the square, heavy ring upon it. Or perhaps the ring only emphasized the qualities he'd acquired since their wedding, the cool dedication and the calm authority.

She wanted him to touch her with the ring on his hand. Badly.

"I hope it will bring us good luck," she said.

"I hope so, too. But should things go ill, at least we will know it is only because of the capriciousness of luck, that we have done everything in our power to seize the opportunity." He placed his hand on her arm. "And whatever the outcome tomorrow, I couldn't have asked for a better partner in this endeavor—or any other, for that matter."

It was not a declaration of love, but one of friendship. Her heart ached—yet at the same time, filled with sweetness. She closed her hand over his, the one bearing the ring.

"It will happen," she said. "If not tomorrow, then another day. Sooner or later the prize will be ours."

*T*he meeting was a theatrical production.

In the five weeks leading up to it, they had discussed and prepared for every last aspect of the encounter, including their personal appearances. Her mourning dress, especially commissioned, was cut large to make her look smaller and younger in it. He'd let his hair grow long in order to look less serious. They both shook hands rather limply.

Once inside her father's old office, he did not take one of the chairs arranged in two semicircles before Mr. Grave's desk, but stood in a corner at the back of the room, looking slightly bored, to give the impression he'd come solely to accompany his wife and was little interested in the goings-on himself.

Lady Fitzhugh, she of the most impeccable posture, hunched forward in her chair and looked as if she had trouble raising her eyes to the assembly, let alone addressing them.

Her voice quivered slightly. "Gentlemen, thank you for coming this morning. It is a pleasure to have all of you in the same room. I am sure you are as grieved as I am that it is no longer my father occupying this chair, but such is the will of God and we must cope as best as we can.

"He has, as you know, left Cresswell & Graves to me as a going concern. I am young and inexperienced, therefore I have called you together and hope you may advise and guide me as to how I may best proceed."

It was vitally important that she, though the rightful owner, did not appear to be a usurper, given that she was a woman and her husband a toff who presumably knew nothing beyond polo and shooting.

Mr. Hawkes, a wizened old man who had been a trusted lieutenant to the senior Mr. Graves, Lady Fitzhugh's grandfather, and who no longer participated in the day-to-day operation of the business, said, "Perhaps it would be best, Lady Fitzhugh, for you to remain removed from the running of the business. A woman's place is at home."

Helena would have demanded whether the man had heard of Queen Elizabeth, who ran the business of England better than any man before or since. But Fitz's wife only nodded timidly.

"Indeed you have read my heart, sir. It is a difficult task, the direction of an enterprise such as ours, requiring much perspicacity and expertise. I would have dearly loved to remain in the comfort and insularity of my home. Alas, I am the last of the Graves, and as such, it would be a complete dereliction of duty were I to turn my back on Cresswell & Graves."

She said it with a steely resignation, a young martyr

facing her doom with serenity and courage, because she knew she was doing the right thing.

From their weeks of practice Fitz already knew her to be a good actress. However, not all actors excelled as much onstage as they did in rehearsal—he'd witnessed classmates seize with stage fright during school performances, sweating and butchering their lines. But he need not have worried. She was outdoing herself.

Mr. Hawkes looked taken aback. It was all very well for him to put a woman in her place, but before such dutiful femininity he certainly could not suggest her father had made a mistake by bequeathing the firm to his only child.

Mr. Hawkes's former protégé and current rival for influence Mr. Mortimer, a balding, thickening man in his late forties, said, "I do believe, Lady Fitzhugh, that the best manner going forward would be for you to continue to devote yourself to your home and your charitable work. And we will keep you informed of our decisions—say, annually."

"It is most kind of you, Mr. Mortimer. I always knew I could rely on the gentlemen in this room to watch out for my best interest. Since you are so generous, there is no reason I cannot find a few days every quarter to dedicate to the business of Cresswell & Graves. I am slightly ashamed, however, of the inadequacy of my dedication— I'm sure my father would have wanted me to keep an even closer eye on things. Monthly briefings, perhaps."

"Oh, I dare say quarterly briefings would stand you in good stead," Mr. Mortimer hastened to say.

The other men around the table echoed his sentiment.

Fitz suppressed a smile. From annual to quarterly, with no resistance whatsoever. His wife was slowly and gently sliding them into her pocket—without giving the least indication what she was up to.

"I am so grateful for your reassurance, gentlemen. You make me feel very well taken care of and I thank you. However, there is one thing that is still on my mind and that is the matter of choosing a first among equals. When my father was alive, he was that person. Now we have a dozen colleagues, but no leader. I have led a sheltered life, but even I know that an unled group, no matter how individually brilliant the members, would disintegrate into factions along lines of disagreement."

The men around the table look at one another, some at their allies, some at their rivals. Fitz had informed her closely of his observations. Her father's lieutenants were split between those who were content to do Mr. Graves's bidding, and those who itched to branch out and grow.

"And yet we face challenging times ahead and it is important that we preserve comity and unity. Whomever we choose to head the enterprise should be someone fair and honest, with both the stature and the experience to lead us across troubled waters."

Fitz's pulse picked up. This was where they'd find out whether his strategy would work. By forcing them to choose a leader before her, without time for behind-closed-doors deal-making and compromises, he hoped that they would select the most neutral person in the room, someone whom both sides had good reason to believe they could influence.

Him.

So far she had performed beautifully, but one could

never account for all the variables that might come into play. It was always possible that the men had met beforehand and already decided on the one they'd choose to lead them. And if that were the case, it was more likely than not one of the old guards.

And that would make his intended course of action incalculably more arduous. Rightful owners they might be, but they would have a difficult time getting their ideas implemented, let alone implemented well.

"Perhaps I could invite some names to be put forward?" she prompted them. "Perhaps this is the time to look around the room and see if there is a man acceptable to everyone?"

He'd written most of the script for her speech. But the last question was her own. As if on cue, the men seated in the first row of seats, the leaders of the two factions, turned around. And whom should they see but the untried youth loitering at the back of the room.

Eaglelike eyes assessed him. He did his very best to appear a blank canvas for other men's ideas, or perhaps a clump of clay for someone else to shape.

"I'd have liked to volunteer myself for the honor—were I thirty years younger," said Mr. Hawkes. "But now that I am an old fuddy-duddy, let it not be said that I do not value the valor and enthusiasm of youth. I move that we invite Lord Fitzhugh to lead us."

Fitz did not need to pretend. He *was* as astonished as the other men in the room. The best-case scenario—the one for which they'd schemed, plotted, strategized—had come to pass.

"Me? But—but I haven't the faintest idea what to do with a passel of tinneries."

Lady Fitzhugh also protested. "I thought we needed a man of experience. I'm sure Lord Fitzhugh is full of fine qualities but his only experience is in cricket."

"And did not the Duke of Wellington himself say that the battle of Waterloo was won on the playing fields of Eton?"

Now Mr. Hawkes was going all out, pushing Fitz's candidacy, no doubt believing he'd enjoy a particular influence over Fitz should he succeed.

The men of the reforming faction looked at one another. Mr. Mortimer, realizing that he would not be elected to lead the company, hastened to put in his own approval of Fitz's fitness for the office. "Experience can be earned. Lord Fitzhugh is a bright, winsome young man and I am sure he will lead us most capably."

"Hear, hear," somebody said.

*M*illie excused herself once her husband had been installed at the head of the company. But the rest of the day she could do nothing except anxiously pace about the house, waiting for him to come back.

He did, late in the afternoon. As soon as they'd closed the study door behind themselves, he enfolded her in a bear hug.

She had not expected it at all—or the swift current of warmth that instantly surged through her. God, he smelled wonderful. And his body was lean and angular—and strong, for presently he lifted her and spun her around.

"Well done, old gal. Well done!"

She squealed with laughter and banged at his shoulders

to be put down. "What happened after I left? Tell me. I'm dying to know."

"The meeting was adjourned an hour after you left. Mr. Hawkes pulled me aside to give me a word of caution on making too many changes too fast. But even men who don't want to make too many changes too fast have an occasional idea or two. So I told him about his bottling plant."

"What bottling plant?"

"Twelve years ago, he had wanted your father to expand to bottled beverages and had prepared a thorough dossier for the construction of a new manufacturing plant dedicated to these bottled beverages. The site, the blueprint for the building, the designs for the machinery were all there. He even had a book of recipes and several prototype designs of the bottles that would be used.

"One could only imagine how disappointed he was to have his proposal rejected. So I told him that with me in charge, he will have his bottling plant—and soon. Norwich & Sons went belly-up during the construction of a bottling plant. I let him know that I'd be quite happy to buy it with my own funds and sign the deed over to the company—a coming-aboard present, so to speak."

"He didn't become suspicious, did he?"

"No, he looked at me as if I were an old friend—the only one in the world who understood him. He was quite helpful the rest of the day and now we've a list of ideas as long as I'm tall to consider. And there will be a number of new products to be taste tested the next time you meet with them."

He hugged her again. "I can't tell you how thrilled I am

that everything went off so well. I couldn't have done it without you."

She was happily proud—of both of them. "You did very well yourself."

A knock came at the door. It was their butler, with the coffee service.

"Shall we open a bottle of champagne for you?" asked Lord Fitzhugh.

"No," she said, "coffee is more than good enough."

Water would have been more than good enough.

She poured the coffee. He raised his in a toast. "To a future of our own making."

They clinked their cups. "A future of our own making," she echoed.

And wished fervently that it would be so.

CHAPTER 10

1896

*T*he invitation—summons, rather—came at the last minute, on the morning of the ball.

Millie was about to look in on Helena's final fitting when a footman presented a silver salver. She recognized the envelope by its embossed stem of a rose at the lower right-hand corner: Mrs. Englewood.

She ducked into an empty room to read.

Dear Lady Fitzhugh,

Let me be the first one to admit that it is terrible form to request a meeting, given that we have never been introduced. But as we are well aware of each other's existence, let us dispense with needless formalities, shall we?

Please let me know if I may wait on you this afternoon at two.

Yours,
Mrs. John Englewood

This was not entirely unexpected. She and Mrs. Englewood were not two bitches tussling over a bone. At some point it behooved them to sit down and hold a civilized conversation concerning the Arrangement. But for Millie that point hadn't come yet and shouldn't come for at least another five months.

Mrs. Englewood obviously believed otherwise.

Millie had the perfect excuse in the ball of course—she was much too busy—but she would not decline the meeting. She'd learned her lesson about putting off till eight years later what she should do today. If the meeting must happen at some point, then let it happen today.

Even if today was the day Fitz became her husband in truth.

Especially if.

*W*ere Mrs. Englewood and Fitz a pair of bookends, they could not be better matched physically. Like him, her build was tall, slender, and tight. Like him, she had dark hair and blue eyes. And like him, she moved with a nonchalant grace.

Millie was neither overly short nor overly pudgy. Before Mrs. Englewood's stately figure, however, it was difficult not to feel squat—even a little dumpy. But it was not as if she was ever going to feel anything but inferior before Isabelle Englewood.

"You are different from how I remember you," said Mrs. Englewood, sipping her tea. "Taller and prettier."

Just like that, no other preliminaries.

Millie took a deep breath. "It's nice to know that I look better now than I did at my wedding."

"The dress swallowed you."

Millie had to agree. "Yes, in hindsight the dress was quite atrocious. Instead of the best money could buy, we went for the most money could buy."

Her acknowledgment of the parvenu tastes of her wedding gown garnered her a surprised glance from Mrs. Englewood.

"All the same," she said, her voice turning wistful, "I'd have gladly worn that gown—or one ten times as hideous— if I could have walked down the aisle to him."

Millie ate her biscuit and said nothing.

"I loved him. I'd planned my entire future around becoming Mrs. Fitzhugh. And when he married you, all my hopes and dreams collapsed. For two months, all I did was sit on my bed, dawn till dusk, dusk till dawn. I barely ate. Slept maybe once every three days. I've never looked the same since."

She did look different, like a broken vase that had been put back together: still beautiful, all the pieces accounted for, but the damage showed. Millie's heart flinched, as if someone had brought a burning match too near.

"My mother and my sister eventually coaxed me out of my exile. They convinced me that it was better for me to go to London and find a husband, instead of fade away at home. So that was what I did the next Season."

"He was there that day at your wedding. He said you looked beautiful—and happy," Millie said, in a futile attempt to remind Mrs. Englewood that not all had gone awry in her life.

"I suppose I was happy enough. But it was not the same—an imitation. Nothing could approach that perfect, unmarred happiness I'd once known."

Every breath Millie drew scalded her lungs, but Mrs. Englewood went on inexorably.

"All I want is to regain what I once lost, to live the life I was meant to live. It's not too much to ask, is it?"

Millie forced out her answer. "No."

"Fitz is a lovely man—and I'm not just talking about his looks. You know he is stalwart and honorable. You know he will sacrifice himself to the call of duty. And—" Mrs. Englewood's voice faltered. "And you are now part of his duty."

"What do you mean?"

"He cares deeply for your well-being. He views you as the blameless party and he does not want any action on his part to injure your future happiness."

Millie began to understand. "You are worried that I won't let him go—that I will resort to tears to keep him with me."

"I am not saying you would," said Mrs. Englewood. "But in your place I might have. It is so easy to fall in love with him and so difficult to let go."

"It is a good thing for everyone, then, I am not bound up in him."

Mrs. Englewood stared at Millie, her gaze as heavy as a boulder. "Do you not love him?"

No one had ever asked her a direct question on this matter—and therefore she'd been spared the lying.

"Lord Fitzhugh and I married because he needed my family's fortune and my father wanted a titled son-in-law," Millie said carefully. "That we get along as well as we do is odds defying enough. Love would have taken it into the realm of fiction."

"You don't find his person appealing?" Mrs. Englewood sounded incredulous.

"He is very agreeable."

"I mean, do you not think he is extraordinarily handsome?"

"He is handsome. But so are a number of his classmates and his new brother-in-law, the Duke of Lexington. If I fell in love with every toothsome fellow I came across, I'd be frequently and needlessly in love."

"But he is also kind. Considerate. Willing to shoulder all burdens. Being married to him all these years, you've never wished that he would have eyes only for you?"

Millie forced herself to hold Isabelle Englewood's eyes. "Not everyone is meant to fall in love. Lord Fitzhugh and I are good friends and nothing more."

"Then, you will let him go?"

"I have never restricted the freedom of his movement, not once in our married life."

"Even though the two of you will have six months of intimacy? That changes things, you know."

"If that alone were enough to make people fall in love, all the wives in this country would be in love with their husbands—and vice versa."

Mrs. Englewood set down her teacup and rose. She

walked to the open window and looked out to the street beyond. It was a quiet street, no hawkers, street musicians, or the constant hoof clacks of hansom cabs looking for custom. Fitz had clearly put a great deal of thought in the house he'd selected for her.

She turned around. "I am afraid, Lady Fitzhugh. I've been at the receiving end of life's caprices and it's not a kind place to be. But I have no choice, do I? I must trust that you are a woman of your word."

Millie had not given her word to Mrs. Englewood. She had not yet conceded Fitz. Did a faithful wife of almost eight years not have some claims to her husband? She deserved a level playing field, at least.

"So he *was* there at my wedding . . ." whispered Mrs. Englewood, as if to herself. She blinked, her eyes brilliant with unshed tears. "I knew I sensed his presence."

How foolish Millie was: There was no such thing as a level playing field. She would always be the usurper, the spoiler of dreams, the one who caused such grief on Mrs. Englewood's part that to this day it was writ large in the very alignment of her features.

"You are the one he has loved all along," she heard herself say. "There has never been anyone but you."

$\mathcal{H}$elena gazed at the adorable ducklings a minute longer—Miss Evangeline South was a talented artist—before rising from her seat, her notes in hand. She opened the door of her office and handed the notes to her secretary.

"I need these typed, Miss Boyle."

"Yes, miss."

Susie was in her spot—Helena could swear the woman never needed to use the water closet. She retreated back into her office and shut the door.

She didn't know why it should be so, after a day and a half with the ducklings and turtles and fish of Miss South's pond, but her hands reached on their own toward the drawer into which she'd stuffed Hastings's manuscript.

And when she had the manuscript before her, she did not begin from where she'd stopped, but opened to a random page.

Her skin is dusky in the candlelight. I trace my fingers up the side of her ribcage, over her shoulder, then along the length of her arm to her wrist, fastened to a slat in the headboard with a silk scarf.

"Aren't you weary of looking at me like this, tied up always?" she murmurs.

"No," I answer. "Never."

"Don't you want to be touched?"

"I do. But I don't want to be scratched."

She licks her lips, her tongue pink, moist. "What is a good time in the marital bed without a few scratches on your back, darling?"

Helena's pulse accelerated. She'd read some erotica here and there. Always the stories seemed to be aimed at titillating male readers, with the female characters completely interchangeable, mere objects to be spanked and poked.

But this was different. The nameless bride of Larkspear was a person in her own right, neither afraid nor given to senseless worship of a man's cock.

"If only I could be sure that a few scratches will satisfy you."

I bend my head and bite her lip. Her breaths caress my chin. Her gaze slides down my body. "Ready again, I see."

"Ravenous."

"Such interesting nights you give me, Larkspear."

"Do you think of me during the day, Lady Larkspear?"

She smiles. "Never, my dear."

"Liar."

"Prove it."

I thrust deep inside her. Her lips part. Her eyes close briefly, but the next moment they are wide open again. She likes to look at me in my animal rut, to witness my weakness for her and taunt me with the unattainability of her heart.

Helena turned the manuscript facedown. It made her uncomfortable, as if he'd pulled a fantasy out of the deepest recesses of her mind, a fantasy she never knew about until he'd set it down in writing. A fantasy about power, *her* power, and a man who pushed back without being fearful of it.

A knock came at her door. She hastily locked the manuscript away. "Come in."

Susie poked in her head. "Miss, the ball is tonight. Lady Fitzhugh asked me to remind you to leave earlier than usual."

Of course, the ball in honor of Venetia and the duke—with Hastings certain to be there.

"Yes, I will leave earlier," she said. "Or Lady Fitzhugh will fret."

*T*he train bellowed. The platform fogged with steam from the engines. A fading swirl of it passed between Fitz and Isabelle.

Her children were already aboard with their governess. Through the windows they waved at him, excited at the prospect of visiting their cousins. He waved back.

"They like you," she said.

"I like them. They are good children." He changed his walking stick—the one with the blue porcelain handle—from one hand to the other. She'd admired it earlier; he did not tell her it had been a present from Millie. "You should probably board. Your train will leave any minute now."

"I'm loath to leave you," she said. "I wish I hadn't agreed to this visit."

"You will enjoy it—you haven't seen your sister in years. Besides, you'll only be gone a week."

"A week is a long time. Everything can change."

Any other day he'd have scoffed at her fear. But tonight something *would* change.

On the face of it, a roll in the hay ought not to matter. He'd sauntered through quite a few beds in his time. Sometimes he grew more fond of a woman, sometimes less. But the change was predicated upon their personal qualities, not because he slept with them.

He already respected and admired Millie. He'd like her even more tomorrow morning, but the fundamental nature of their firmly established friendship should remain the same.

More or less.

"A week is only seven days," he said.

He noticed he did not reassure Isabelle that nothing would change. Her lips tightened: She'd noticed, too.

The steam whistle blew, a sharp-pitched warning, followed by a deep rumble that rattled the tracks.

"Hurry," he said, leaning forward to kiss her on her cheek. "Or your children will be in Aberdeen without you."

She gripped his hand. "Think of me."

"I will."

She turned toward the train, then turned back again. "You once told me that no matter what happened, you'd always, always love me. Is that still the case?"

"Of course," he said, perhaps a little too fast.

"I'll hold on to that, then."

"I'll be here waiting, when you come back."

She threw her arms about him. "I love you. I will love you till my last breath."

CHAPTER 11

The Bench

1890 ∼

Millie knocked on the door of her husband's study and pushed it open. "You wish to see me, sir?"

"Yes. Come in, please."

She took her usual chair across the table from his, but he was not in his chair. Instead, he was before the mantel, a poker in hand, prodding at the coals in the grate. Something in the set of his jaw alarmed her.

"What's the matter?"

He shrugged.

"Tell me."

He dropped the poker into its holder. "I opened a letter from Gerry Pelham just now. He informs me he has become the proud uncle of a baby niece."

Gerry Pelham, Isabelle Pelham's brother. It had been little more than a year since Miss Pelham became

Mrs. Englewood—and now she had a child. A familiar pain gnawed at Millie's chest—Fitz had been once again reminded of what he'd lost.

He sat down in his chair. "I'm sorry. I was surprised by the news, that's all."

Ambushed by the news, more like it. "Would you prefer that I came another time?"

"No, I'm glad you are here. Help me take my mind off it."

He used to want to be away from her when he had such news from his beloved. The pain in Millie's heart was now mixed with a slow, bittersweet pleasure. "Anything," she said.

He opened a dossier on the desk. "Your father advertised very little. He believed that the quality of Cresswell & Graves products spoke for themselves. When we first began to expand into bottled beverages, my instinct was to advertise, but Mr. Hawkes felt otherwise. He was more concerned with wooing the retailers to stock these new products. Once the products were in view, he believed they'd fly off the shelves.

"I gave him one quarter to prove himself right. When he did not, and our new beverages collected dust in shops, I commissioned an advertising campaign. Since women are responsible for the majority of the household expenditures on food and drink, I thought I'd ask your opinion on these placards."

She was immensely flattered—and almost as nervous. "I'd be honored to help, if I can."

He passed the drawings to her. She spread them before her. The designs were black and white. "Are these the finished designs?"

"Yes."

She hesitated. "You know I have no particular artistic eye."

He smiled slightly. "In other words, you don't find them appealing?"

"Not particularly," she said slowly. She'd hoped to tell him otherwise.

"Don't look so apologetic. If I thought you'd say yes to everything I wouldn't ask your opinion. Now tell me why you don't find them appealing."

Encouraged, she said, "Well, raspberry soda water, orange soda water, and strawberry lemonade are pretty and vibrant in person. A black-and-white placard does not convey their attractiveness. And the image of a bottle surrounded by words extolling its virtues is too matter-of-fact, almost as if we are selling a tonic when we are doing nothing of the sort."

"What would you do, then?"

"We want young people to take these bottled drinks on picnics and to the seaside on holidays, don't we?" she said tentatively. "Then, why not let us suggest that in the advertising itself? Young ladies sitting under the shade of a tree, a nice spread of a picnic, raising our bottles in toast. Or young ladies at the beach, blue sky, blue sea, everyone in white dresses, holding our bottles."

He jotted down a several lines of notes. "All right. I'll recommission the artworks."

"On my words alone?"

He looked up. "Of everyone involved with Cresswell & Graves, you are the one I trust the most. And if I've learned anything since we married, it's that you have good instincts. So yes, Lady Fitzhugh, on your words alone."

She scarcely knew what to do. It was difficult to remain seated, yet a lady simply couldn't leap wildly about the room, even if her husband had just told her that yes, indeed, she was his closest advisor.

She swallowed the lump in her throat. "Thank you. Do you need me to look at anything else?"

*H*er ideas were exactly right. Introduced the next spring, the advertising placards, with their lush, striking contrasts of colors and idyllic images, were so wildly popular that they were stolen wherever they were put up. Fitz, encouraged, sent shopkeepers posters to display inside their stores and ordered tens of thousands of handbills to be passed out by sandwich-board men. The bottled beverages sold and sold.

Fitz, not one to let such excellence go unremarked, bought a set of jeweled hairpins for his wife. He'd taken both of his sisters with him to the jeweler's, but he'd known, the moment he'd seen the amethyst-and-diamond pins, that they were what he wanted. They reminded him of the lavender at Henley Park, an apt symbol for his wife—handsome, adaptable, and endlessly beneficial.

The first time he saw his gift on Lady Fitzhugh was on the occasional of Lady Knightbridge's ball.

He attended very few balls. For one thing, his presence was beside the point. The function of a ball was to put into proximity young men and women who might someday forge matrimonial alliances. He, a married man, would waste the young ladies' time. Also, a man at a ball was expected to dance, as there were always ladies in want of a partner. And he didn't exactly fancy dancing as the night was long.

But he was at Lady Knightbridge's ball for a purpose. Venetia, now in a platonic marriage with Mr. Easterbrook, an old family friend, and very much back in Society, wished to present Helena to the elusive Duke of Lexington, whispered to be expected. Fitz, who'd played cricket against Lexington when he was at Eton and Lexington at Harrow, was to make the introductions, as he was the only one in their party already acquainted with their quarry.

Venetia was disappointed: The duke did not attend after all. But the ball did have the piquancy of having in attendance Fitz's current mistress.

Mrs. Dorchester wanted to dance; Fitz obliged with a schottische. Mrs. Dorchester would have preferred a waltz, but Fitz felt strongly that for a man and a woman already conducting an affair, there was no need to further broadcast the relationship by engaging in any activity that would have them pressed together in public.

The dance done, he walked Mrs. Dorchester back to her friends, and returned to his wife and sisters. Not five minutes later, Mrs. Dorchester sauntered past their group, smiled at him, then shot an utterly superior look at Lady Fitzhugh.

Fitz turned toward his wife. "Did she do what I think she did? On the occasion of your return to Society no less."

Her year of mourning for her father had excluded her from all the goings-on of the previous Season. It was the first time in nearly two years that she'd attended a London festivity.

"Anne Dorchester knows she has something I don't.

And she has always enjoyed lording over the less blessed of us."

"I did not know that about her."

"Some women are very nice to men but not so much to other women."

"Well, she picked the wrong woman to not be nice to. No one is allowed to disrespect my wife, least of all some woman with whom I am temporarily keeping company."

His wife shrugged. "What are you going to do? Make her come here and apologize to me for looking at me the wrong way?"

"I will no longer keep company with her."

She angled an eyebrow. "You cannot do that. It would be kinder to take her out back and shoot her."

He laughed. She had the driest sense of humor. "Moreover, I am going to dance with you."

"You can't dance with your own wife at a ball."

"Let them arrest me for it, then. Come, the next dance is starting—and Mrs. Dorchester is watching."

She studied him. Her eyes were a light brown, the color of the hazelnuts beloved by his Alice. And then she smiled—she had a nice smile. "They will call me bourgeois for it, but I have always been proudly bourgeois."

He led her onto the floor. She promptly stepped on his toe on the first turn. "Sorry!"

He laughed. "Don't worry. I just might return the favor—I'm completely out of practice. And I can't remember any of the fancier steps."

"Better not. Or I might find myself facedown on the floor."

Beyond this initial mishap, however, they danced quite well together. His more cautious quarter turns and half turns gave away to ebullient full revolutions. They spun around the ballroom, everything at the edge of his vision streaks of color and light.

"Wait. Dance slower," she suddenly said.

"Are you dizzy?"

"Not in the least. I just realized you are right: Mrs. Dorchester is watching. I want to enjoy the sight of her fuming."

"And I, of course, will very pointedly *not* look her way."

"She is fanning herself hard," reported Lady Fitzhugh, delighted. "Now she just snapped at someone."

"Excellent, I say we keep dancing until she pulls out her hair."

"No, she loves her hair too much. We'd be here all night."

"Until she pulls out someone else's hair, then."

Not that his motives were entirely altruistic. He enjoyed dancing with his wife: They moved well together, their sense of rhythm in perfect unison. And she smelled good, the scent light yet distinct.

"What perfume are you wearing? I like it."

"I don't wear perfume, but my soap is made with extract from our own lavender."

As it had turned out, the soil and climate of Somerset were perfect for the propagation of lavender. A few cuttings had grown to over two acres of lavender and she planned to keep expanding. Not long ago they'd discussed acquiring a hive of bees to make lavender honey. And perhaps even purchasing an apparatus to steam distill essence of lavender on site.

Henley Park, once a wasteland, was now a thriving estate. According to his housekeeper, tourists applied regularly to see the interior of the house and to picnic at the edge of the lavender fields.

He looked down at the amethyst-and-diamond pins sparkling in her hair. "Why don't we plan a house party for August?"

She missed a step. He had to tighten his grip on her so that she didn't stumble. "Careful now."

"I'm sorry. Did you say you want us to host your friends at Henley Park?"

"For a bit of shooting and fishing, yes. And invite plenty of eligible men for Helena, even though she'll most probably turn up her nose at all of them."

She said nothing.

"You don't like the idea?"

"No, no, I adore it. Just that—I wasn't sure this day would ever come."

"At some point I have to give up sulking."

She raised her face, her eyes shining. "And now they can at last snicker at your blue daisy commodes."

He chortled. "Don't mention them. You'll make me reconsider."

"Sorry. What was I saying? We only have strapping, manly commodes. They gurgle if you look at them wrong."

They were still laughing when the music stopped.

"Mrs. Dorchester looks like she is about to break the slats on her fan," she observed gleefully.

"Let's see if she'll do it."

They danced a second waltz. Then a third waltz.

"Oh, my, she is leaving," Lady Fitzhugh murmured halfway through the third waltz. "And . . . she has left."

"We'll dance one more just so that somebody doesn't

run to her and say we pulled apart the moment we drove her away."

"Four waltzes. Shocking, Lord Fitzhugh."

"My pleasure. And please, call me Fitz—all my friends do. And we've been friends for a while, haven't we?"

"Yes, I think so."

He raised a brow. "You don't know for certain, Lady Fitz? Has anyone else ever insulted you? Tell me and I'll bring down my wrath upon them to prove my devoted friendship."

Her cheeks turned pink. "You don't need to prove anything. I know we are friends."

"Good," he said. "I don't want you to think of me as just the man you had to marry to please your parents."

"No, not that," she said softly. "Not a chance."

Sometimes dreams did come true.

The country house party was a roaring success. The grouse was plentiful, the trout endlessly abundant. They organized a cricket match, a cycling competition, and an excursion to the spectacular Somerset coast. Millie, in a moment of inspiration, hired a photographer and gifted each guest with a sitting and a handsome portrait.

On the last night of the party, in a crowded drawing room, full of laughter and high spirits, Lord Hastings raised his glass and cried, "To our delightful hosts!"

His toast was taken up by all the guests. Millie, at the center of all the cheer and goodwill, her husband by her side, did her level best to commit every last detail of the moment to memory. The kiss Venetia blew toward her,

Helena's arm around her shoulders, her mother's proud smile, all under the golden light from the new chandelier which had been hoisted into place only two days before the house party began.

The next morning, however, she learned that Mrs. Englewood had given birth to another child, a boy this time. And if she knew, Fitz must also know. As they waved good-bye to their departing guests, she observed him rather nervously.

He turned to her and smiled. "Would you like a similar party for Christmas as well?"

He was genuinely pleased. It was as if the increasing size of Mrs. Englewood's family now had very little—if anything at all—to do with him.

"Yes, absolutely," she said, her tone fervent.

"You are sure? You look a little tired."

She had been feeling bleary-eyed, but not anymore. "I can climb the Matterhorn with nothing more than a stick and a canteen."

"Then, come with me. You've had your fun and games, Lady Fitz. Time to get back to work."

"Aye, aye, Captain!"

They traipsed all over the estate. Now that the house had been largely taken care of, their attention turned to the grounds. The kitchen garden's west wall needed to be rebuilt—its big gap let in too much cold air and some of the fruit trees had not survived the winter. The man-made lake not far from the entrance of the estate was a great big bruise on the land. Next to it, the Greek folly that must have once been someone's pride and joy had become what the French might call a *pissoir*.

Always so much to do.

After a whole morning of planning and note-taking, they shared a sandwich next to the lavender fields, listening to the buzz of the bees and talking about a new bridge across the trout stream to replace the old one, which had become too rotted to use.

Millie would not have minded if the day had gone on forever. But eventually, they walked back toward the manor. Once they crossed its threshold, he would seek his own rooms and expect her to do the same.

But before they returned to the house, he guided her toward the gardens. She'd been extravagant with the lavender, but she had not neglected the rest of her gardens. The roses were past their best, but the honeysuckles and hydrangeas were still in fine fettle. And now, in her favorite corner of the garden, just past a bed of chamomiles and a laburnum avenue that had been restored in the spring, was something that had not been there before: a garden bench.

"I know you've always liked the bench behind our town house. Consider this one a slightly early birthday present."

"It's . . ." Her voice caught. "It's very fine."

It was a near exact replica of the one in the garden behind their town house, large, sturdy, sun warmed.

"I'll leave you to enjoy," he said, and walked away with a wave.

She sat down and enjoyed indeed. A garden and a bench—and a hope that ever bloomed.

CHAPTER 12

1896

$\mathcal{C}$hristian de Montfort, the Duke of Lexington, enjoyed watching his wife when she was less than perfectly illuminated. The room was thick with the blue shadows of twilight.

She slipped into her combination, then came back to bed and looped an arm about his shoulders. "You are not getting ready?"

"My dear Venetia, it doesn't take as much time for me."

"All right, I see diplomacy is of no use. What I mean to say is that if you don't decamp, sir, I cannot summon my maid."

"In other words, I can profitably leverage my presence here." He caressed her still-bare arm. "How about this? I will remain, duchess, unless you favor me again."

She laughed and slipped away from his grasp. "Later. After the ball—maybe."

A sense of déjà vu came over him. "My God, I'd dreamed of this."

She waggled one brow. "Of being a squatter in my bed?"

"Of this whole tableau. You dressing, me ogling, a salacious invitation from me, and this exact reply from you. *Later. After the ball—maybe.*"

"When did you dream it?"

"The night before my Harvard lecture, which quite upset my apple cart."

The lecture had been several months earlier. Unbeknownst to him, she'd been in the audience. And the things he'd said from the podium had led their lives to collide in a way he'd never expected.

"And sent you down a path that led directly into my evil clutches," she teased.

"Which is not a terrible place to be at all—juicy, snug, h—"

She threw a small jar of something at him. He ducked hastily. "What have we come to? A man can't pay his wife a compliment anymore?"

She winked. "Not when he is no longer in said evil clutches. Now off with you. I must bathe and dress."

He hopped off her bed and pulled on his trousers. "You'll pay for that summary dismissal after the ball, *mein Liebling.*"

"Maybe," she said saucily.

He ran his hand through her unbound hair—which fell to the small of her back, as he'd dreamed. "We were meant to be, weren't we?"

She pressed a kiss upon the palm of his hand. "Yes, darling, we were."

* * *

The giving of a ball was an art rarely mastered by the average London hostess. She invited too many guests to fit into a space that was hardly bigger than a drawing room. She covered the windows and alcoves so that her three hundred sweltering guests asphyxiated inside an airless prison. Then, to add insult to injury, she stinted on the musicians and the refreshments.

Fitz's wife did not make such mistakes. Her guest list was always capped at precisely one hundred and seventy-five. Her ballroom remained properly ventilated from beginning to end. And she never pinched pennies at the expense of her guests' comfort or enjoyment.

Tonight the Fitzhugh ballroom bloomed with monuments of roses and lilies. Between the flower arrangements stood ice sculptures in the shape of Corinthian columns, faintly iridescent under the light of the electric chandeliers—electric light gave off less heat than flames and the ice sculptures would keep the ballroom cool when it brimmed with vigorously dancing guests.

Lemonade and chilled punch had been laid out. Tiered platters bore small iced cakes, piped with buttercream roses and lilies to match the flowers. And unique to the Fitzhugh balls, pyramids of Cresswell & Graves chocolate bars, cut to precisely bite size, in the brand's most popular as well as newest flavors.

Millie stood before the punch bowl, in a plum-colored ball gown, lavishly studded with crystal drops. The amethyst-and-diamond pins he'd bought her twinkled in her hair. Her bare shoulders gleamed.

Tonight. After all these years.

But it must not change anything. His future lay with Isabelle. This was only his duty, to the title and to Millie.

She turned around at the sound of his approach.

"Everything is ready," he said.

She smiled but did not meet his eyes. "Yes, I believe so. But it is always nerve-racking, giving a ball."

"You'll do just fine. What time is carriages?"

On the cards she sent out for her balls, she always specified the hour at which carriages would be ordered for the guests—when she didn't, their guests, having such a good time, stayed till dawn, something she did not entirely approve.

And before a ball started, he always inquired after the time for carriages, so he had an idea how long he needed to man the fort. But tonight, after the carriages left . . .

He ought to be thinking of Isabelle's ardent declaration of love. Of the past, the future, anything but the present. But tonight, after the carriages left, there would be Millie, her scent like a breeze from their lavender field at the height of summer, her skin as smooth as the finest velvet.

Their eyes met. She flushed. Desire tumbled through him.

"That's—that's the first carriage arriving." She picked up her skirts, already walking away. "I'd best take up my position at the head of the stairs."

He watched her—and tried to think of Isabelle.

*U*nlike Fitz, who rarely danced when he didn't need to, Hastings enjoyed a ball and took part in every set. And Helena had to credit him: He always remembered the wallflowers, girls who waited, hope mixed with embarrassment, for a partner.

A dance request from him gave the wallflowers much pleasure. Even with an illegitimate child under his roof, he remained highly eligible—he had inherited from his uncle not only a title, but a substantial industrial fortune. Helena wondered what the wallflowers would think if they knew he wrote erotica—with a female character who would send their mothers into fainting spells. Who made love with her eyes open.

Strangely enough, for all the kisses Hastings had attempted to steal from Helena over the years, he had never claimed a waltz. This ball was no exception. Instead of a waltz, he was her partner in a lancers set, which involved three other couples.

Still, the dance offered enough privacy for him to bend his head to her ear. "Mrs. Monteth is on the warpath, I hear. I would be careful if I were you."

"Mrs. Monteth is always on the warpath."

It was not an exaggeration. Mrs. Monteth, Andrew's wife's sister, was not so much a gossip as a self-appointed guardian of virtue and righteousness. She spied on the servants, opened random doors at country house parties— for which reason she was seldom invited to any these days—and did just about everything in her power to expose and punish the private moral failings of those around her.

"Should Mrs. Martin discover a stray love letter from you to her husband, who would she go to first?"

They joined hands with the two dancers to either side and advanced toward an opposing line of dancers. The gentlemen bowed; the ladies curtsied. The lines drew apart and formed again into four couples.

"Mrs. Monteth will be wasting her time. I am constantly watched."

"I don't trust you, Miss Fitzhugh. You *will* somehow create a path to trouble."

"And drop myself into Mrs. Monteth's lap at the same time? I think not."

"You look at the situation and consider only your part in it, Miss Fitzhugh. But there are other players involved. You cannot predict what they will do."

"As long as I am all but a prisoner, they can do whatever they like."

Hastings made an exasperated sound. It was rare that he allowed a show of frustration, this man who was always smooth and slippery. The demands of the dance interrupted their conversation. When they'd put some distance between themselves and the rest of the couples again, he said, "I am beginning to think you are hoping to be caught."

She snorted. "And why would I do that?"

"So I'd have no choice but to be your knight in shining armor."

"You are not a knight in any kind of armor if you prefer your women always tied up, Hastings."

He *tsked*. "Fiction, my dear. Know the difference between the author and a first-person narrator.

She glanced up. It still felt odd to have to tilt her head back to look him in the eye—she'd towered above him during their adolescence. "*Is* there a difference in this case?"

"I'd say there is. I haven't fettered my wife yet—in fact, I don't even have a wife yet. But if you get caught, I'd have to marry you out of obligation to Fitz, and then maybe truth will come closer to fiction."

Heat pooled in her. "It won't happen."

"Not if you watch yourself." His voice was velvety. "But if you continue to be reckless, who knows what will happen?"

*F*itz opened the ball dancing with Venetia, the guest of honor, and he closed the ball dancing with her. Now, arm in arm, he walked her to her waiting carriage.

"Am I not to have my wife back, Fitzhugh?" said Lexington, smiling.

"Seniority, sir. When you've been her husband as long as I've been her brother, you may claim her more readily."

Venetia laughed heartily. Fitz loved seeing her delighted. She deserved every good thing in life.

"Come to Algernon House in August," Lexington proposed. "I have been abroad a great deal and my grouse population has exploded. I'll need all the help I can get."

"Excellent idea," enthused Venetia. "Fitz is a marvelous shot. As is Helena, by the way. And we really ought to teach Millie to shoot."

Fitz's throat tightened. There was hardly time.

A footman held the carriage door open. Fitz shook hands with Lexington. Venetia kissed Fitz on the cheek.

He didn't let her go immediately. "I'm happy for you," he whispered.

"And I hope to be just as happy for you, my love," she whispered back. "Choose carefully."

*M*illie gazed at Fitz. He was so beautiful, a protective hand around his sister's waist, then handing her into the carriage himself.

The Lexington brougham pulled away, but De Courcy and Kingsland, a pair of his school friends, wanted a word. De Courcy, who'd played cricket with Fitz at Eton, had become engaged not too long ago. He probably wished Fitz to take part in his wedding. Fitz was wildly popular for such endeavors; every man who'd gone to Eton during remotely the same era considered him a chum.

"You look at him as if you are a baker and he the last sack of flour in the world," said a voice behind Millie.

Hastings. They'd never spoken openly of her unrequited love for Fitz—or his for Helena. "You mean, the way you look at my sister-in-law—the unmarried one?"

"Tragic, isn't it? The pair of us."

Sometimes she thought so, but never enough to quit altogether. "I noticed an animated conversation between the two of you during the lancers set."

"I'm worried about her."

"Me, too. But we are keeping a close eye on her." So close that she felt rather awful for Helena. "Has this been a trying time for you?"

"No worse than what you've had to endure of late, I imagine." Hastings took her gloved hand in his. "But don't worry, Fitz will see the light."

"Will he?" It was what her mother had said, too.

"Like Paul on the way to Damascus." Hastings lifted her hand and kissed it. "You'll see."

Fitz, who'd dispatched De Courcy and Kingsland, came and slung an arm about his friend. "It's three in the morning, David. Stop flirting with my wife. She's had a long day—and she won't touch you with a ten-foot pole in any case."

Hastings winked at Millie. "We'll let Fitz think such

comforting thoughts, won't we, Lady Fitz? I'll see myself out."

Now Millie and her husband were alone in the ballroom. Her knees grew weak. She couldn't quite look at him.

"Are you tired?" he asked solicitously, standing all too close.

Her fear and her imagination both ran amok—it seemed as if she could already feel his touch upon her. She shook her head slowly.

"Shall we go up then?"

She inhaled—the deep breath before the plunge. "Yes, of course. Do let us."

CHAPTER 13

The Airship

1892 ∼

itz was not a man who gave gifts on a set schedule. Millie was just as likely to receive something in November that counted as her Christmas present as getting something in January, for her birthday the year before. She greatly encouraged Fitz in his casualness. "Venetia always has a gift for me from you," she told him, "because you are so careless about the exact dates. If you became more diligent, then I should have to turn down that second gift—which would quite sadden me."

Therefore, she was not at all surprised when he announced one day at dinner, when she still had a good while of being twenty years old left, that he had a present for her twenty-first birthday.

"What is it?"

"I'd like to take you to Italy at the end of the Season."

She was dumbstruck. *Just the two of us? Alone?*

Those were not acceptable questions. Yet she must say something. Peeling her hand from where it was splayed over her heart, she reached for her glass of water to moisten her suddenly dry mouth.

"Why Italy?"

"I made you come home early when you were there the last time."

"For a matter that was of deep personal concern to me. Thinking back I'd have been insulted if you didn't ask me to return."

"Nevertheless, shall we?"

"But what about—ah, so that was why you said you would take care of the invitations for the shooting party. There is no shooting party."

He grinned. "Unless you'd prefer a shooting party instead."

She remembered a time when weeks, or even months, would pass between his smiles. He smiled much more often these days, but she could never take them for granted. Each one still surprised and delighted her anew.

"No, I dare say I'd prefer Italy."

"Italy it is, then."

Now the most important questions. "What about Venetia and Helena? Are they coming with us?"

It seemed unlikely, at least for Venetia, whose second husband, Mr. Easterbrook, had passed away not too long ago.

Fitz shook his head. "Venetia doesn't want to travel while she is still in first mourning and Helena plans to keep her company."

"Hastings?"

"He is shooting in Scotland. It will be just the two of us."

Alone. For weeks and weeks. In scenic, romantic places.

She had to take another sip of water before she could speak. "I suppose I must tolerate it if my husband wants to drag me all over the Continent."

He grinned again. "Oh, rest assured he does."

And for the rest of the night, it was as if she held a sugar cube in her mouth, a slow, constant melt of sweetness.

They traveled through Switzerland, took the train through the Gotthard Tunnel, scaled the Splügen Pass in a diligence, and descended to Lake Como, their first stop.

Lake Como, with its perfumed air, its red-roofed villas, and its sweeping vista of high slopes and blue, glacier-fed lake, was surely paradise on earth. For a fortnight Millie and Fitz hiked, rowed, played occasional games of tennis, and ate themselves silly. But alas, the romance of the locale failed to spark him to kiss her—or do anything else remotely of the sort.

At their hotel in the commune of Bellagio, they kept separate rooms, just as they did at home. He was considerate and companionable, just as he was at home. And just as it was at home, his nights belonged to himself.

Millie suspected him of having a lover. Her suspicions were confirmed one night when a pretty dark-haired woman, her throat sparkling with diamonds, winked at him during dinner, which they took on the hotel's large terrace overlooking the lake.

"You are sleeping with her," she said.

"I am not," he answered, smiling down at his plate. "I pay her a visit, if you must know, before I go to sleep in my own bed."

"Is she staying at this hotel?"

"My dear, I would never be so crass as to have my mistress under the same roof as my lady wife."

"Hmm, doesn't the Prince of Wales always have his mistress present when he goes to a country house party, even when the princess is also in attendance?"

"I am far more respectable than the Prince of Wales, I will have you know. The House of Hanover was nothing but a gaggle of middle-class Germans before we ran out of royals to put on our throne."

A waiter came and served their next course, filets of lake fish in sage butter.

"Tell me how it works," she heard herself say, "finding a paramour. I'm curious."

He shot her a look of surprise: She'd never before been so forward. There was something in his eyes—a new awareness perhaps, or an existing one that had suddenly expanded. "Every man is different. Hastings, for example, walks into a room, sees a woman he wants, and approaches her immediately."

It was just like him to shift the discussion onto someone else. Reticent about his private life, this man. But she wasn't about to let him off the hook so easily. "And you?"

"I am not so industrious."

"And yet you are no less successful than Hastings."

He shrugged good-naturedly, but the gesture also indicated that he was not about to discuss the specifics of his moves any further.

"I know how you do it," she said.

He raised a brow.

"When you walk into a room of mixed company, you never head for the prettiest ladies right away. You will talk to the gentlemen for some time, or maybe one of the dowagers. But at the same time, you are perfectly aware of where the candidates are, and you know which ones are looking at you."

He smiled very slightly, and took a sip of his mineral water. "Go on."

She was abruptly aware that what he was listening for was not her analysis of the mechanics of his seduction, but an account of just how much she'd observed him, closely, while pretending not to. She could not, however, bring herself to stop.

"You are not that different from Hastings: You know exactly which woman you want. And you are no less a predator than he; but you are like the spider, content to wait for your prey to come to you.

"So the ladies take note of you, young, gleaming, and assured. With their fans, they beckon you to approach. You never oblige them immediately. You speak with the hostess. Share another joke with the gentlemen. Only then do you pretend to notice the ladies signaling you.

"You start with the one in whom you have the least interest and end the night chatting with the one you'd decided on in the first place, when you walked into the room. And then a few days later the gossip will get around to me—but I already know."

He drank some more of his mineral water, then some more. The sun had set, the sky was indigo, the torches on the terrace cast a muted golden light upon him.

"It's quite possible," he said, "that you know me better than anyone else."

She certainly paid the most minute, constant attention.

"I don't know you half as well," he continued.

"There is not much to know about me."

"I beg to differ. There is not much you wish to be known about you—and that is not the same thing at all."

Sometimes she wondered whether he studied her as she studied him. Now she had her answer: He did. And she had no idea what to do with that knowledge.

Tamping down the fluttering in her stomach, she went after the fish on her plate. "Why, this is delicious. Don't you agree?"

*T*hey left Lake Como two days later, spent a week in Milan, then traveled east to Lombardy for more mountains and more lakes—Lake Iseo, this time, arriving at their destination late in the day.

The innkeeper was full of apologies. A large wedding party had descended and he had only one room left—a very nice room, but only one.

"We'll take it," said Fitz.

"Did you not hear him?" Millie said when they were out of the innkeeper's hearing. "It's only one room."

"I heard him. But it's late. We haven't had our supper and I'd rather look for another inn tomorrow."

"But—"

"I remember exactly what our pact entails. You are in no danger from me."

And why, exactly, was she in no danger from him? Why didn't he want her with the fervor of a thousand overheating engines? She ought to be constantly ogled and groped, having to beat him off with her parasol, her fan, and maybe one of her walking boots.

"All right, I suppose," she said reluctantly.

They were shown to the room, which was nice but *small*, and the bed laughably tiny.

She was speechless. He cast a glance at the bed and turned away. But he stood in front of the washstand and she saw a lopsided smile on his reflection in the mirror. Her face heated.

"It's only for one night," he said.

*T*hey ate a quick supper. She retired directly afterward; he did not join her until the clock had struck midnight.

The light from his hand candle preceded him. He set the hand candle on the mantel and pulled off his collar and his necktie. From beneath her lashes, she watched him. She'd seen him stripped to the waist, bathing in a stream, but she'd never seen him disrobe.

He drew out his watch and laid it on the mantel. His jacket and waistcoat he draped over the back of a chair. Then he pushed off his braces and took off his shirt. She bit on the inside of her cheek. The one time she'd seen him, he'd been skin and bones. Now he was fit and sinewy, as handsome unclothed as one of those garden statues in Versailles.

She'd laid out his nightshirt for him before she went to bed. He picked it up, put it on, then pinched out the candle flame. In the dark, she heard him remove his trousers.

The mattress dipped beneath his weight. She held herself very still and did not even breathe.

"You might as well breathe. You have to breathe at some point," he said, a smile to his voice.

What?

"I know you are awake."

"How do you know?"

"If I'd never had anyone in my bed before, I know I'd still be awake."

She pulled her lips. Out of bed they were equals: She was just as well-spoken and poised as he. But in this particular arena he was vastly more experienced than she, an arena in which theoretical knowledge counted for nothing.

"When did you sleep with a woman for the first time?" she asked, her voice clipped.

"At my gentlemen's party, supposedly."

"Supposedly?"

"I was three sheets to the wind. Can't remember a thing."

"When was the first time you remember? Mrs. Bethel?"

"No, it was her sister, Mrs. Carmichael."

She didn't say anything.

"I can hear your disapproval."

"I can hear your smugness."

"I wouldn't say I'm smug about it. Mrs. Carmichael passed me on to Mrs. Bethel because she knows Mrs. Bethel likes her men young and inexperienced—so you can also say that Mrs. Carmichael found me an inferior lover."

"I assume you are not an inferior lover anymore since you've had a bit of practice since."

"I am passably competent," he said modestly. Then he chuckled. "I never thought I would lie in bed in the dark and discuss my competence or lack thereof in this matter with my wife."

The bed creaked. Had he turned toward her? "I don't wish to presume, but you sound curious."

"I don't know what you are talking about."

"I don't mean that you are curious about me or that you are itching to try something yourself, but you sound intrigued about the matter as a whole."

She bit her lip. "Do I?"

"Nothing wrong with it. You are of an age to be curious. Do you still have news of your fellow?"

So he still remembered. "Yes."

"Ever think of him?"

She grimaced. "From time to time."

"Have you two ever—"

"Of course not."

"I don't question your virtue. But have you two ever kissed?"

"Once."

"How was it?"

You were there. What did you think? "I'm not sure I can describe it. I was in such despair. As was he."

"Is he married now?"

"Yes."

"Are you ever jealous of his wife?"

And how did she answer that? "It's late. Let's sleep."

The bed creaked again as he shifted and put another few inches between them. "Just make sure you don't kick me out of bed. I don't like sleeping on floors."

"I've never kicked anyone out of bed my entire life."

"True, but you've never had anyone in it either. So . . . watch yourself."

* * *

*H*e fell asleep long before she did, his back turned toward her, his breathing deep and even.

She lay in a nameless agitation until she too finally dropped off.

Only to awaken with a start as he flung his arm around her midsection. One hand over her open mouth, she tried, with her other hand, to move him. But his fingers, when she touched them, were completely slack.

He'd turned in his sleep. Nothing else.

Her hand lingered on his, coming into contact with the signet ring she'd given him, warm with the heat of his body. Someday, she thought, someday . . .

Suddenly he yanked her toward him. She gasped—but made barely a sound, her shock stuck in her throat. Now they touched from shoulders to thighs. He buried his face in the crook of her neck. Dear God, his lips grazed her skin. And his stubbles, the sensation of it against her skin—

Things ran riot in her. Heat, want, confusion. What was he doing? Was he even aware of what he was doing? And did she want him to stop this moment . . . or not to stop at all?

He certainly wanted to go on. Behind her he was now rock hard. She heard herself pant in a mixture of astonishment and desire. She wanted him. When she heard about his satisfied lovers, she'd always wanted to be one of them. To enjoy him for blind pleasures, without entertaining any other thoughts.

But she couldn't. She could never be content just to sleep with him.

A sound of lust came from the back of his throat. His

hand came up to her chest. Before she knew what was going on, he'd cupped her breast.

Her mute shock translated into a frantic thumping of the heart.

He nuzzled her neck. His fingers found her nipple. His thumb rubbed it through the linen of her nightgown.

She leaped out of the bed, knocking over the glass of water on the nightstand in her hurry. The glass fell on the rug. It didn't break, but it did roll off the rug and make a clear clink upon coming into contact with the leg of the armoire.

"What the—" he said sleepily.

She made not a sound.

After a while, she thought he'd gone back to sleep. But he asked, "Why are you out of bed?"

"I . . . I can't sleep when there's someone right next to me."

"Come back. I'll sleep on the floor."

"The floor is wet now."

He sighed. "I'll sleep in the chair, then."

His footsteps. She shrank back. He brushed past her and felt for the chair. "Go."

"I think I should—"

She yelped—he'd picked her up. He crossed the few feet to the bed and deposited her squarely in it. "Sleep."

A thin light crept past the curtains. She lay on her side, facing away from the chair where he sat— facing so much away that her face was almost nose first in the pillow.

It was cool in the mountains, but she'd kicked off the

bedcover from her legs. And he had a good, if poorly lit, view of her ankles. In fact, he could see halfway up one delectable calf.

Delectable. An odd word to use on one's wife. But everything in view was fresh and pretty. And everything not on display . . .

He turned his mind away from that unprofitable direction: Everything not on display would remain out of sight for years to come. Six years she'd proposed, but he had to extend it to eight. How stupid he'd been, to believe that he'd always feel the exact same way about her, about everything.

She stirred faintly, his woman of mystery.

He kept no particular secrets from her. But she, she was like a castle from another era, full of hidden passages and concealed alcoves, the full knowledge of which she revealed to no one and at which he could only guess.

Until her detailed recital the other night, he'd never given much thought to his modus operandi with regard to getting women in bed. It was true he preferred to achieve his objective discreetly, with the least amount of energy expended, but she was mistaken in comparing him to a spider.

Appearances to the contrary, he'd always been shy where women were concerned. Even with Isabelle, she'd been the one to take the initiative and tell him that he vast preferred her to every other girl on the planet—he'd only needed to agree.

Looking for a woman to gratify his lust was hardly the same thing as baring the contents of his heart. But the same reticence prevailed. He'd rather they came to him, and let "young, gleaming, and assured" be the only advertisement of his intentions.

She stirred again and turned onto her back. Her toes wiggled slightly. One foot slid up along her other leg. He watched with avid interest. He would not mind at all for her sleepy, unmindful motions to hike the hems of her nightgown farther north—a great deal farther north.

She stilled. Then, slowly, deliberately, she drew her legs up and pulled the blanket over them.

"Good morning," he said.

She sat up, obviously about to pretend that he hadn't seen her unclothed almost up to her knees. "Good morning."

She glanced about the room. Even though he'd put on his trousers and his shirt and was presentable enough to his own wife, she seemed intent on not looking at him. He was not, as a rule, terribly excited by primness in a woman. But somehow, her primness seemed not so much stuffiness as avoidance. As if she herself did not want to know how she'd conduct herself in a more charged situation. And that made him curious: How would she conduct herself?

"Did you sleep well?" he asked.

"Passably. Did you?"

"Let's see. In the middle of the night, I had to get up and go sit in a chair because my wife doesn't like to sleep with me. How do you think I slept?"

She stared at her knees, now tented up beneath the bed-cover. "I would have taken the chair."

He scoffed. "As if I'd let you sleep in a chair while I took the bed."

"Sorry about that."

"Did I do something?"

Her hand had been tracing random patterns on the sheets. She stopped. "Why would you think you did something?"

"I don't have any precise recollections. But the bed is small and a man's impulses strong. Besides, you knocked over a glass of water while fleeing the bed. That would be a pretty good indication."

"It was nothing particularly egregious. Probably wouldn't have alarmed anyone but an old maid like me."

"You were alarmed?"

"I fled, didn't I?"

Why didn't you give in?

And with that thought came a sudden memory, of arousal, her body pressed against his, her breast in his hand, warm and pliant, her nipple hard with excitement.

He sucked in a long breath. "You know you have nothing to fear from me."

"Of course not," she concurred all too readily.

He left the room for her to dress. Then he returned and banished her. "I need to sleep another hour or so."

He locked the door and laid down on the bed. He would doze some, but not yet, not until he'd exorcised this unwanted lust that had abruptly taken hold of him.

So for now, he would allow himself not only to remember what had taken place during the night, but to imagine what would happen in slightly less than four years, when he'd have her naked and open beneath him.

Just this once.

"*F*itz, are you there?" Millie rapped loudly on the door. It was ten o'clock, two and a half hours since she left him. "Wake up, I need to talk to you."

"I'm not sleeping. I'm in the bath. What is it?"

"My mother—" She swallowed. "She is not well."

"Give me one minute."

Millie looked down again at the telegram in her hand.

Dear Lord and Lady Fitzhugh,

I regret to inform you that Mrs. Graves has taken ill. She wishes to see you most urgently. Please make your way back to London at your earliest convenience.

Yours, etc.,
G. Goring

She could not believe it. Not her mother, too—she was far too young. But Mr. Goring, Mrs. Graves's personal solicitor, would not have taken it upon himself to cable unless the situation was critical.

Fitz opened the door. His shirt clung to his person and he was still toweling his hair, the abandoned bathtub half visible behind a screen.

He took the cable from her hand and scanned it. Giving the cable back to her, he tossed aside the towel and pulled out a book of schedules from his satchel.

"There is a train that departs Gorlago in three hours. If we leave right away, in a fast carriage, we might make it."

They were twenty miles out of Gorlago. The road was decent, but narrow and steep at times. Three hours seemed a very optimistic assessment.

She did not argue.

"Have Bridget pack our things but we are not taking the trunks—they will slow us. Arrange with the innkeeper to send the luggage and take only what you can carry in hand. I'll find us that fast carriage. Be ready when I get back."

He was back in a quarter hour with a lightly sprung *calèche* and a child of about eleven. Millie climbed in with a picnic basket, Bridget followed her with a satchel stuffed with a change of clothes for everyone.

"Where's the coachman?"

He flicked the reins. The horses eased into a trot. "I'll drive."

"What about directions? And the changing of horses?"

"That's what this young gentleman is for—he will tell us where to go. And when we reach Gorlago he will stay with cattle and carriage until his uncle comes for them. He is six stones lighter than his uncle, so I chose him."

The boy's slighter weight and their lack of luggage made the difference—as did the Italian railway's tendency to run behind schedule. They arrived at the Gorlago station ten minutes after the published departure time for the train to Milan via Bergamo, but had just enough time to purchase tickets and catch the train—Fitz, the last one up, had to run and leap onto the steps.

By the middle of the afternoon they were in Milan. Thanks to the modern marvel that was the Mont Cenis Tunnel, twenty hours later their express train pulled into Paris.

Now they only had to hurry to Calais and cross the English Channel.

Someone gently shook Millie by the shoulder. "Hot air balloons—do you want to see?"

Millie opened her eyes—she didn't realize she'd nodded off.

There were indeed seven or eight hot air balloons in an open field, most of the envelopes still limp tangles of bright colors, in the process of being inflated. "Is this a competition of some sort?"

"Maybe. Look, there is even an airship."

"Where?"

"It's behind the trees now. But I saw it, it had propellers."

Millie rotated her neck. It rather ached from her nap. "*Calèches*, trains, and hot air balloons, I feel as if we are attempting *Around the World in Eighty Days*."

"The current record is sixty-seven days, so you will have to do a little better."

"How far are we from Calais?"

"Seven miles or so."

The sky was clear, but she could not help worrying. "I hope the Channel stays clear. Last time I had to wait overnight."

He touched her hand briefly. "You'll see her again. I'll get you there in time."

*T*he weather, however, did not wish to cooperate. A heavy fog stuffed the entire channel; all ferries remained in port.

"How long before it lifts?" Millie asked anxiously. Fitz had been talking to ferrymen and fishermen.

"Nobody thinks it will lift today. Half of them don't expect anything to happen before tomorrow afternoon, and the rest believe it's one of those that will stick around for at least forty-eight hours."

Her heart sank. "But we can't wait that long. She might not last."

"I know," he said.

"Why haven't they built the tunnel under the Channel yet? They've only been talking about it for as long as anyone has been alive."

He gazed back toward the direction they'd come. Then he looked at her, one thumb pressed into his chin. "If you have the stomach for it, we can go above the Channel."

"Above?"

"Remember that airship I saw? Crossing the Channel in a balloon has been done before. But it's a dangerous undertaking—especially going from east to west."

She stared at him for a second. She'd never been on an aerial device before—never even read Jules Verne's *Five Weeks in a Balloon*. The idea of being thousands of feet above the ground did not hold any particular appeal for her, but desperate times called for desperate measures.

"Well, what are we waiting for?"

*T*he airship was very peculiar looking.

Millie was familiar with a hot air balloon's lightbulb-like shape. But the airship's envelope looked more like an overfilled sausage. A rectangular wicker basket was suspended beneath. And from the back of this basket, two long poles protruded, each outfitted with propellers at the end, the blades almost as long as Millie was tall.

"Yes, she is safe as can be," said the pilot, Monsieur Duval, to Fitz, in French. "The propellers are powered by batteries, none of that gasoline engine nonsense the Germans are trying. Just you wait. They will set themselves on fire yet."

Millie was not sure that was what she wished to hear just now, even if they didn't have a gasoline engine. She was beginning to envy Bridget, who'd chosen to stay behind in Calais until she could cross the Channel by steamboat.

"How do you heat the air?" she asked.

"The air is not heated. That is hydrogen inside the envelope, madame."

"Hydrogen is lighter than air, isn't it? How will we descend?"

"Ah, very intelligent question, madame. There are two air sacks inside the hydrogen envelope and these we can fill or empty. And when they are filled, the entire weight of the airship becomes slightly larger than the lift provided by the hydrogen and we will come to a very gentle landing."

She glanced at Fitz.

"Only if you wish to go," he said. "But you must make up your mind soon. Or it will be dark before we reach the English coast."

She expelled a long breath. "Let's hurry, then."

The moment they'd settled themselves inside the basket, which Monsieur Duval called a gondola, his assistant began tossing bags of earth overboard, while Monsieur Duval coaxed his battery-powered engine to life. The propellers rotated, at first lazily, then with vigor.

The basket lifted so gradually that Millie, absorbed with Monsieur Duval's handling of valves and gauges, didn't even notice they were airborne until the basket was three feet off the ground.

"Last chance to jump," murmured Fitz.

"Same goes for you," she said.

"I'm not afraid of falling into the English Channel."

"Hmm, I am quite afraid of falling into the English Channel. But if I jump now"—she looked down; the ground had receded dramatically—"it is a certainty I'll break my limbs. Whereas it is only a probability that I will need to swim."

"Do you know how to swim?"

"No."

"So you have entrusted your life to this mad venture."

She exhaled. "I trust I will be all right with you by my side."

For a moment he looked as if he didn't quite know what to say, then he smiled. "Well, I do have a compass on my watch. Should we hit water, I'll know which direction to push the gondola."

The fog. She'd forgotten about the fog altogether.

Above them was a clear sky, beneath them the French countryside—dotted with sheep, cows, and hamlets. Children pointed and waved; Millie waved back. Two boys threw stones that fell far short; Fitz laughed and shouted something that sounded like French, but did not contain any French words Millie had ever been taught.

The airship kept rising. The livestock were now pin-pricks; the land a parquet of tracts in varying shades of green and brown.

"How high are we?" Fitz asked.

Monsieur Duval consulted a gauge. "The barometric column has dropped almost two inches. We are about fifteen hundred feet up—half again as high as the top of the Eiffel Tower—and we are still ascending."

After some time, Fitz shaded his eyes with his hand. "I can see the fog now. Are we approaching the coast?"

"*Oui, monsieur le comte.*"

The fog was the most spectacular sight Millie had ever seen, a sea of cloud upon which the airship cast its elongated shadow. The thick vapors erupted and writhed, with currents and climates of its own. And as the sun lowered toward the western horizon, the peaks and ridges turned into mountains of gold, as if they were being given a tour of heaven's own bank vault.

Fitz draped his coat around her shoulders. "Magnificent, isn't it?"

She stole a look at him. "Yes," she said, "in every way."

"I'd once hoped my marriage would be an adventure—and it has turned out to be just that." His gaze still on the fog, he placed his arm around her shoulders. "If something should befall us this day, know that of all the heiresses I could have married four years ago, I'm glad it's you."

At times she'd wondered how her life might have turned out differently had she been given a choice in the matter of her marriage. Now she knew: There would have been no difference, for she'd have chosen the very path that led her to this precise moment. She gathered her courage and put her arm around his waist.

"I feel the same," she said. "I'm glad it's you."

*T*here was just enough light for Monsieur Duval to set down the airship on an empty field, causing much excitement to several Sussex villages. Millie and Fitz arrived in London by midnight.

Millie spent the next week by her mother's bedside. At first it seemed that Mrs. Graves might make a miraculous recovery, but Millie's hopes were dashed when her condition further deteriorated.

Mrs. Graves slipped in and out of consciousness, sometimes awake long enough to take some nourishment and exchange a greeting with Millie, sometimes falling unconscious again before she'd even quite oriented herself.

Mrs. Graves's sisters and cousins sometimes sat with Millie during the day; Fitz was there every night, keeping her company. They did not speak much during these long nights, each dozing in a chair, but his presence was a source of immeasurable comfort.

One morning, just after he left to have his breakfast, Mrs. Graves came to.

Millie leaped up. "Mother."

She hurriedly reached for the glass of water kept on the nightstand and fed her mother several large spoonfuls.

"Millie," Mrs. Graves murmured weakly.

Millie had not meant to, but she found herself weeping. "I'm sorry. Forgive me."

"Forgive *me*, for leaving you much sooner than I'd intended."

Millie could deny it, but they both knew Mrs. Graves had not much time left. She wiped her eyes. "It's not fair. You should be as long-lived as the queen."

"My love, I've lived a wonderful, enviable life. That it will be a little shorter than I'd liked is no cause for complaint."

She coughed. Millie gave her another three spoonfuls of water. Her breathing was labored, but she waved away the tonic Millie offered. "No, my love, the only unfairness here is what your father and I asked of you—that you give up your own happiness so that we could have a grandson who would one day be an earl."

"I am not unhappy." Millie hesitated. She'd never spoken aloud the secrets of her heart. "I do not wish to be anyone's wife except Fitz's."

Mrs. Graves smiled. "He is a lovely young man."

"The best—like you, Mother."

Mrs. Graves caressed Millie's still-wet cheek. "Remember what I said years ago? No man can possibly be more fortunate than the one who has your hand. Someday he will see the light."

"Will he?"

But Mrs. Graves's arm slackened. She was again unconscious and passed away the same day, late in the afternoon.

Fitz was by Millie's side. He kissed her on her forehead. "I'm so sorry."

Her eyes welled again with tears. "It was too soon. She was the last of my family."

He handed her his handkerchief. "Nonsense. *I* am your family. Now go have a lie down; you haven't slept properly for days."

I am your family. She stared at him, her vision blurred. "I haven't even thanked you, have I, for giving me more time with Mother?"

"You don't need to thank me for anything," he said firmly. "It is my privilege to look after you."

Her vision grew ever more watery. "Thank you."

"Didn't I already tell you not to thank me?"

She mustered a small smile. "I meant, for saying that."

He returned her smile. "Go rest. I'll take care of everything."

He left the room to speak to Mrs. Graves's butler. She stood against the door frame and watched him disappear down the stairs.

I'm glad it's you.

CHAPTER 14

1896

*F*itz had not been in the mistress's rooms since he walked through the town house upon inheriting it. A great many renovations had taken place since then, to turn the house from a near hovel to an airy, comfortable home. Their marriage, in fact, could be traced plank by plank, brick by brick.

Even now the enhancements continued: The draining of the lavender fields had been improved in the spring; a second beehive had been commissioned for the kitchen garden—it was to be a scale replica of the manor at Henley Park; and, the servants' quarters, which had been overhauled once four years ago, were being worked on again.

Her room was light and pretty, with wallpaper the summery, crisp green of a sliced cucumber. Potted topiaries stood guard at either side of the fireplace. Above the fireplace hung a painted landscape that looked rather familiar—not the painting, but the landscape.

She stood in the center of the room, still in her full evening regalia, her fan held before her like a plumed breastplate. She glanced at him, but did not otherwise acknowledge his presence.

He did not want to make her more nervous than she must be. Instead of approaching her, he crossed the room to take a better look at the painting. "Is this Lake Como?"

"Yes."

His gaze dipped to the mantel. Upon it were a row of framed photographs that had been taken in summers past, at their country house parties. Each photograph contained the two of them, though never alone; sometimes they were in a large group, sometimes with only her mother or his sisters.

At the edge of the mantel, another familiar object. "Is this the music box I gave you for your seventeenth birthday? Looks much better than I remember."

He lifted the lid of the music box. It emitted the same thin, slightly discordant notes. Still worked. Who would have thought?

She watched him. But when he looked at her, she glanced away immediately.

"Where is your maid?"

"I told her not to wait up for me."

She dropped her fan onto the seat of a nearby chair. The gesture was determinedly casual. Yet as she stood next to the padded armrest, her throat wobbled with a swallow. The sight of it—the implication of it—made his blood hot.

"It won't be disagreeable," he said. "It can be made quite enjoyable."

"Oh, it had better be," she said tartly. "I've heard plenty over the years on your amatory prowess. If I'm not on the roof crowing, I will consider myself disappointed."

He smiled and put the music box back on the mantel. "Into the bedchamber with you then, lady."

For a few seconds she stared at her dropped fan without moving. Then she went for the switch and turned off the electric sconce on the wall. The lamp in the bedroom had been left on, illuminating the path. She walked past him and disappeared inside.

So, we come to it at last.

A mundane marital task, was this not? An obligation he'd put off for too long. Why then, as he advanced toward the bedroom, did he feel as if he were being swept out to sea? That the tides and currents would be unlike anything he'd ever known in the calm estuary that had been his marriage?

She turned off the light the moment he'd closed the door behind him. He supposed he shouldn't be too surprised— he was dealing with a virgin after all. But they knew each other so well it seemed she shouldn't be shy at all.

"Wouldn't you want me to see what I'm doing?"

"No."

He smiled. "Not even when I have to wrestle with tricky bits of your gown?"

"There is nothing here you haven't encountered enough times elsewhere."

The darkness was impenetrable: Her windows had been shut and shuttered, the double curtains tightly drawn.

"This will be a first for me," he murmured. "Fumbling about in the dark. I ought to have you sing a hymn so I can find you."

She snorted. "A hymn?"

"The heavenly host rejoice tonight: At last I am doing something ordained by God and immortalized by Christ's love for his Church—et cetera, et cetera."

"What should I sing? 'Hosanna in the highest'? Or maybe we ought to really make our rector proud and recite the Lord's Prayer, too."

He knew where she was now: by her vanity table. She jumped as his hand settled on her shoulder. Had she not heard his approach in the dark?

"All right, so you found me. Your turn to hide now and mine to seek," she said, her voice just a bit squeaky.

"Some other day. We've business to attend to, Lady Fitzhugh."

She wore long kidskin gloves that extended well past her elbows. They were fastened at the top with three ivory buttons each. He popped the buttons—one, two, three—pushed one glove down and pulled it off.

"I forgot to say so earlier, but you looked quite lovely tonight," he said. He slid his palm along her now-exposed arm. So much of her was a mystery to him.

"Thank you," she said, her voice barely audible.

He removed her other glove. "Did I ever tell you, when we first married, I never quite knew what you looked like? Your face changed every time I saw you. And when you came back from America, I had to look twice to make sure it was you."

Ruffles on her gown brushed the back of his hand.

"So . . . if I'd been away for a little longer, I'd have been able to walk past you without you recognizing me?"

"I quite doubt it. Your eyes do not change. Your gait

does not change. And your footsteps—I can always tell when you pass by my door."

She let out a breath.

He touched her hair, the careful crown of it her maid had constructed earlier in the evening, pulled out two of the amethyst pins, and tossed them aside. They landed with small, muffled thuds against the carpet and the lace cloth spread upon her vanity table.

How long had he been curious about this day, this hour?

Since the Italian trip, certainly. Though if he had to be precise, he would guess it to have been that crucial meeting during which they wrested control of Cresswell & Graves from Mr. Graves's subordinates.

He'd firmly buried that curiosity: A pact was a pact. They'd shaken hands on eight years and eight years he intended to keep his hands to himself.

But buried things had a funny way of sprouting roots and feelers just beneath the consciousness. So that when he did at last acknowledge it, he found himself facing not the same small seed of desire, but a jungle of lust.

And she, who felt as deeply and relentlessly as any other mortal, but kept such a serene facade, had she, too, hidden nuggets of yearning in the least frequented corners of her mind?

She kept a decided silence, but beneath his fingers there were tremors: She, with her ladylike, tightly laced ways, did not want to give in to something as common and vulgar as lust.

But he wanted her to. He wanted to break apart her facade piece by piece.

The very thought of it took his breath away. Eight years

of platonic friendship, of keeping to affable yet firm limits of conduct, of not thinking about how it would be when they at last came together—

A subtle perfume rose from her skin, rich, golden, and mouthwatering. Lavender honey, that must be it: Their soap was made with not only distilled lavender essence, but also the lavender honey from their fields.

He inhaled her. It was only natural that next he bent his head and kissed her on her bare shoulder.

A white-hot heat pulsed from her shoulder to her fingertips. The intensity of it stunned Millie. Had he wrought permanent damage to her nerve endings? Would she wake up in the morning with no sensation at all in her extremities?

But no, he kissed her again, at the base of her neck, and liquid fire scorched her once more.

Faintly she became aware that he was still extracting her jeweled hairpins. They fell soundlessly upon the carpet. Equally faintly she saw the need to ask him not to do that. Or she'd have to remember to gather them up before Bridget came in the morning with her cocoa.

It would be too embarrassing for Bridget to know what had taken place during the night, especially as in six months' time he would be doing exactly this with Mrs. Englewood, touching her arm, kissing her shoulder, taking down her dark, glossy hair.

Except he'd be at it with much greater fervor and impatience, wouldn't he, driven by a desire that had smoldered for more than a decade? None of this courtly consideration, these deliberate little touches that annihilated her but affected him not at all.

She was thankful for the dark. He might yet feel the tremors beneath her skin, but at least he would not glimpse the parting of her lips, or the closing of her eyes—involuntary reactions that she could not quite control, which would completely give away her pretense of amiable indifference.

He kissed her on her ear, a kiss with the barest hint of moisture to it. She could not breath for the electricity of it, a violent spark of pleasure that shook and scarred. His fingers caressed her shoulders. His lips pressed into her exposed nape. Dark, hot sensations spiked into her.

She clenched her teeth tight. *Make no sounds. Do not, under any circumstances, make any sounds.* If she remained as silent as the night, he would not know how she felt. He would not.

The buttons on her back gave away as if before a Mongol horde. The small cap sleeves at her shoulders sagged. He pushed them down, his hands lingering on the inside of her elbows.

The skirt of the ball gown was a monument of ruching and pleating. It contained so much understructure that even with the bodice of the gown hanging limply in defeat, it still stood upright on its own, stalwartly defending her virtue with silk ramparts and chiffon moats.

He simply lifted her bodily and—good Lord—did he *kick* her magnificent and costly ball gown out of the way?

Now he turned her around to face him. "Should be easy from here on," he said.

She shuddered. Indeed, it was easy for him. Her corset

cover evaporated. Her stockings melted away. He passed his hands down the front of her corset; the steel busk fasteners split apart as if he'd said "Open sesame."

"Stop," she said, as he undid the first button on her combination. "I would like to keep it on."

And not just for modesty, but for pretense. There was too much honesty in nakedness. Skin heated, heart pounded, and God knew what other reaction he'd provoke from her. Best keep a layer of deniability between them, however thin.

He paused, as if considering. "Certainly."

She was struck dumb. By relief, of course. And perhaps, a bit of chagrin that he did not even want her naked.

"You may keep your combination," he continued. "And in exchange I will turn on the lights."

"No! No lights." No lights under any circumstances.

He undid another button on her combination. His thumb traced a line down the center of her cleavage, his knuckles brushing against the side of one breast, his signet ring coming dangerously close to her nipple.

A kiss landed lightly on her jaw, just below her ear. Then he bit her on her earlobe; the pressure of his teeth singeing her. She clamped down on her lower lip and barely managed to swallow her gasp.

He dropped kisses on her cheeks, her chin, and at the corners of her lips. She could scarcely breathe, but with each breath she inhaled his scent of open fields and wide skies. He went on unbuttoning her, his finger trailing down her torso. Dear God, he dipped one fingertip into her navel—she was practically naked.

Ten seconds later she *was* naked, the combination pooled at her feet. Darkness was the only thing that separated them. A moment of hush descended; neither of them moved—or breathed, it seemed.

Then his palm slid across her nipple.

Make no sounds. Do not, under any circumstances, make any sounds.

She faltered. A whimper of unutterable pleasure escaped her tightly clenched teeth.

Deep inside her, a dam that had been ceaselessly reinforced crumbled. Years upon years of pent-up desires flooded her. Suddenly she couldn't care less that she must remain quiet and pliant.

She wanted. She wanted. She wanted.

She gripped him by the lapel and yanked him to her.

But he kissed her before she could kiss him—hard, the way he'd kissed her in his long-ago hallucination, when he'd thought her his Isabelle. She whimpered with pleasure and gratification. She wanted this ferocity, this vehemence.

His hands cupped either side of her head, holding her in place for the onslaught of his lips and tongue. She thrilled to it: It was exactly how she wanted to be secured. And the kiss, God, wild, unrefined, full of raw, barely leashed needs.

She did not know until she heard the pinging of buttons flying everywhere that she was ripping off his waistcoat, tearing apart everything that separated them. He pulled away from the kiss to help her. She slapped his hands away: *She* would do it.

He tumbled them both into bed.

His rasping breaths aroused her. His ungoverned hands aroused her. And his erection, pressing insistently into her thigh—*oh, yes.* She'd thought she'd be afraid of it. Or at least wary. But she only gloried in its dimensions and its hammer-hard rigidity. This was how it ought to be. He ought to want her this much. He ought to swell and extend to the limits of his endurance.

She pushed off his braces and yanked his shirt overhead. And then she went for his trousers.

"My God, Millie."

Yes, every utterance of her name should be preceded with such an imprecation, an uttering of the Lord's name in vain.

He certainly did not slap her hands away, but helped her to release the fastenings and get rid of both his trousers and his linens. Immediately she set her hand on his cock. It pulsed in her grip. He sucked in a breath.

"Take me," she ordered, impatient, imperious.

He touched his hand to the seam between her legs. She was utterly sleek.

"Take me now."

"Shut up, Millie."

"But I want—"

He silenced her with a harsh kiss. "Shut up or I'll make you wait longer."

She shut up.

He stroked, teased, and plucked her. Every touch was unbearable pleasure. She wanted more. She wanted him. She wanted this emptiness inside her pounded to oblivion.

She kissed every part of him she could reach. She bit his shoulders and his neck. She plunged her hands down the length of his back and grabbed his firm buttocks.

He retaliated by licking her nipple. She moaned, a long, keening admission of enjoyment. He rolled her nipple around his tongue, grazed his teeth across it, and pulled it deep into his mouth. Her cries of pleasure ricocheted about the room.

His fingers, which had not been idle a moment since they descended between her legs, chose this moment to flick a most gloriously sensitive spot. Her breath hitched, snagged, and disappeared altogether. He flicked the spot again and she convulsed involuntarily, a fast, juddering slide of pleasure.

On the heel of that, he centered himself between her knees and pushed into her.

It was the most incredible sensation, a splitting open of her person, widening, deepening. But he was so frustratingly *slow*, as if advancing against an opposing army. At least he sounded as impatient as she felt, his breath catching with each minute movement forward.

The thrust came all of a sudden. One moment he was on the cusp, the next moment he was deeply embedded in her, the two of them locked together by the force of it. He gasped. She gasped, too.

It hurt. But she welcomed the pain—good riddance to her virginity. And the pain was nothing compared to the *rightness* of it. This was what they should be doing, nightly, daily, hourly.

She raised her hips, wanting more. He held her still with his hand on her abdomen. "Are you not hurt?"

"Not enough to stop," she answered in complete honesty. "Not even enough to want a reprieve."

Still he withdrew. Just as she was about to cry out at the unfairness of it, he drove back into her.

How did one describe a sunrise to the blind? Or the sound of rain to the deaf? How could words ever adequately express the pleasure of lovemaking? Each thrust was a voluptuous surge of sensations. Each plunge both compacted her and expanded her.

"Don't stop. Don't stop."

She didn't know whether she was issuing a command or a prayer. But he must not stop, not yet. Not when the pleasure was so new and acute, and she so ravenous.

Six months.

Suddenly she was convulsing, her back arched, her person shaking, her heart in pieces.

*T*hey'd barely started. And yet here he was, on the verge.

Don't stop, she begged.

Everything about her was such pure decadence. Tight, sleek, hungry—an overload of sensations. Her skin was too soft. Her legs, clamped about him, too smooth. Her mouth, which he couldn't stop kissing, too delicious.

Don't stop, she begged again.

All those rampant urges threatened to crash upon him. He held back. Slow. Slower. But though he moderated his pace, he couldn't help taking each stroke to the hilt.

His climax began gathering again, rising toward a point of no return. He didn't know if he could restrain himself this time: He was too close, too near to being overwhelmed.

She cried out, trembling exclamations.

He lost all control, his release hot, violent, and endless.

*M*illie touched her husband's hair—a first time for her, after all these years. It was thick, a little wavy, and just slightly damp at the roots with perspiration. His heart beat fast and hard against hers. His breathing, like her own, remained tattered.

So . . . this was how one made babies.

No wonder the population was ever increasing.

Her fingers continued their exploration: his ear, his eyebrows, the bridge of his nose. He nuzzled her on her shoulder, her throat, her cheek—and claimed her mouth once more.

The kiss was slow and leisurely. He'd never left her, now he hardened again inside her.

Yes, she thought, *more. As much as possible.*

He located innumerable obscure nooks and crannies of her body that needed only a caress to reveal themselves superlatively sensitive and starved for attention. Each touch was luxuriant, every nibble unhurried.

But this was lovemaking for people who had years—decades—ahead of them. They did not have that luxury. Each slow brush of his hand reminded her of the ticking clock. Every measured path he kissed only made her that much more aware of the end drawing nigh.

She did not want to remember; she only wanted to forget.

She bit into his shoulder. She touched him most indecently. She writhed against him, pagan, shameless, driving him—and herself—into a renewed frenzy, a dizzying peak of obscene delights.

And then, at last, the next all-obliterating paroxysm.

CHAPTER 15

*C*onsciousness returned with a vengeance. Millie's eyes flew open. The room was still somber, but it was definitely morning.

She'd best hurry. There were all her amethyst pins to be collected from the carpet, not to mention the buttons she'd ripped off his clothes. And of course the sheets must somehow be made pristine again—baby-making was a messy business.

"Good morning."

Her head jerked toward the foot of the bed. Fitz, in his riding jacket and breeches, gloriously stylish in the dusky light.

"Morning." She yanked the blanket higher over her person and thanked God that he could not see her flush. "What time is it?"

She'd given instructions to her maid to wake her at

eight—an hour and half later than usual. Fitz typically left for his ride as she was drinking her cocoa in bed. But since they were up quite late, engaged in rather exhausting activities—her face heated again—perhaps it was half past seven rather than half past six.

"Half past nine."

She bolted straight, barely remembering to hang on to her blanket. "What? But Bridget was supposed to wake me up at eight."

"She came by at eight. But you were still fast asleep so I dismissed her."

She blinked. "You still were *here* at eight?"

"Yes, sleeping."

"Bridget saw the two of us *together*?"

He tapped his riding crop against the top of the footboard, his tone mock patient. "It's quite forgivable these days, you know, to be found in bed with one's spouse. I'm sure Bridget would find the strength to accept it."

She only heated more, feeling flustered and gauche.

At least she didn't need to hide the hairpins or the buttons from Bridget anymore, as the latter had already seen what all that pin-tossing and button-ripping had led to.

"Well," she said—and didn't know what else to say.

Tongue-tied, too.

Fitz tilted his head. "Are you quite all right?"

Would he be, if he knew he had only six months with Mrs. Englewood?

And what did she have to say for herself, going after him like a pack of wolves?

"I—" She looked down to see strands of her hair tumbling over her shoulders. Such a strange sight: She never had her hair loose except for drying it after a bath. "You were right all those years ago, when you suggested that I was curious about the act itself. I guess it was past time for me to have a go at it."

"Sore?"

"Negligibly so. You?"

She realized the stupidity of the last word the moment it was uttered, but it was too late.

He tried not to smile and didn't quite succeed. "Not at all. I'm perfectly well."

The playful curve of his lips, the teasing light in his eyes—she'd always wanted him to look at her like that. She didn't know whether the pain in her chest was the anticipation of losing him or the expansion of new hope cracking through the barricades.

She cleared her throat. "I was just asking since you didn't seem to have left for your ride yet."

"I was waiting for you to wake up. Didn't seem right to go anywhere before I'd spoken to you."

He rounded the corner post of the bed and came toward her. She hiked the blanket up to her nose. He pushed it down, but only so that he could take her chin between his fingers and turn her face.

"Best choose something with a high collar today," he said.

She did not understand him until she was alone again, sitting before her vanity. She examined her reflection in the mirror for any outward differences, something that might cause pedestrians to stop on the sidewalk and whisper to each other, *Look, there goes a woman freshly plucked.*

And that was when she saw the lover's mark on her neck.

Look, there goes a woman laid something proper.

*M*any newlyweds' first dinners were disasters. But Venetia was an old hand at managing a household and the Duke and Duchess of Lexington's first dinner, a small, intimate affair for family and select friends, proceeded without a single snag.

Venetia and her husband had invited Helena to stay with them, starting this very night. Helena had accepted, her mind already busy, trying to think of a way to take advantage of the change.

"You are scheming something," said Hastings.

The man was beginning to read her all too easily, as if she were a children's alphabet primer. She looked longingly toward the other occupants of the drawing room, hoping someone would saunter by. But as was usually the case, once Hastings had cornered her, no one else came.

"I don't advise you on how to live your life, Hastings. You should return the same courtesy."

"I would. Except if I were to set off a scandal, you wouldn't need to marry me. If you did, however, I wouldn't get off the hook so easily. I'm practically part of the family and people will look at me and wonder why I didn't step in and save you." He paused dramatically. "But I'd rather not marry you."

"Oh, you wouldn't?"

"I'm an old-fashioned man, Miss Fitzhugh. The little woman ought to be, well, little, to start. She ought to agree with everything I say. And she ought to look at me with stars in her eyes."

"And yet your fictional bride would have had you for breakfast."

His gaze raked her. "That's why I keep her hands bound," he said slowly. "And her person fictional."

Her breaths came in shallowly. "Then don't marry me. I won't cry my little heart out."

"But I will, when it comes to that. I won't have any choice. So don't push matters to their logical end, I beg you, Miss Fitzhugh. You are the only one who can stop our marriage from taking place."

And with that, he rose to accost the dowager duchess at the other end of the room.

*F*itz had never thought his wife beautiful—pretty, yes; lovely, at times; but not beautiful. How blind he'd been, like a novice gardener who only understood the gaudy spectacle of roses and dahlias.

The light lingering on her smooth, fine-grained skin. The way she held her head, her throat, slender and elegant. The courtesy and interest in her eyes, as she listened to her neighbor.

He couldn't look away from her.

She was not a showy blossom, good for a few days—or at most a few weeks. She was more like the hazel tree beloved by Alice: In summer one found shelter and peace under the green shade; in winter the bare limbs were still shapely and durable. A woman for all seasons.

Their eyes met. She colored and looked away, the very

model of decorum. When she'd been anything but in the dark, when she'd been all indecent touches, hot kisses, and rapturous whimpers.

Her ear, exposed by her upswept hair, was delicate and comely. Her profile was as exquisite as any he'd seen on an ivory cameo. And her eyelashes, had they always been so long, curved as dramatically as scimitars?

At the end of the evening, with Helena staying behind at the Lexington town house, Fitz and Millie traveled home alone.

They were silent inside the carriage. He didn't know what to make of his reticence to speak to her. He certainly didn't feel physically bashful—he'd disrobe this minute if his nudity in a moving carriage with all its windows open wouldn't offend her. But it was shyness all the same, a shyness of the mind, perhaps. He was not yet accustomed to the reality of their marriage, not yet accustomed to going home with a woman he held in such high esteem—and making love to her, too.

Her maid took an eternity to get her ready for bed—the queen did not need this much time before her coronation. The moment she left, Fitz opened the connecting door.

Millie sat before her vanity, in her dressing gown, turning her hairbrush in her hand. At his entry, she glanced up at the mirror and watched as he approached her.

Could she see his hunger in his eyes? The entire day he'd thought of nothing but the untrammeled creature she became when all her clothes had been stripped away.

He lifted the end of her pleat and loosened the ribbon that kept the strands tied together. How small such things usually were: the restraints and fastenings that held together order and modesty. Without the ribbon, he easily unraveled the braid.

Unbound, her hair was still neat—it dropped in a straight-edged cascade down her back—but it was far from the simple light brown he'd always assumed it to be, instead full of nuances and variations, with threads of gold, bronze, and even coppery red.

"Will you turn off the light?" she murmured.

"Eventually."

Now he wanted to see her, her hair, her skin, her intricate, interesting face.

He parted her hair at the nape, traced her vertebrae one by one, and watched her reflection in the mirror. Five years ago, perhaps even three, he'd have thought she reacted not at all. But now he'd become much more fluent in the language that was her expressions. He perceived the minute fluttering of her eyelids. He also caught the fact that she was biting the inside of her lip, because her lower lip pulled ever so slightly toward the seam of her mouth.

He undid the sash of her dressing robe. Her fingers tightened around the handle of her hairbrush. He lifted her out of the chair and flicked the dressing robe from her shoulders.

He'd never paid much mind to women's nightgowns, except to know that they were made to make any woman appear twice her girth. Hers was no exception, pleated and puffed with all the trickery known to garment-making.

He gathered fistfuls of the nightgown's skirt. Her lips parted, as if about to protest. But she said nothing, emitting only a breath of air.

"Arms up."

She obeyed. He pulled the nightgown over her head and cast it aside. For a moment, it seemed as if she wanted to shrink, to hunch down. But all those years of walking with books on her head prevented her from doing anything, anything at all, to sabotage her posture. She stood very straight, her breasts high and pink-tipped, her hips full and round.

"Please, turn off the light."

He looked at her for another minute, mainly her face, the caught breaths, the licked lips—the interplay of shyness and abandon.

And then he turned off the light, found her in the darkness, and kissed her.

*T*heir third night together he did not turn off the light when he had her naked. Instead, he laid her on the bed, parted her legs slightly, and touched her in that hidden place and watched her face.

This should have mortified her, to be so intensely observed when she was so entirely exposed—and at his mercy. But it only made her pleasure more searing.

He did not extinguish the light until after she'd come to a shaking climax. Then he made love to her not only as if he had never experienced lovemaking before, but no one had.

CHAPTER 16

*T*he next afternoon Fitz and his wife had to sit down together and review a batch of advertising prints.

Ever since the success with the soda waters, he'd charged Millie with formulating and improving the messages, visual and verbal, that the company conveyed to the public. And she had proved to be an enormous asset. He kept the factories and the chains of supply shipshape and efficient. But without her golden touch, Cresswell & Graves would be nowhere as successful as it was.

Today's tête-à-tête was but a routine meeting between two partners, discussing business matters. Why then did he again feel overwhelmingly bashful, as if he'd never been alone in a room with a girl?

"These are for the autumn campaign for preserved vegetables and fruits, no?" she asked.

"They are."

She pulled her chair closer to the desk and bent over the prints. Her afternoon calls over, she'd changed into a powder blue tea gown. He'd peeled away any number of tea gowns in his time—ladies often devoted the hour between four and five in the afternoon to entertaining their lovers. Hers was rather ordinary, made of a sturdy broadcloth, with none of the seductive drapes and shimmers he'd seen on some of his former paramours. Yet he itched to undo the buttons and expose her beautiful body. He knew what she looked like now, every inch of her skin. And if he closed his eyes, he'd see her head thrown back, her eyes shut tight, her lips parted, as he brought her to pleasure.

He forced his gaze away from her face, onto something safer: the advertising prints spread before her, which they'd already assessed once before.

The first, done in the style of a *Punch*'s cartoon, depicted a hostess in pearls and plumes instructing her daughter, "Now, when our guests compliment us on the crisp asparagus and the beautiful strawberries, under no circumstances will you reveal that they come courtesy of Cresswell & Graves. No, they arrived fresh this morning from our estate in the country."

The second, aiming not so much to amuse as to reassure, showed a woman dressed simply but respectably, gazing with both contentment and relief upon her children, who tucked enthusiastically into a dessert dish of pears. The caption on top read: *This winter, let Cresswell & Graves, always top quality, always affordable, be your greengrocer.* The bottom caption stated: *All fruits vacuum processed and solid packed.*

"What do you think?" he asked, unscrewing the cap of his fountain pen.

She did not like for their secretary to be taking notes during these discussions, as she did not want her participation in the business to become public knowledge.

"The wording is fine on both," she said slowly. "But the ladies' gowns"—she pointed at the first print—"we last saw the artwork in April, before it had become quite obvious that sleeves would collapse this Season. They must be reduced. I'll send along a fashion plate so that the artist will know what they ought to look like: with only very small puffs at the shoulders, none of that leg-of-lamb ballooning."

She examined the print further. "And their hair needs to be dressed higher. There is no such thing as a coiffure that's too high these days."

He jotted down her instructions. Strange, he never quite thought of it this way before, but these private meetings of theirs were his favorite part of his involvement with Cresswell & Graves. He relished listening to her talk about how she wished their products to be perceived. She became impassioned—and wickedly shrewd.

They moved on to a color lithograph advertising poster for preserved cream, fresh cream being a luxury out of the reach of a large swath of the population. This one was straightforward, showing simply a crystal dish of strawberries drenched under lovely, thick cream.

Summer is more summery with Cresswell & Graves Potted Cream.

"They finally have the color right," he said.

First the cream had been the white of leaded paint, then it had been almost currylike. But now it was a pale yellow, full-throttled richness.

She regarded the poster with a critical eye. "I suppose

I'd better let it go. Or we won't be able to use it until next summer."

They dispatched several other posters—for jams and jellies, ox tongues, and curried chicken—and now it was time to discuss ideas for advertising the new chocolate bars, several of which sat on a plate on his desk.

He handed her an orange crème, her favorite, and chose a raspberry delight for himself. They sat in silence for a minute, busy eating.

"We could do something like this," he said, the tart sweetness of the raspberry delight lingering on his tongue. "A man and a woman, sharing chocolate."

Immediately he regretted the suggestion. Of course she'd guess what he really wanted was to kiss her with the chocolate still melting in her mouth.

Her brow knitted and unknitted. "We could, starting with the gentleman offering the lady a chocolate."

She rose and began pacing. This meant a Tremendous Idea had struck—she would not even realize until a few minutes later that she'd left her seat in the excitement. His true intentions remained safe for now.

She stopped midstride. "The gentleman should offer the lady chocolate on a number of occasions, at a tea, at a picnic, on a rowing excursion—fewer and fewer people around them as their acquaintance deepens.

"We should intimate the first time he offers her a choco-late to be the occasion of their first meeting. They will both be a little shy and the chocolate offers a good excuse to exchange a few words. At the picnic they will know each other better. Their postures will be less stiff, they will lean into each other without quite noticing that they are doing so. By the third image—on a rowing boat—they know each other even better, but they have never been in such close proximity for so much time. It is as exciting as it is taxing: They'd like to be closer, but of course they must restrain themselves."

He wondered now how he'd ever thought of her as bland and bloodless, when she was both quick-witted and inventive. "We can run these first three images together—in the same magazine issue, for example, separated by a few pages of text each. We should make it clear, by the end of the third image, that we intend to tell a story, this couple's story. And that it will continue in future installments."

Her eyes sparkled. "Yes, you read my mind: I did intend it as an ongoing story. But your idea is marvelous; a quick succession of vignettes would achieve greater interest faster. After that, we will present new developments in the courtship at regular, but not too close, intervals. And of course our young lovers must overcome a gauntlet of challenges on their way to happiness. But at each step along the way, our chocolates are there to help cement their attraction, comfort their heartbreak, and eventually, celebrate their happiness."

"We will introduce new varieties when our couple's children arrive one by one," said Fitz. He was invariably swept away by her enthusiasm and her barrage of interesting ideas. "And should our chocolates be a success, they will also accompany those children through the ups and downs of childhood and adolescence."

"Not to mention each milestone anniversary of our couple." She smiled. "Chocolate is such fun. Would that asparagus were half as enjoyable to think about."

"The last asparagus advert was quite genius, if you ask me."

The advert had shown individual asparagus spears in tartans and plaids, in a good-natured parody of the images of the Highland regiments famously used to advertise Huntley & Palmers biscuits. People had chuckled all over Britain and the sales of preserved asparagus had jumped sky-high.

"You've always been very uncritical of me," she murmured.

"The very thought of those bagpipe-playing, bearskin-wearing asparagus still makes me snort."

She blushed and bent her neck, a gesture of immense modesty. If he hadn't experienced it, he'd never be able to imagine her thrashing beneath him, her hand between his legs. But it was all he thought of these days, her heat, her temerity, her abandon.

"I think we did well today," she said. "You can pass on the ideas to Mr. Gideon and I'll be glad to look at the first sketches when you have them."

Without waiting for an answer, she rose. He rose, too, and walked her to the door.

He'd meant to open the door for her, but instead he blocked it. Before she could say anything he took hold of her face and kissed her, pressing her into the nearest wall.

All these years. *All these years.*

Her mouth was chocolaty, her tongue eager and nimble. She dug under his waistcoat and dragged at his shirt, pulling it free of his trousers. He flicked open the buttons on her bodice, pushed down everything in his way, and captured her nipple in his mouth.

His trousers, her skirts, all obstacles were shoved aside. He lifted her and drove into her. The sounds she made, rough, beautiful, sounds of the loveliest distress. And her face, her exquisite face.

"Open your eyes," he ordered.

She only squeezed her eyes shut tighter.

"Open your eyes or I'll stop."

He did stop. She whimpered in protest. Her eyelids fluttered then raised—slightly. She kept her gaze down.

"Look at me."

Reluctantly, she did.

And in the depth of her eyes were all these years—seasons they'd known, paths they'd trod.

Slowly he entered her again. Everything reflected in her gaze: shyness, yearning, ripples of pleasure.

The pleasure turned fierce, then ferocious. He labored to draw breath. In the wash of her climax, she closed her eyes. He closed his own eyes and yielded to the moment.

*B*ut even when they'd restored their clothing to a semblance of decency, he still found it difficult to breathe—an oppressive weight had settled over his chest.

This was not procreation. This was not even simple lust. He sought something—an echo of his own heart, perhaps, a consonance—and he found it in her.

No, no, it had been only an illusion, a moment of make-believe.

And never mind what he thought he'd found, what made him think it was *acceptable*, in the first place, to look for it in his wife?

He'd promised himself to Isabelle.

He opened the door for Millie.

"Booting me out now that you've had your way with me?" she said without quite looking at him, but with a small smile lingering at the corner of her lips.

The very faint note of flirtation in her voice was a sharp pain through his lungs. She never flirted otherwise. He'd given her the wrong impression.

"Just stepping aside so as not to be in your way any-more."

"You weren't in my way. In me, perhaps, but not in my way."

She flushed and bit her lower lip, as if shocked by her own bluntness.

He was no less shocked: He'd thought her only capable of prurience in the dark. He wanted her this way, shyly raunchy. He wanted to—

He'd promised himself to another.

"I need to speak to Gideon before he leaves for the day, about the changes we want to make to the advertising prints."

"Yes, of course. I'll make myself scarce."

She kissed him on his cheek—which she'd never done in the entire course of their marriage—and showed her-self out.

He closed the door quietly, shutting himself inside.

Never mind what a man says; watch what he does, an exasperated chaperone had once said within Millie's hearing.

If she were to go by this excellent advice, then she would disregard Fitz's stated plan—that in six months he would leave her for Mrs. Englewood—and pay attention only to what he did.

On the surface of it, what he did might not seem so terribly significant: He'd taken their lovemaking out of her bedroom and into his study—and from night into day. But Fitz was a discreet man who understood nuances and who conducted himself accordingly. For him to be so carried away, like a balloon in a storm, was indicative of an enormous lust, at least.

And quite possibly much, much more.

She tried not to let her hopes get the best of her, but she burst at the seams with anticipation. Any day now, he was going to see that he had not waited eight years for Mrs. Englewood, but for Millie.

Since Helena was under Venetia's chaperonage, Millie had the evening free. She quite looked forward to a nice dinner at home with Fitz, an interlude to let their desires build to a new ascendancy. And tonight she would not ask him to turn off the light. She liked the undisguised covetousness in his eyes when he looked at her naked form. He could look as much as he wanted.

For dining at home, she could have worn her tea gown. But it was a bit too brazen to wear the same dress in which he'd ravished her, so she changed into a pretty marigold dinner gown. No sounds came from his room, but she was not particularly concerned. She'd heard him in his bath earlier; he'd probably already changed and was again in his study.

But when she arrived at the drawing room, a few minutes late, he was not there.

"Is Lord Fitzhugh still in his study?"

"No, ma'am," said Cobble, the butler. "Lord Fitzhugh has gone to his club. He said not to expect him for dinner."

She blinked. That he'd have gone out in the evening was not so strange. He enjoyed seeing his friends at his club and occasionally dined there. But why tonight? He'd given no indication in the afternoon that he was headed anywhere.

"Shall I serve dinner?" asked Cobble.

"Yes, of course."

A minute ago she was walking on clouds, now she was in a dungeon, with screws in her thumbs. She forced herself to eat normally. She must keep a sense of calm and proportion. Chances were she had overreacted both in her earlier euphoria and her current despair. The truth was probably somewhere in the middle: Their lovemaking in his study was not as significant as she'd made it out to be; and neither was his absence this evening.

He would be back at night. And he'd come for her again.

*E*leven o'clock. Twelve o'clock. One o'clock.

He was having fun with his friends. She was glad.

No, she was not glad in the least. His friends were not going anywhere. They'd still be his friends when he was old and grey. She had less than six months and he chose to spend his time elsewhere.

Six months, dear God, not those words again. Just hours earlier she'd thought it would be a lifetime.

How quickly happiness shrinks to nothing.

He entered his room at a quarter past one. His lights turned off at half past one and he went directly to bed.

She shouldn't be too greedy. It already happened once this day. She ought not expect more.

But she wanted more. More of the incandescent pleasures, more of the stark hunger in his eyes, more of this connection, this intimacy unlike any she'd ever experienced.

They were good friends, weren't they? The best of friends. She ought to be able to walk into his room and ask him the reason for his absence this evening—and the reason for his absence from her bed.

But she couldn't, because it was all a sham, their friendship, at least on her part, a disguise for her true feelings, an awful solace for not being his one and only.

A thing without wings.

CHAPTER 17

*A*fter eight years, how did a woman take over a man's life overnight?

And why couldn't it be a simple case of lust, an itch that could have been scratched on any post?

Instead Fitz felt split in two, his other half on the far side of the door. But he couldn't open that door, walk inside, and make himself whole again. He could only wait for the end of the night.

In the morning he rode and took his time bathing and changing. She should have already left the breakfast parlor when he descended at last, but she was very much there, in her customary spot, a stack of letters and a cup of still-steaming tea before her.

Once upon a time he'd dreaded it, the prospect of sitting across from her at ten thousand breakfasts. Today he could not think of anything more felicitous. She was daily sustenance, like bread, water, and light.

"Good morning."

She looked up and did not smile. "Good morning."

She thought he'd rejected her. But it was not true. He'd stepped back because he could not in good conscience continue to mislead her—or himself.

"You've a letter from Mrs. Englewood," she said.

It was to be expected. He pulled out the letter and sliced it open. "She is back in town."

A few days ahead of schedule. This, too, was not entirely unexpected.

"She will want to see you," said his wife.

"She does. I will call on her in the afternoon." He took a sip of his coffee. "And what do you have planned for the day?"

"Nothing much. A call on Venetia in the afternoon."

How he envied Venetia. "I'm sure she will be delighted to have your company."

"As I'm sure Mrs. Englewood will yours." She rose. "Good day."

*I*sabelle's parlor suffocated.

It shouldn't be the case at all—Fitz had made sure that the house was well ventilated. And it had rained midmorning. The sky was clear, the window was open, the white dimity summer curtain danced in the light breeze.

Yet he felt as if he'd been locked into a cupboard.

She talked about her sister, her niece, her children, gesticulating with great animation—as if by the motions of her arms and hands she could stir the air enough to save him from asphyxiation. As if she knew her house was choking the air from his lungs.

"From everything you say, you enjoyed Aberdeen very well," he said. "You should have stayed longer."

Why must you return so soon?

"I missed you."

She waited a beat, waiting for him to echo her statement. When he didn't, for a brief moment, it seemed as if she'd ask outright whether he shared her sentiment. And what would he do if she did? He could not lie. He'd tried; but in the end he'd thought only of Millie.

Millie, his mainstay, his solace, his coveted companion of the night.

His lack of a response was a void, an absence, an empty chair at dinner that everyone tried not to notice.

Isabelle broke off a piece of cake. "So . . . what did you do while I was away?"

A less awkward question, but not by much. *Slept with my wife. Which I've given up.*

"I've kept busy."

"Well, tell me more. I want to know how you spend your days in the course of an ordinary week."

But this had been no ordinary week, had it?

"It will bore you."

"It won't."

"Well, yesterday I looked at some advertising prints for Cresswell & Graves."

Of all the things he could mention, why must he bring up this particular episode? Why did he keep remembering Millie's quick kiss on his cheek? How happy she'd seemed.

Isabelle glanced at him with some astonishment. "You

have hirelings to do that sort of thing for you, surely? You don't need to get your hands dirty."

He understood her reaction: It was not good form to be actively involved in business. But he could not quite put out his irritation. "I'm not exactly working in the factories."

"But advertising is"—she grimaced—"vulgar."

"It makes a significant difference in profits."

"Profits are vulgar, too. Profits are what shopkeepers and merchants think about."

He understood that a preoccupation with wealth and its generation coarsened the soul. It was the reason that landed gentry had always held such sway in this country: For a long time they'd made a convincing argument that gentlemen who did not need to muddy their thoughts with the provenance of their next sou were better suited to loftier things like justice and governance.

But it never felt vulgar when he discussed matters of business with Millie. It felt—intricate, like tinkering with the inner workings of a fine watch. And a hefty percentage of their profits went into schools, parks, and hospitals. He'd be a far richer man if he believed in improving only his own lot.

"Then I must admit to being vulgar."

She turned her face one way, then the other, agitated. "Don't be like that."

"I cannot pretend my land is enough for my upkeep. My houses, my dinners, the shirt on my back—everything I have is thanks to profits from tinned goods."

She looked pained. "Must we introduce tinned goods into our conversation? They are so déclassé."

He could not blame her. Once upon a time, he'd held

exactly the same views. The gentry was ever dismissive of those who made their fortunes in commerce and manufacturing. And Cresswell & Graves didn't even have the cachet of grandeur or luxury. He'd had plenty of potted chicken for his afternoon tea when he'd been a student and bottled beverages had made good inroads among the young, but there was no denying the fact that enormous quantities of tinned goods were consumed by those who could not always afford greengrocery and freshly butchered meat: the poor and the working class.

And therefore, déclassé.

"I oversee the management of the firm on my wife's behalf," he said. "By my own choice. And I quite enjoy it, advertising component included."

"This is so unlike you." Her eyes pleaded with him to change his mind. "I can't imagine the old you would ever take up something like this. It isn't gentlemanly."

Gentlemanly it might not be, but it was fascinating, an ever shifting challenge. From the sourcing of the ingredients to the manufacturing processes to the allocation of capital, a hundred variables must be considered, a thousand decisions made—many of which he delegated to his lieutenants but for all of which he remained ultimately responsible.

"It is my life now."

Her chair scraped and wobbled as she shot out of it. Her momentum carried her to the window, where she had no choice but to stop and turn around. "I can't imagine life with someone who is involved in the making of canned sardines."

A cleverer, more opportunistic man would have seized on the opportunity to tell her good luck and farewell. But he was not that man. Her expression had a measure of her old impetuosity, but so much of it was ravage and anxiety. How could he run out on her at a moment like this?

He rose, went to the window, and placed his arm about her shoulders.

"What's the matter, Isabelle? You've known about the sardines. It's not about the sardines."

She turned her face into his sleeve, but it was less a gesture of affection than one of desolation. "You've changed, Fitz."

"It's been eight years. Everyone changes."

"I haven't changed."

The insight came to him like a match flaring. "I can see how you've tried to remain the same. But no, you have changed, too. Once you thrilled to new horizons. Now all you want is to live in a monument to the way things might have been."

She jerked, as if he'd handed her a live wire.

"Is that what I am doing?" she asked, a question for herself. "You think there is something wrong with it? Is that why you aren't the least bit interested in returning things to the way they might have—should have—been?"

"You cannot go back in time, Isabelle. You cannot re-create a past that never happened. You—all of us—must move forward."

She clutched his lapel, her voice muffled. "The future terrifies me. All the best years of my life are behind me. Now I'm just a widow with two children and no idea what to do with myself."

He lifted her face. "You must not think like this. You still have all your life ahead of you."

"But I do think like this. I've thought like this for a

while now." She touched his cheek, her hand cold as fear. "Don't let me be alone, Fitz. Don't let me be alone."

$\mathcal{V}$enetia had such a glow to her, whereas if Millie were to look into the mirror, she'd see a face from which the light had gone out, except for perhaps one or two sputtering flickers.

"I was hoping Fitz would come with you," said Venetia.

Millie steeled herself. "He is calling on Mrs. Englewood this afternoon."

"She's already back from Scotland? I thought she was staying an entire week."

"So did I."

"I hate to pry—well, actually, that's not true. I would pry with a crowbar if I could—I'm terribly concerned that Fitz may not be thinking quite right just now."

Millie poured tea for them, glad for a legitimate excuse not to meet Venetia's eyes. "He has made up his mind to take up with Mrs. Englewood."

"I'm sorry to hear that. I don't consider Fitz a foolish man but this is a foolish choice indeed."

Millie bit the inside of her cheek. "Is there ever such a thing as a wise choice in love?"

"Yes, I'm sure of it. I refuse to believe that every happy marriage under the sun is simply a matter of luck. At some point someone must have weighed the choices and chosen well, whether it is a choice of mate or a choice of conduct within the marriage."

"He loves Mrs. Englewood."

"I used to believe so—not anymore. He *loved* her, many years ago, when they were children. Had they married then, they'd probably have suited each other well. But they didn't and their paths diverged. And I'm not sure whether what he believes to be love isn't simply the throb and echo of cherished memories, of nostalgia masquerading as a blueprint for the future. But with you, he has built such a strong foundation of affection, of common interest and common purpose. I cannot believe he'd cast it all aside for something almost entirely illusory."

Millie was beyond grateful for Venetia's support. But in such matters the opinion of a sister, however beloved, counted for little. She raised her head. "We've only ever been friends. Friendship is love without the wings and who would ever choose something without wings?"

There, she'd done it. She'd let her bitterness and discontent leach through to her words. Even her skin must be green with bile.

Venetia gazed at Millie, her beautiful face saddened but no less radiant. "No, my dear Millie, you are wrong. Love without friendship is like a kite, aloft only when the winds are favorable. Friendship *is* what gives love its wings."

*F*itz found Millie in her sitting room, fiddling with her supper plate.

He dropped into the chair opposite hers, stretched out his legs, and tilted his head back. Her ceiling came into view. A pretty ceiling, papered with a design of—his eyes widened—hot air balloons and airships.

He smiled at the memories—what a grand adventure that had been.

She didn't say anything. It was a comfortable silence.

He had his eyes half closed. Her silverware clinked gently against her plate.

"So what's the matter?" she asked after a few minutes.

He realized he'd been waiting for her to ask just that question, even if she were the last person to whom he should unburden himself—on this matter at least. "I'm at a loss."

"About?"

He sighed. "Mrs. Englewood."

"I'm listening."

"She's had a difficult time of it—upheavals of all sorts. She now looks to me as an antidote to change, a known, fixed entity. I cannot help but think she will be dreadfully disappointed. I am not my nineteen-year-old self and I can never be again."

"Is that what she wants, the you she once knew?"

"I want her to be happy. But I don't know how to give her what she wants. Worse, I don't know what she truly needs, whether it's a hothouse to protect her for the rest of her days or simply a hand to help her over a rough patch."

She had spoiled him, his Millie. He was used to a self-sufficient woman now, not one who depended on him to ensure her happiness.

"I want to do the right thing by her," he said. "If I only knew what that was."

*A*s his lover, she did not want to hear about his concern for another woman. But as his friend, she was not offended that he'd come to her with his worries.

Far from it. She was glad.

"You will," she said. "You might make a mistake or two along the way. But I know you. In the end you always do the right thing."

He smiled, a tired smile, rose from his chair, and kissed her on her forehead. "What would I do without you?"

Her gaze followed him as he left, closing the door softly behind himself. Perhaps friendship was what gave love its wings, perhaps not. But she understood now that she'd been wrong earlier: There was nothing the least sham about their friendship.

It was true—and it had wings of its own.

CHAPTER 18

"I am going to see a place in the country day after tomorrow, will you come with me?" asked Isabelle. "Doyle's Grange. It's not far from Henley Park, from what I understand."

Doyle's Grange was only twenty miles—three stops on a branch line—from Henley Park. "Doyle's Grange is for let?"

"It is and it sounds rather perfect for our purposes. Not too big, not too small, close enough to Henley Park for you to keep an eye on things. And a shorter trip to London than from Henley Park, for when you must see to business matters and such."

This was her way of conceding that his involvement with Cresswell & Graves would not cease—or even be curtailed—as a result of his involvement with her.

She bent her head to the map and he spied a single white

hair on her otherwise raven head. Long ago she'd told him that because her mother had needed to dye her hair from her midthirties, she, too, expected to be prematurely grey. They'd joked that when it happened, he'd call her Gran and she'd call him Sonny.

His heart filled with a painful tenderness. He wanted so much for her to be happy, to be once again fearless and vibrant, not this shadow of her former self, this adrift vessel desperately in search of an anchor.

But was a man who thought far more often of another woman the right one to accompany her on the path back to confidence and joy?

Outside her house, he sent away his carriage and walked. There was no doubt which choice he *wanted* to make—every fiber of his being yearned toward Millie. But that would be putting his own happiness above Isabelle's.

As much as she had suffered eight years ago, she had not blamed him. This time there were no external forces acting against her desires, only the changes that had taken place in the intervening years.

Only the man he'd become and the wife he'd come to cherish.

But was it too selfish to want to hold on to what he had when Isabelle needed him so? Could he possibly derail her dreams again?

He was no closer to an answer when he arrived at his own house. Cobble informed him that a report he'd been waiting for had been delivered from Cresswell & Graves. He sat down in his study, opened the report, but could not understand a single sentence therein. After a quarter hour he tossed aside the report and crossed the room to the mantel.

Alice was in her spot. He gazed upon her as if she might have the answer, she who'd been with him through some of the most difficult months of his life. But she, in her eternal rest, could not help him. He sighed, lifted the bell jar that covered her, and stroked her along her back.

"Does she feel soft?" Millie asked from behind him.

He stilled—he almost did not trust himself to turn around. But he did. She stood at the exact spot where he'd ravished her. Heat rose in great coils from his soles to the back of his neck. "You've never felt her?"

Millie shook her head. Of course, he'd never offered her Alice to hold while Alice yet lived and Millie was not the sort to take the liberty just because now Alice was dead.

He picked up the hazel-wood base on which Alice rested and extended it to her. "Go ahead."

She came forward. He could not take his eyes off her: her hair, pulled back ever so neatly; her neck, slender and elegant; her simple tea gown, small roses printed on white silk, that had been a part of her wardrobe for years, He'd never told her the dress was one of his favorites.

She extended her fingers tentatively toward Alice—and drew back, surprised, when she came into contact with the dormouse: Although Alice gave the impression of being warm and pliant, in fact she was quite rigid, her body the same temperature as the room.

"She's gone," he said, "as dead as the pharaohs."

And would that he'd understood it sooner. What he'd felt for Isabelle, in those first moments of seeing her again, had been as lifelike as Alice. But like Alice, they, too, were but a preserved relic of an earlier age.

*H*e replaced the bell jar and put Alice back on the mantel. "And how are you, my dear Millie? Were you looking for me?"

He looked weary. She knew he hadn't been sleeping well. In the week since he stopped coming to her bed, nightly he would leave his own bed for his study, return some time later, then repeat the same excursion again.

She, too, had been lying awake, staring into the dark. But unlike him, she had come to a decision.

This impasse could not be blamed entirely—or even largely—on him. Nor on Mrs. Englewood. If anyone should have acted different, it was Millie. Sometimes changes happened imperceptibly; he could be excused for not quite realizing that he had fallen in love with someone he'd considered only a very good friend. But she, she'd known from the very beginning that she loved him.

She should have done something about it years ago. Instead, she'd been too proud and too afraid to let him know how she felt, for fear that should things not go well, she would be left without even her hope, her mainstay all these years.

No more. No more cowardice. No more holding back. No more hanging on to a hope without ever putting it into action.

"Everything still proceeding as you'd planned?" she asked.

He looked at her and did not answer.

"I am going to Henley Park for a few days," she said. "And when I come back, we should give serious consideration to going our separate ways."

He blenched with shock. "What do you mean?" His voice rose; he almost never raised his voice. "We are not about to go our separate ways, Millie. We—"

She put her hands on his arms, the wool of his jacket warm beneath her palms. "Listen to me, Fitz. Listen to me. Think of Mrs. Englewood's children. How will you explain your arrangement to them? What will other people say?"

He opened his mouth but made no response.

"At least they are legitimate children, their parents properly wed. What if Mrs. Englewood should conceive by *you*? What will happen to those children?" She took a deep breath. "If you want to spend the rest of your days with her, you must marry her."

His face was obdurate. "I can't marry her. I'm already married."

"We'll obtain an annulment."

"Absolutely not. You might be with child."

"I'm not." The beginning of her menses, six days ago, had dithered and fudged, dragging out a thin, frayed hope, before snapping it altogether. "Are you going to sleep with me again?"

"I . . ."

"Then, I won't be with child and we can safely proceed to the annulment. The Leo Marsdens did it: They put their marriage behind them. There is no reason we cannot."

"I don't care what the Marsdens did. We are not getting an annulment."

"If you are concerned about the maintenance of Henley

Park, I will gladly sign over half of the shares of Cresswell & Graves. The firm is four times the size it was when we married, so it's still a good bargain for me."

He stared at her as if he couldn't even recognize her. "I will burn down Henley Park before I'll let you think I'm keeping you for your money."

"Then, why are you keeping me?"

He pinched the bridge of his nose. "Your fellow already has a wife. What purpose does an annulment serve for you, when you cannot marry him in any case?"

She dropped her hands from his person and took a step back—she was still afraid of the consequences of speaking the truth at last. But she would no longer delay it. "There is no one else. There never was."

He looked disoriented. "But you said you were in love with him. You said you had to give up your chances with him when we married. You—"

"I know what I've said over the years. But the truth remains: There was never anyone else—never anyone other than you." She stared down at her hands. "I fell in love with you the moment I saw you. When you were angriest at Fate, so was I, because it made me the last girl you'd ever love."

A long, long moment of silence passed. He gripped her arms. "My God, Millie! Why did you never tell me?"

She raised her face and met his eyes. "I should have, shouldn't I? I'm sorry I didn't make my confession sooner, but now you know."

If he loved her, this was the time to reciprocate her declaration. And he did love her, of course. It was only a matter of how much.

He gazed at her, his eyes like the dawn sky, full of the

heat and promise of a new day. Her heart ached with this wordless communion of hope and desire. He didn't need to say anything. A kiss would be enough.

But he didn't. He left her and walked to the window, his fingers on his temples. "You should have told me," he said. "Years ago."

"Had Mother lived, perhaps she'd have advised me differently." She bit her lip. "I'm sure you see now that it will be impossible for me to remain married to you after you set up your arrangement with Mrs. Englewood."

He turned around. "Millie—"

There came a knock at the door. It was a footman, come to inform Millie that her carriage awaited.

After the door closed again behind the footman, she approached the window. "You've spoken much of fairness of late. I think it is only fair that if you choose Mrs. Englewood, you let me go so that I have a chance for a true marriage, and perhaps, someday, a family."

"Millie—"

"I have said everything there is to say on the subject. Now I must catch my train." She kissed him on his cheek. "You know where to find me."

CHAPTER 19

$\mathcal{F}$itz couldn't stop looking at the photographs.

It was night, only hours to go before he and Isabelle visited Doyle's Grange, the house in the country that she wanted for the two of them. Millie had been gone for more than a day, and her absence was a sharp emptiness in his heart.

Except for her sojourn in America at the beginning of the year, as co-chaperone to Helena, they had not been apart in years. During her absence, he'd written almost daily, skipping a few days here and there not because he wanted to, but because it seemed embarrassing to be constantly pelting one's wife with letters.

And now he was in her rooms, missing her, missing the part of himself that had left with her.

He lifted his favorite photograph from the mantel and brought it closer. It was from the previous summer. Likely the photographer had intended only to capture Hastings, who sat at one end of a chaise longue, looking rather serious. But just beyond the other end of the chaise stood Fitz and Millie.

He'd bet good money they were discussing nothing more significant than the evening's entertainment for their guests, but it felt far more intimate. Their heads were bent toward each other, their expressions intent. And the way he'd positioned himself, with his hand on the back of the chaise, from the angle of the camera it looked almost as if he had his arm around her waist.

She loved him. She'd loved him all along.

What a fool he'd been, to not have realized it sooner.

Had he a better understanding of his own heart, when Isabelle asked whether it was too late to reclaim some of what they could have had, he'd have answered differently. She'd have been disappointed, but not overcome. Now, after he'd raised her hopes with his pledge for a future together, she would be furious—and heartbroken.

He could not bear to break her heart again.

He could not bear to lose Millie.

Millie had said that he always did the right thing. He clung to that praise like a poor fisherman to his tattered net. But was there a right thing to do here? And if there was, how would he know it?

*D*oyle's Grange was a pleasant surprise from the first sight: The property was separated from the country lane that passed before it by a hedge of rhododendron, in raucous, purple bloom.

The gate was whimsical and charming: finials in the

shape of grape leaves; wrought iron vines meandering across the pickets. Pines lined the gravel drive. Somewhere in the distance, a stream babbled.

The house was constructed of brick, with large bay windows and gabled dormer windows. Ivy climbed over the portico. The interior, full of books and low furniture upholstered in creams and yellows, was bright and comfortable.

Isabelle was clearly enchanted. But in every room, she'd cast an uncertain glance at him, gauging his reactions. After they'd inspected the interior, they went out to the gardens. The roses had faded but the pinks and the delphiniums were going strong. Bees buzzed. The air was English summer at its finest, a dash of warmth, a hint of hay, and a garden in bloom.

"Can you picture yourself here?" she asked.

Suddenly the right thing to do was there in front of him. To keep Isabelle happy, he would have to lie, and that was no way to begin a life together. She deserved better. She deserved a man who was thrilled to share her house and her life, a man in whose heart she would always be first and foremost.

He was not that man. And he hadn't been for a very, very long time.

"I'm sorry, Isabelle, but I picture myself elsewhere," he said.

The corners of her lips quivered. "You mean you'd like to look at a different house?"

There was such fear in her eyes he almost could not continue. "No, I picture myself at Henley Park."

Some of her old fire came back. "That hovel? I never told you but I went to see it before you married. It was a horrible place."

"It was. But it isn't anymore."

Her face took on an obdurate set. "I don't believe you."

"Then come with me," he said gently. "And see it for yourself."

*W*hen had Fitz fallen in love with his house? A long time ago, most likely. But he'd realized it only the year before, coming back after a London Season.

They'd never stopped working on Henley—decades of accumulated neglect could not be reversed by any single bout of renovation. The renewal of the estate was steady and ongoing.

Perhaps because there were always works in progress, something else in need of attention, perhaps because the two previous years his return to Henley Park had taken place at night, but it was not until that particular day that Fitz had a long, continual view of Henley Park, as if he were a tourist, seeing it for the first time.

Double rows of hazel trees hugged the drive. Through their canopy fell a light almost as green as the leaves, a clear, cool light with flecks of gold that shook with the rustling of the branches.

There, at the turn of the drive, he'd come across the eyesore that was the dilapidated Grecian folly—and not fallen into ruins in a rustic, isn't-it-quaint manner, but dumpy and ugly, promising to reek of things one couldn't mention in mixed company.

But no, the restoration was at last complete. Gleaming white and slender columned, the folly seemed not to touch the grassy slope on which it had been built, but float above it, its reflection rippling in the man-made lake below.

And the lake, once reed choked, was now clear as a mirror. The jetty, so long falling into the water, had been rehabilitated. Tied to the jetty was a rowboat painted a brilliant blue, a pair of oars laid across the bow.

The road rose, dipped, and rose again. And spread before him were the lavender fields, a sea of purple spikes swaying in the breeze.

"My God," he murmured.

"I know," said Millie, in the carriage with him. "I love coming back to it."

He was struck by a fierce gladness. This beautiful place belonged to him and he belonged to this beautiful place. He would never again think of it merely as the estate he'd inherited. It was home now—and would be till his dying day.

*H*enley Park was as lovely as Fitz had ever seen it. The drive, the lake and the folly, the lavender fields, and at last coming into view, the house he shared with Millie, a trim, compact Georgian, its walls faintly lavender from the fading of the bricks, asymmetrical from the demolishing of the north wing, and yet, harmonious in every aspect.

"This is where I picture myself," he said to Isabelle, "my favorite place on Earth."

He'd come to it by fate; but now he held it by love.

He signaled the driver to stop. They alit and walked in silence, arm in arm, until they came to the new bridge crossing the trout stream: a Japanese bridge made of stone, perfectly arched.

A pair of swans glided past the bridge.

"I should have realized it sooner, but I've been a fool. We have built this place together, my wife and I. And we have built a life together. She is a part of me now, the greater part of me, the better part of me."

Isabelle turned away. He caught her by the shoulders. "Isabelle."

"I understand now—and it is not as if I haven't felt the future I'd imagined for us slipping away these past weeks," said Isabelle, her voice breaking. "It's just that I—"

"You will not be alone, Isabelle. I cannot be your lover, but I *am* your friend. And I am far from your only friend."

She had tears in her eyes. "I hope you are right, Fitz. I wish you all the joy in the world."

He enfolded her in his arms. "And I wish the same for you. I love you and I always will."

But the love of his life was the one with whom he'd built his life.

*M*illie walked, hoping to find solace, but what solace she found was lanced through with a painful longing, for imprinted on every square foot of Henley Park was their collaboration: She and Fitz had massaged every last nook and cranny of this land, to soothe the tantrums of an estate made temperamental by neglect.

They'd once stood not fifty feet from this path, discussing what to do with a vast quantity of cleared underbrush—eventually discarding a bonfire in favor of making mulch. At the next bend she'd come upon Fitz a good many years ago, tossing small bulbs out of his pocket—she'd bought too many for her garden and he'd wanted to see whether some of them might naturalize in the woods. Some of them had, piercing the soil every spring to bloom afresh, dots of yellow and purple and white against the previous year's fallen leaves. And of course, farther ahead was the spot where the trout stream had overflowed on the eve of their Italian holiday, flooding the old bridge and a greenhouse in the process. They'd spent the days before their departure trudging up and down the banks, debating the merits of widening versus straightening.

Sometimes she'd been harried. Many times she'd been resoundingly annoyed by yet another creaking wheel needing her attention. They'd both marched in on each other, demanding the purchase of dynamite to blow up a particularly irksome part of the estate.

But looking back, she could see nothing but wonderful moments, the threads of two separate lives gradually, imperceptibly weaving into one.

The path turned. The new bridge came into view. She stopped, her heart falling into an abyss.

A man and a woman stood on the bridge, in a tight embrace. And then, even after they drew apart, he kept his hand on her shoulder, and she leaned her head on his.

Millie slowly backed away. And when she was sure they could not hear her, she turned and ran.

She ran until she could no longer run. Then she walked—until she could no longer walk. And when she sat down on a mossy rock, her tears overcame her at last.

She would be all right in the end, she supposed. She was an enviably rich woman, and still quite young. And if a place as wretched as Henley Park could be brought back to life, anything could.

But she could not see the future, she could only weep for her loss. Day by day, year by year, kindness by kindness they'd built this life together, its foundation an unshakable affection, its walls partnership, and its pinnacle passion. All she wanted was to add to it, strengthen it, and cherish it.

Now she would have to leave it behind to disintegrate and fall into ruin.

Her tears streamed anew.

*A*s daylight faded, she started for home—she would never not think of it as home.

Not wanting anyone to see her, she entered through the door that opened to the side terrace and slipped upstairs via the service stairs to her bath. In the mirror, her face was almost livid in its splotchiness.

She splashed her eyes with cold water, toweled her face dry, walked into her bedroom and lit the lamps. She didn't believe Fitz would invite Mrs. Englewood to dine at Henley Park, but she was not about to take herself down to the dining room to find out. She'd have her dinner upstairs, by herself.

The sound of running feet stormed down the passage toward her room. Her door blew open. Fitz braced one hand on the doorjamb, breathing hard, as if he'd run across the breadth of Henley Park.

"You idiot. Where the *hell* have you been?"

"I was—out on a walk."

"Mrs. Gibson told me you left for a walk in the morning, before eleven o'clock. It's half past nine at night now. We've been searching for you for the past four hours. God, I just gave the order to dredge the lake. I was afraid—I was afraid that—and then I saw your light come on—"

She was suddenly lifted up and pushed against the bed-post. He kissed her as if the entire world had become a vacuum and she its last remaining conduit of oxygen.

"Don't ever do this to me again," he growled, when he pulled away for a minute to pant.

"But Mrs. Englewood, you are—I saw you, the two of you together."

"What?"

"On the new bridge. You were holding her—tight."

"Of course I was. I'd just told her that I belong here—with you."

"Oh," she said.

He had chosen her in the end. She could not help it. She wept again. "And was Mrs. Englewood all right?"

"I think so. She said she'll return to her sister's place in Aberdeen—her children are still there. She didn't want me to accompany her back so I cabled Hastings to wait on her when she got off at London. He already cabled back. They'd had tea together and he'd seen her off at the rail station."

"I hope she'll be happy," Millie said through her tears. "I hope she'll be as happy as I am now."

He crushed her to him. "I've been such a fool."

"So have I. If I'd let on earlier, if I hadn't been so afraid—"

His kiss swallowed the rest of her words.

"Let me go and call off the search, so people aren't stumbling about in the dark looking for nothing." He kissed her again. "Better get some rest now. After I come back I'm not letting you sleep a wink."

"All right, go," she said, a great big smile on her face, tears still falling.

* * *

*O*ww," said Fitz.

"Are you all right?"

He'd returned some time ago and she'd pushed him into bed and leaped on top of him. She was still on top of him, running her hand over his arm, nipping him on his shoulder.

He dug out a framed photograph from under his back. "I must have left this on your bed when I was here earlier, waiting for you to come back from your walk."

She sucked in a breath. "I'm sorry, darling. I didn't know you were hurting all this time. I'm so—"

He put a finger over her lips and grinned raffishly. "Trust me, I didn't feel it at all."

They spent a moment looking at the photograph, with the two of them standing together at the edge of a picture that should have included only Hastings. It was her favorite—she had a framed print in every house and several unframed prints stashed in her dressing room.

"Let's cut Hastings out," Fitz suggested. "So it will be only the two of us."

She giggled. "Poor Hastings."

"I'm sure he'll volunteer to leave us alone."

The photograph safely out of the way on the nightstand, he kissed her. "So, this is what it feels like to be married to the woman I love."

The woman I love. She would never tire of the sound of it. "Satisfactory, I hope."

He cupped her face. "For years I'd wondered how my life might have been different—better—had I been able to go back in time and change certain crucial events.

Extending the previous's earl's lifespan, for example, or causing the north wing to never have been built. After a while I stopped such speculations because I was busy and there was no point. But now I know: I wouldn't change a thing, because only this life I've lived could have led me here, with you." He traced a finger over her brow. "And I'm beyond glad to be here, with you."

Her eyes turned moist again. "I love you."

"I love you." He kissed her again. "And I love everything about you."

Smiling through her tears, she kissed the signet ring on his hand. Then, she licked it as she'd wanted to do for years and years. "Now, Lord Fitzhugh, I give you a choice: supper or me?"

"You, my love." He pulled her toward him. "Always you."

AUTHOR'S NOTE

Because women made many of the decisions in the purchase of household items, manufacturers and other companies had long sought to appeal to them. As a result, women achieved access and success in advertising far earlier than they had in many other professions, managing advertising agencies by the 1890s.

And for readers who want to know what happened to Isabelle Pelham Englewood, you will find her story in *Midnight Scandals*, an anthology by Courtney Milan, Carolyn Jewel, and Sherry Thomas.

Read on for a sneak peek of the next
irresistible romance from Sherry Thomas

Tempting the Bride

Coming October 2012 from Berkley Sensation

PROLOGUE

January 1896

*D*arkness was like a lover's embrace, Helena Fitzhugh had heard it said.

Bollocks.

Nothing was like a lover's embrace, with its warmth, strength, and passionate need. But a lover's embrace made one look favorably upon the entirety of the universe. As Helena entered her unlit bedroom, surrounded by darkness, she sighed in contentment.

Or rather, as much contentment as possible given that her particular lover's embrace happened through her chemise and Andrew's nightshirt. But still, how new and thrilling it was to kiss and touch in the comfort and privacy of a bed, almost enough to pretend that the past six years never happened and that the only thing that separated them were two layers of thin, soft merino wool.

"Hullo, Miss Fitzhugh," came a man's voice out of the darkness.

Her heart stopped. David Hillsborough, Viscount Hastings, was her brother Fitz's best friend—but not exactly a friend to her.

"Mistook my room for one of your paramours'?" She was proud of herself. Her voice sounded even, almost blasé.

"Then I would have greeted you by one of their names, wouldn't I?" His voice was just as nonchalant as hers.

A match flared, illuminating a pair of stern eyes. It always surprised her that he could look serious—intimidating—at times, when he was so frivolous a person.

He lit a hand candle. "Where were you, Miss Fitzhugh?"

"I was hungry. I went to the butler's pantry and found myself a slice of pear cake."

He blew out the match and tossed it in the grate. "And came back directly?"

"Not that it is any of your concern, but yes."

"So if I kiss you now, you would taste of pear cake?"

Trust Hastings to always drag a discussion in this particular direction. "Absolutely. But as your lips will never touch mine, that is a moot point, my Lord Hastings."

He looked at her askance. "You are aware, are you not, that I am one of your brother's most trusted friends?"

A friendship she'd never quite understood. "And?"

"And as such, when I become aware of gross misconduct on your part, it behooves me to inform your brother without delay."

She lifted her chin. "Gross misconduct? Is that what one calls a little foray to the butler's pantry these days?"

"*A little foray to the butler's pantry*, is that what one

calls gross misconduct these days? Or is that how one properly refers to the territory inside Mr. Martin's underlinens?"

"I don't know what you are talking about."

"Should I use the scientific names?"

And wouldn't he enjoy doing that. But as it was her steadfast policy to never let him enjoy himself at her expense, she declared, "Mr. Martin and I are friends of long standing and nothing more."

"You and I are friends of long standing and—"

"You and I are *acquaintances* of long standing, Hastings."

"Fine. Your sister and I are friends of long standing and yet she has never come to spend hours in my room. Alone. After midnight."

"I went for a slice of cake."

He cocked his head. "I saw you go into Mr. Martin's room at forty minutes past midnight, Miss Fitzhugh. You were still there when I left twenty minutes ago. By the way, I also witnessed the same thing happening for the past two nights. You can accuse me of many things—and you do— but you cannot charge me with drawing conclusions on insufficient evidence. Not in this case at least."

She stiffened. She'd underestimated him, it would seem. He'd been his usual flighty, superficial self; she wouldn't have guessed he had the faintest inkling of her nighttime forays.

"What do you want, Hastings?"

"I want you to mend your ways, my dear Miss Fitzhugh. I understand very well Mr. Martin should have been yours in an ideal world. I also understand that his wife has been praying for him to take a lover so she could do the same.

291

But none of it will matter should you be found out. So you see, it is my moral obligation to leave at first light and inform your siblings, my dear, dear friends, that their beloved sister is throwing away her life."

She rolled her eyes. "What do you *want*, Hastings?"

He sighed dramatically. "It wounds me, Miss Fitzhugh. Why do you always suspect me of ulterior motives?"

"Because you always have one. What do I have to do now for your silence?"

"That will not happen."

"I refuse to think you cannot be bought, Hastings."

"My, such adamant faith in my corruptibility. I almost hate to disappoint you."

"Then don't disappoint me. Name your price."

His title was quite new—he was only the second Viscount Hastings after his uncle. The family coffer was full to the brim. His price would not be anything denominated in pound sterling.

"If I say nothing," he mused, "Fitz will be quite put out with me."

"If you say nothing, my brother will not know anything."

"Fitz is a clever man—except when it comes to his wife, perhaps. He will learn sooner or later, somehow."

"But you are a man who lives in the present, aren't you?"

He lifted a brow. "That wouldn't be your way of saying that I am empty-headed and incapable of thinking of the future, would it?"

She didn't bother with an answer to that question. "It is getting late—not too long now before someone comes to lay a new fire. I don't want you to be seen in my room."

"At least I can marry you to salvage your reputation should that happen. Mr. Martin is in no position to do so."

"That is quite beside the point. Tell me what you want and be gone."

He smiled, a crooked smile full of suggestions. "You know what I want."

"Please don't tell me you are still trying to kiss me. Have I not made my lack of interest abundantly clear on this matter?"

"I don't want to kiss you. However, I'll settle for you to kiss me."

Her, kissing him?

"Ah, I see you were hoping to stand quiescent and think of Christian martyrs mauled by the lions of the coliseum. But as you always tell me, I am a man of unseemly tastes. So you must be the lion, and I the martyr. I shall expect exceptional aggression, Miss Fitzhugh."

"If I were a lion, I'd find you a piece of rotten fish, not at all to my taste and hardly edible, whereas I've just dined on the finest gazelle in the entire savannah. You will excuse me if I fail to summon any enthusiasm to fall upon you."

"Quite to the contrary. I cannot excuse such failure. Not in the least. You will somehow summon the enthusiasm or I shall be on the earliest train headed south."

"And if I do manufacture enough false zeal to satisfy you?"

"Then I shall say nothing to anyone of Mr. Martin."

"Your word?"

"*Your* word that the kiss will be more debauched than any you've pressed upon Mr. Martin."

"You are a pervert, Hastings."

He smiled again. "And you are just the sort of woman to appreciate one, Miss Fitzhugh, whether you realize it or not. Now here is what I want you to do. You will seize me by the shoulders, push me against the wall, reach your hand in under my dressing gown—"

"I feel my bile rising already."

"Then you are ready. Onward. I await your assault."

She grimaced. "How I hate to spoil a perfect record of repelling you."

"Nothing lasts forever, my dear Miss Fitzhugh. And remember, kiss me passionately. Or you'll have to do it again."

She might as well get it over with.

She closed the space that separated them in two big strides and gripped him by the sleeves of his dressing gown. Instead of pushing him backward as he'd instructed—as if she'd allow him to dictate the specifics of her ordeal—she yanked him toward her, fastened her mouth to his, and imagined herself a shark with hundreds of razor-sharp teeth.

Or perhaps she was a minion of the underworld, her mouth a swelter of burning acid and sulfur fumes, devouring his soul, savoring all the idle immoralities he'd committed in his lifetime as a palate cleanser between courses of more substantial sins.

Or a Venus flytrap, full of delicious nectar, but woe was he who thought he could dip a proboscis inside and sample her charms. Instead, she would digest him in place, the stupid sod.

Vaguely she sensed something hard and smooth against her shoulder blades. They'd been in the middle of her room, why was she being pressed into a wall? And why, all of a sudden, was she the one being devoured?

The muscles of his arm were tight and hard beneath her hands. His person was as tall and solid as a castle gate. His mouth, instead of tasting like a furnace of greedy lust, was cool and delicious, as if he'd just downed a long draught of well water.

She shoved him away and wiped her lips. She was panting. She didn't know why she ought to be.

"My," he murmured. "As ferocious as anything I've ever imagined. I was right. You do want me."

She ignored him. "Your word."

"I will say nothing of Andrew Martin to anyone, you may depend on that."

"Leave."

"You will invite me into your room someday."

"When they hold skating parties in hell."

"Sooner than that. Much, much sooner." He smirked. "Good night, my dear. You were well worth the wait."